I0583085

The Echo
of Others

S.D. Rowell

S.D. Rowell

First published in 2017

ISBN-13: 978-0-646-98074-4

Skuda Enterprises Pty Ltd
PO Box 662
Kyneton,
Victoria, 3444
Australia

Cover Photography - Adam Neylon (instagram.com/adam.neylon). Used with permission.

S.D. Rowell

For Karen, for her love and unwavering support.

&

For my sister, Joanne, remembered always.

S.D. Rowell

we are like trees;
our form shaped by weather endured, both fine and foul.

S.D. Rowell

Prologue

Grace's foot was jammed flat on the accelerator. The old Ford's engine screamed. The beams from the other car's headlights cut through the row of eucalypts that bordered the paddocks around them, making tortured shapes in the darkness.

Helen sat rigid in the passenger seat, gripping both the seat and the door. Grace could see a track up ahead, running off the road at an angle. *Maybe we can lose him.* She flicked off the car's headlights, pulled her foot off the accelerator for a moment, and yanked the steering wheel to the right. The car bounced, suspension creaking, as it found its grip on the dirt track. Now driving by moonlight, Grace again kicked her foot down flat against the accelerator.

They were a hundred metres along the track when the beams of light of the car chasing them turned. Helen twisted herself in the passenger seat and watched as the headlights came up fast through the dust of their wake. Grace suddenly knew making that turn was the worst decision she had ever made. She flicked the headlights back on, keeping her foot hard on the pedal.

1

The purple, yellow and orange hues teased a slow dance on the horizon. Dawn was close. It would be a beautiful autumn Sunday. Cloud-free. Peaceful. Warm. And the last for Steve Lawrence.

A duck landed on the swamp with a long splash. Joab had picked his spot early, hidden on top of a small rise, about a body's height above the surrounding ground, a concave indentation at its peak. Like a small meteor crater. There were shrubs and long grass growing around its edge. It would be easy. Just took patience, planning and a few seconds of activity. Simple.

As the sun burned into view, the tribes started to arrive. The ones in camouflage with shotguns, broken open and slung over shoulders. The protesters and rescuers with their thermoses and cameras. The game wardens with deflated looks. A couple of young uniformed police for when things got ugly. They all gathered in their respective groups.

Joab looked for him through the scope, though Steve was hard to spot in the soft light, in the crowd of camouflage. He lay flat, quietly conjuring memories to pass the time.

At ten past seven the shooters started walking out into the water in their waders. Joab knew that in ten minutes they would get the signal to begin their carnage. Through the scope, he watched them smiling, like children on Christmas morning.

Then he saw him. Steve was red-faced, struggling to slosh through the water. Through the scope, Joab could see the broken capillaries of a heavy drinker on his face; the loose jowls flopped as he walked. He watched Steve pull up the sleeve of his jacket to scratch his elbow, a tattoo from his navy days prominent on his forearm. Steve was smiling as he looked around, his glasses propped up on his forehead, his hair sculpted with hair gel, the last trace of his vanity on show.

Joab was perfectly still, lying flat against the ground, watching. Steve was now only one hundred metres away.

'Great shooting yesterday, Steve. You fucking nailed them,' his friend called across, with a smile on his face that could have been a snarl. Eyes squinted, his top lip pulled up as he spoke, teeth showing. The voice amplified off the water.

'Thanks, Gavin, yeah, you did all right too,' Steve said more quietly as he loaded his gun, not looking at his friend. He took a deep breath. 'Nothing but fresh air and the smell of gunpowder out here.'

Joab took a look at Gavin. He was a few years younger than Steve, gaunt and pale, and wore a camouflage jacket that appeared to have been bought for him to grow into. His hair looked as if he had fallen out of bed just seconds before. As a pair they were opposites, some comedy duo from another time.

The shooters spread out all over the swamp, all with an eye on the most senior game warden, awaiting the signal. Protesters were now in the water as well, waiting to rescue the downed birds that were still alive. They would try to rescue the protected ducks and the swans, as none of the shooters would claim them.

The game wardens trudged around in their blue vests. Officially, their job was to stop the shooting of protected birds, but as they would not be able to prove who shot what, their job was really more about keeping the protesters and shooters apart. Joab could already hear the arguments starting in the distance.

'Look at them fucking greenies,' said Gavin, nodding towards the protesters. 'Do-gooders, one and all.' He lowered his gun with one arm, pointing it casually at a protester eighty metres away. He liked to do this whenever one looked his way. She stood defiant, staring back at him.

Joab instinctively took aim at Gavin's head, his finger firm against the trigger.

Steve looked towards the protester. 'Yeah, if they'd just fuck off back to their communes, we could have some real fun. Raise that gun though, or she'll get the wardens and cops to hassle us.'

Gavin raised his gun towards the sky, leaning it back against his shoulder. Joab swung his aim slowly back onto Steve.

'Hey, did you see me on the news last night? There was a TV reporter here to cover the opening day who interviewed me,' said Steve.

'Nah, what did you say?'

'I told her that the protests were all for nothing. Told her that we shot the birds, they fell down and we finished them off humanely, so there is no suffering at all. She lapped it up.' They both laughed. Too loudly.

Steve checked his watch. 'Come on, come on,' he said.

Joab shut his scope eye, opened his left and looked down at his watch. Seven-twenty.

A game warden gave a signal and the thudding boom of shotguns shook the air.

There were shrieks of laughter as ducks started to fall from the sky. Some fell like stones, but others attempted to right themselves with one wing, or flailed desperately as they fell.

With his eye an inch behind the scope, Joab aimed the SR-98 just as Steve lifted his shotgun high towards a target. Instinctively he breathed out and held it there, waiting a moment. In one smooth action, he pulled the trigger, absorbing the recoil. The soft-pointed bullet hit the target's stomach. Through the scope, Joab watched a halo of pink mist surround Steve for his last, spectacular moment of life. He dropped the shotgun and fell forwards into the water.

His friend just stood there staring.

Joab breathed in again. He dismantled the rifle methodically, placing all the pieces in his bag. He retrieved the shell casing and picked up the shotgun that was lying off to one side. Sliding backwards, he used a branch to sweep the area clean. Halfway back he stopped, took a note from his bag and placed it on the ground, resting a small rock on top. Then he swept the rest of the area.

To his front, Joab could hear people screaming and frantically splashing their way towards Steve Lawrence, where he floated in the cool water. Joab picked up the bag containing his rifle and slung it on to his back. He pulled off the latex gloves and put them in his pocket. Carrying his shotgun over his shoulder, he wandered away, using the mound as cover against the crowd gathering on the other side.

Just another hunter.

2

Rachael shook as her muscles suddenly released, quivers rippling throughout her body. She dropped her hands to her sides and lay there warming for a few minutes in the early sunlight, as the last aftershocks pulsed down her legs all the way to her toes. She was completely at peace. She kept her eyes closed and enjoyed the warmth of the early sun across her body. *Nice way to start a Sunday*, she thought to herself.

After another five minutes of lying in bliss, she got up and took a warm shower. Once dry, she put on a T-shirt and an old pair of yoga pants. Barefoot, she grabbed yesterday's suit jacket and placed it flat on the table. Pulling the lefthand side of the jacket open, she found the pocket of lining, held closed by a Velcro strip. She pulled it open and removed the tiny digital recorder and thin white cord threaded through the inside of the jacket to where the microphone and switch were attached to the underside of the lapel. She left the cord and recorder on the table and hung the jacket up in her walk-in wardrobe with the others, all almost identical, either black or various shades of dark blue. She had decided years ago that a simple wardrobe would best allow her to blend in.

An old-school tailor in Carlisle Street had altered her

jackets for the recorder. *If I ask no questions, I can tell no tales*, he had said conspiratorially, with a whimsical smile.

Looking down at the wall, she double-checked her gun safe was locked. It always was, but she always had to check again, and then double-check once more.

Back at the table, Rachael connected the digital recorder to her laptop, created a dated folder on the hard drive, transferred all the files and deleted the originals from the recorder.

Pulling her bag onto the table, she took out the new cold case file. She opened it and placed all of the various sections across the table. She found some Moby on her phone and hit play, adjusting the volume to low. The first read of any new case was important and was much easier to do at home, without the constant interruption of phones and people in the office. She had to do it methodically and absorb it into her mind.

The new case involved two young women who had come off a dirt road at high speed about twenty kilometres from Bendigo a decade before, on 6 April 2007. The old Ford Falcon they were driving hit a tree head-on at about two in the morning, and Grace Blackwood and Helen Ng had died instantly. The car did not have airbags.

Rachael was stationed with the Bendigo Crime Investigation Unit at that time. She remembered hearing about the crash, but she had been in the middle of an investigation into a car theft racket—one or more vehicles stolen per night from Bendigo and sent to Melbourne to be stripped for parts—so it had barely registered at the time.

Grace Blackwood was twenty-four years old, born and raised on a large fruit and vegetable farm near Ballarat. She was a final-year law student at the University of Melbourne. Grace was single and was survived by her parents and two sisters.

Helen Ng was twenty-six, and had been born in Melbourne. She was the only child of Vietnamese refugees who ran a fruit shop in Springvale, in Melbourne's southeast. Helen was completing a PhD in Environmental Science at La Trobe University. Rachael could feel the mixture of pride and grief in her parents' statements, which read like a eulogy for their lost girl. Helen was also single.

Both women were dressed identically in black when they died—jeans, T-shirts, even their shoes and socks were black. Rachael made a note of this.

A witness had come across the crash site and called it in at five am. The first unit on the scene had sealed off the road when they confirmed both women were dead. By seven-thirty, the Major Collision Investigation Unit arrived from Melbourne to examine the scene and collect evidence. They found a second set of fresh skid marks in the dirt near the spot where the women's car had first lost control.

The collision team's preliminary report, dated a week later, concluded that the victims' car was travelling at around one hundred and twenty kilometres an hour on impact. *The kind of accident that takes teenagers, not academic types in their mid-twenties.*

Rachael read that the analysis of the second set of tyre tracks found they most likely came from a Holden Commodore VZ. The particular tyres were factory fitted to these models; and from the quality of the tread patterns, it was concluded that the tyres were most likely less than two years old. The report stated that about one hundred and seventy-five thousand Commodore VZs had been sold in Australia since the model was launched two and half years before the crash. The forensic reconstruction showed that the second car had cut violently in front of the victims' car, causing it to skid and crash. There had been no contact between the vehicles so there was no paint transfer. With no physical evidence from the second car, the case required witnesses or informants to come forward. None had.

She looked at the crash scene photographs. Apart from the trauma to the women's bodies and the car itself, Rachael noted the row of mature eucalyptus trees that lined the edges of the dirt road before cleared farmland began. The road itself looked only one and half car widths across in some parts—the kind of road where drivers would pull over to allow each other to pass. With trees growing right alongside the road there was little margin for error.

Rachael sat back in her chair to collect her thoughts. The second car must have been going much faster to overtake and cut in the way it had. It was almost certainly intentional—and, as the second car's driver didn't notify police, it became a criminal act.

There had been interviews with one hundred and four local people who owned Commodore VZs, none of which resulted in any leads. The summary said that all the people interviewed were either home in bed or away from the area when it happened. The reports stated that no one stood out as looking suspicious. She set the folder of those interviews to one side.

Rachael read through all the statements given by family, friends and local residents. Through the statements of friends, she started to get a picture of the two women. They were both members of an animal rights group, Animal Action, which had been exposing cruelty for many years. The group would be tipped off about perpetrators and find ways to enter premises and document the conditions through photos and video, which would then be broadcast on the internet and sent to the media to raise public awareness.

Family and friends had been consistent: both women were passionate about the cause and put animal welfare before their own safety and security.

The file contained some photographs of the victims together with other activists at protests. Rachael could see that many of the photographs were shot from above, most likely from nearby rooftops. *Police surveillance shots.*

Apart from a couple of minor police cautions from their activism, neither woman had any criminal record. They seemed to be happy, healthy young people at the start of their lives. No drugs, little drinking, no jealous partners or exes, no hidden secrets that investigators could find.

None of their families or friends knew why the women were out there, two hours from Melbourne, in the middle of the night. They all assumed it was for Animal Action, but no one the original detectives spoke to, including the organisation's other members, had any specific details.

Rachael read through the statements from locals, of which there were few, as the crash happened in a remote area. One person recalled having heard a noise around two am, but assumed someone must have hit a kangaroo and hadn't thought any more about it.

The autopsy results showed that neither woman had drugs or alcohol in her system. Hair samples were also analysed and found to be negative for past drug use.

Rachael swallowed. The locals were all interviewed by local detectives from the Bendigo Crime Investigation Unit, Detective Sergeant Mark Cullen and Detective Senior Constable Johannes Petra. Rachael had worked with Mark when she was first starting out as a detective at Bendigo CIU. She and Mark had a bad history, but there was no avoiding it. She'd have to track him down in the morning. *Hopefully he's retired by now.*

She placed the files back in order and stood up, stretching her back and looking around. Her eyes were drawn past the paintings on her wall to the framed photograph sitting next to the television. She smiled at the seventeen-year-old Rachael staring back at her, her take on a Jennifer Aniston hairstyle not working quite as well as she had thought at the time. Her parents were standing behind her, beaming, proud. It was the only thing she had kept from when she was younger, this large photograph taken at her school graduation. It was her most prized possession and she had it sitting where she could see it from most parts of the apartment.

They all looked so happy. Rachael was on her way to law school and all their hard work had paid off. She shook her head when she thought that just two weeks after the photo was taken, her parents would be dead. The people closest to her had not known what to say or how to act, and she had spent the next year mostly alone, dragging herself slowly forwards, inch by inch, her life blurry and forgettable. A year later she would join the police force. Nineteen years after that, here she was.

Rachael blinked; she stretched her arms towards the ceiling and walked out on to the balcony. The view from her apartment on St Kilda Road took in the expanse of Port Phillip Bay. She watched a container ship in the distance as it pushed its way through the water. She felt the last warm trace of summer in the autumn air. Rachael decided she would try and race the ship to Port Melbourne and went back inside to find her running shoes.

3

Detective Sergeant Mark Cullen got the call to head out to Frogmore Swamp—he was on-call for the weekend. He put on a suit and grabbed the keys for the unmarked car. Revving the engine, he skidded off down his street in the suburbs of Bendigo, the siren blaring, shattering the peace of Sunday morning.

He was a tall man, lean, and proud that the skin under his chin was still firm and that he had kept his looks, despite his hair now starting to go grey. Mark felt he had always done all the right things, but his career had never quite properly taken off in the way he thought it would. He put it down to politics. Other times it was feminism. Or equal opportunity. Or diversity. Without political correctness, he would have been a detective inspector by now. Being a white male nowadays means you're fucked, he would tell anyone who would listen.

Half an hour later, he passed the ambulance heading back towards Bendigo. No lights and sirens, going at the speed limit. 'Shit,' he whispered.

Mark pulled off Baringhup Road and drove onto the dirt track that led to the swamp. He saw the crowd of people, jammed his foot on the brake and slid the car to a stop, throwing dust into the air.

A young police officer jogged towards the car.

'What have we got?' asked Mark gruffly, getting out of the car.

'Duck hunter got shot in the back. Looks like he was dead before they shut the ambulance doors. The hunters are all fired up so the ambos decided to move the victim out of the area straight away while everyone thought he was still alive. Reckon it's a shotgun blast close up. It was messy,' said the constable.

Mark let out another sigh and looked down, shaking his head. *Paperwork*, he thought. The young constable smiled sadly, as though they were sharing grief for the victim. 'Okay, who got shot?'

'Steve Lawrence, forty-eight years old, married father of three, duck hunter obviously, from Ballarat,' said the young officer.

'And who is who here?' he asked, as he pointed to the large crowds of people, who stood shouting at one another.

'Well, the ones with the guns are the hunters,' the constable said, half-grinning. Mark stared back flatly at the younger officer. 'Right, okay, well the ones in the orange vests are either protesters or rescuers, or both. And the people in blue are the game wardens.'

'Okay, looks like fun,' said Mark, wondering why he had to be the one called out to this shitfest.

The crowd of hunters were screaming at the protesters that they had shot one of the duck hunters. The appearance of a senior police officer seemed to encourage them and their screaming became more animated.

Mark placed his fingers in his mouth and whistled a high pitch that lifted the birds from nearby trees. Everyone turned. 'Okay, hunters head off to that tree, protesters go that way. And hunters, break those shotguns open immediately and unload. Right now.' Mark's bellowing voice made them take notice.

Mark scribbled a phone number on the pad in his black folder and tore it off, handing it to the young officer. 'Okay, call Dave Boucher on this number and tell him to inform the coroner that we've got a probable accidental death and then to get his arse down here pronto. And tell him to rustle up four more detectives, else we'll be here all day.' Mark walked slowly towards the group of hunters. About fifty people all started to yell that he should be off arresting the protesters.

'Shut it,' he said sharply. He pointed at the group of protesters. 'How many of those hippies did you see carrying weapons today? Come on, out with it.' Mark waited a moment for a response. Everyone was mute. 'So, let's just say that it was an accident. You know, accidents happen with guns all the time. Malfunctions. All sorts of things can go wrong. So, does anyone want to be the brave one and own this fuck up, so we can all go home?'

The shooters shifted on their feet, looking at Mark or at the ground in front of them. He waited a few seconds, before letting out a sigh.

'Right, who was with the guy who got shot?'

A man stepped forwards, a grim look on his face. 'That would be me.'

'Come this way,' said Mark, pointing towards his car. 'Everyone else, stay put and someone will be along to talk with you soon.'

4

At four in the afternoon, Mark was driving into the outskirts of Ballarat when he got the call from his partner.

'I just spoke to the hospital,' said Detective Senior Constable Dave Boucher. 'Steve Lawrence wasn't killed by a shotgun blast to the back. He was shot with a soft-nosed bullet to the front, which mushroomed and fragmented on impact, and tore a big hole in his back as it exited his body. That's why they thought it was a shotgun blast when they first saw him. Doctor up there used to work for Médecins Sans Frontières, and recognised it straight away from the war zones in Africa. He said that if the bullet had been a hollow point it would probably still be in the victim—the shooter probably used a soft point to mimic a hunting accident. This one is going to Homicide. Where are you?'

'I'm in Ballarat now. I'll grab something to eat and drive back. See you later.'

Mark pushed the button on the steering wheel, ending the call. He had no intention of giving up the case yet. He would still go and see the victim's wife, he thought, and just say he spoke to her before Dave called.

Up until then it was a probable accidental death, with the victim's mate, Gavin Smyth, the most likely shooter. Now it was a murder and he knew that Homicide would be coming to snatch it away. By tomorrow he and Dave would be back investigating stolen cars and burglaries. Mark's rate of clearing cases was consistently the best in the Bendigo CIU, so maybe he'd get lucky with this interview and get a confession or lead that would solve it quickly. That could only help his case for promotion.

Mark arrived at the victim's address at Banksia Road in Ballarat. The street was full of neat, older-style homes. Gardens were uncomplicated and the grass was short. He could tell straight away that the Lawrence household was the one that neighbours would discuss when walking their dogs. Long grass and weeds.

The statements from the witnesses at the swamp had resulted in no leads. No one saw anything, except the victim's friend, who saw him fall into the water. The shooters continued to blame the protesters, despite their lack of weapons. Things had become heated and the police had seized many of the shotguns as the hunters hyped each other up, on their way to deciding a lynch mob might be a quicker solution.

Mark sat in the car and composed himself after the drive. He looked up the victim's details on the police database on his laptop. Steve Lawrence had no police record.

Local police had informed Steve's wife of his death just before lunch, meaning Mark was at a disadvantage: witnessing her reaction to the news would have been a good pointer. He got out of the car and walked down the driveway, past discarded bikes strewn across the grass.

Pulling open the flywire screen, he knocked twice on the door. He could hear children yelling inside. After a few moments, he knocked again, this time more forcefully.

'Shut the hell up, you kids,' he heard a coarse voice scream from behind the door.

The door opened and a woman stood there, looking him up and down.

'Cop?'

'Yes. Are you Mrs Lawrence?'

'Yep.'

'Mrs Lawrence, I'm Detective Sergeant Mark Cullen from Bendigo CIU. Can I come in to have a chat?'

Mark noted the light blue of a fading bruise under her right eye and several fresher fingerprint-shaped bruises on her upper arms below where her T-shirt sleeves ended.

'Call me Charni,' she said wearily, cocking her head towards the inside of the house and standing aside so he could enter.

The passageway ran down the centre of the dark house, with rooms off to each side. Charni Lawrence wore sweat pants that were a size too small, her hair was limp and her forehead had a crease that had become permanent from, Mark suspected, years of being disappointed by life.

She indicated to Mark to go into the front sitting room and yelled down the hallway for the children to watch television. Her body jiggled under her clothes as she settled herself in an armchair. Mark looked away.

'So, you investigating Steve getting himself shot?'

Mark's ears pricked up. 'Yes, that's correct. Mrs Lawrence, I am very sorry for your loss.' He waited a moment before continuing. 'I believe the local police came by earlier to inform you. What did they say happened?'

'They said there'd been some accident and that Steve had been shot by another hunter. Told me they were getting to the bottom of things and that someone would be in touch. That was it. Haven't worked out how to tell them yet,' she said, pointing over her shoulder towards the room where the children were watching television.

'What would you say if I told you that we now believe that Steve was not killed by accident, but that he was murdered?' Mark watched Charni Lawrence's reaction carefully.

Charni said nothing, her eyes narrowing as she stared back at him. Mark waited; many people cannot stand any periods of silence and have an overwhelming need to fill them with talk. If they were feeling stressed they would sometimes make an admission or react in some other way that would tip him off. Or even start to confess.

'I'd say that sounds crazy,' said Charni finally. 'No way.'

'I was wondering if you had any idea who might want to kill your husband?'

'No. No one.'

'Did he have any enemies?'

'No.'

'Did Steve have any issues with drugs?'

'No, nothing at all like that.'

'What about gambling?'

'No. Look, Steve just liked to go to the footy and go hunting. That's it.'

'What about your relationship with your husband, Charni? How would you describe that?'

'It was good.'

'So no issues at all?' asked Mark, looking at the bruises on her arms.

Charni Lawrence saw him staring. 'No bloody problems at all,' she said dourly.

'Okay, well what about the bruises, Charni? What's the story there?'

'There is no story. I tripped and fell in the kitchen over one of the kids' skateboards for this one,' she said, pointing to her eye. 'And I like it rough in the sack. That ain't a crime, is it?'

'So you have no clue why someone would want to kill your husband?'

'No. Next question?' Her tone had quickly turned sharp.

'Why did you ask when I first came in whether I was investigating Steve getting himself shot? Why do you think he got himself shot?' asked Mark, staring directly into Charni's eyes.

'I didn't mean it like that. It's just the way we speak around here, okay,' she said, stubbornly. Everything about her now said *Fuck you, copper*.

'So, where were you when Steve "got himself shot"?'

'I was visiting Melbourne, seeing my old friend, Kirsten. From high school days. She lives in Melbourne now. I left the kids with Mum for the night.'

'I'll need Kirsten's details.'

'Sure. Name's Kirsten Capinello. Lives in Melbourne. Used to be one of us, but then she met a bigshot who told her she was special, bought her a boob job and taught her to speak posh. She's got some marketing job. Shaking her arse for the corporate dollar now.'

'By details, I meant her phone number, to alibi what you were doing together. And what was that, by the way?'

Charni picked up her phone and found her friend's number. She held the screen towards Mark and he wrote it down.

'Steve was away hunting, so I went to Melbourne for the night. Kirsten and me went to the cinema down at the casino and then sat around having a few drinks and reminiscing about the old days. Stayed at her place. Then I caught the train this morning back to Ballarat. Got home around ten and realised I hadn't turned my phone on after the movie, so I switched it on and had about a hundred messages about Steve. Went and got the kids from Mum. Then I came back here and the local coppers showed up. That enough for you?' Charni pushed herself up out of her chair.

'You don't seem all that upset, Charni.'

'That a question?' she asked, standing up.

'More an observation.'

'We all grieve different. This is my way.'

'Is there something you're not telling me?'

'Nope.'

Mark knew he was getting nowhere. He got up out of the chair.

'Okay, Thanks for all your help, Charni,' he said, trying not to sound too pissed off.

They walked to the front door. 'We'll be in touch,' he said as he marched down the path to the driveway.

'Yep, you do that,' Charni said to his back.

It was just before six when Mark got back to the

Bendigo CIU. Dave Boucher was typing up reports. He looked up at Mark and then down at his watch.

'Somewhere to be?' asked Mark.

'Kind of. Sarah's been stuck at home with the baby all day and I wanted to give her a break.'

'Right,' said Mark, not commenting further as he sat down.

Dave took a deep breath. He knew Mark wasn't too sympathetic towards the partners of cops. He said they knew what they had signed up for. Meanwhile, Mark was halfway through a divorce from a woman he had married thirty years back, who he now called *that bitch*.

Dave guessed he would be stuck with Mark as his partner until the older man retired. They had worked together for just over two months, since Mark's old partner transferred to Professional Standards Command. To Dave, it felt like a lot longer. He was hoping he wouldn't feel driven to join internal affairs as well to get away from Mark.

'So, did the victim's shooting buddy remember anything else when you went back to him this arvo?' asked Mark.

'No, nothing substantive to add to what he'd told you this morning,' said Dave. 'He said they had started shooting and the next thing he knew his mate had a big hole in his back and was floating in the swamp. I got the call from the hospital halfway through taking his statement. Gavin seemed stunned when I told him Steve had been murdered with a high-powered rifle. He should have been relieved. Right up until then I had him pegged for being the shooter. I went through all the usual lines of enquiry. Drugs, gambling debts, angry husband of someone his mate was shagging. All drew a blank—at least that's what he's saying. I asked about Steve's relationship with his wife. He said it was *peachy*, although he said it with a dopey grin on his face. I reckon he's a couple of stubbies short of a six pack.'

Mark nodded. 'Yeah, I thought the same when I spoke to him. Well, I had finished with Steve's wife when you called,' he lied. 'She was a piece of work. Old bruises on the face and arms, but she said that there was no domestic violence involved.'

'Just clumsy, eh?' said Dave.

'Yeah, something like that. I checked Steve out on the database before I interviewed the wife. No record. No DV call-outs either. But who knows? Hardly ever gets reported. She's got no record with us either.'

'Any chance Gavin could have been slipping it to Steve's missus? Maybe Gavin led Steve into an ambush,' said Dave.

'Maybe, but she is rougher than fresh sandpaper. Can't see anyone wanting to slip anything near her. Stranger things have happened though, so he should stay on the list.'

'And her as well, obviously,' added Dave.

'Let's get as far as we can before Homicide get here.'

'Agreed,' said Dave.

'It was a high-powered rifle using a soft-point bullet. A rifle like that would make a distinctive sound, very different from a shotgun. No one heard anything weird, so I'd say the rifle had a suppressor attached to deaden the sound of the shot. Looks like a professional hit to me. Steve did something bad to end up like this. Best we check out everyone connected with the victim and his missus first up. Look for a gun nut. If we find a likely connection who knows high-powered weapons, we'll start there.'

'Got it. When you came in, I was just about to start a search on social media to see who Steve and Charni know,' said Dave, turning back to his computer.

As he said it, the head of the Bendigo CIU, Detective Inspector Max Martinez, came through the open door, followed by two detectives, an older man about Mark's age and a younger, tall Asian-looking woman.

Mark could tell they were from Homicide as easily as he could tell you the sky was blue. 'Time to hand over the baby,' he said under his breath.

5

Rachael woke. A helicopter was flying low over her building, the thumping sound of its blades reverberating through the walls. She knew it was an air ambulance heading in to land around the corner at the Alfred Hospital, and thought a prayer for the person inside. Coming in by air, they were always going to need it.

She lifted her head to see the clock on the bedside table. Four-thirty. Sighing, she shut her eyes, listened to the melodic tapping of the rain against the window and drifted back under. *She was standing in a long curved corridor, painted hospital white. She walked along, passing plain doors on either side. She wanted to hurry. She had somewhere to be, but couldn't remember where. She was carrying documents, but couldn't remember what they were. It was her first day there and she was in a panic.*

Rachael came around the bend and saw a man facing away from her. She could sense he was older— someone in charge. She strolled towards him, relieved. As Rachael got close, the man turned and smiled at her, but not in a friendly way. He looked her up and down, stepped forwards and backed Rachael against the wall. Tightly holding the documents against her stomach, she couldn't use her hands to push him away. He roughly grabbed at her breasts, while using his hips to hold her there. She tried to yell, but no sound came from her mouth. Rachael suddenly let go of the documents and pushed her palm up hard against his nose. He reeled back and she ran off around the curved corridor. The man stood laughing.

She was trying to open doors to her left and right. All were locked. Rachael ran until she could no longer hear him laughing behind her. She slowed to a walk, now worried about the documents she had left behind on the floor. She walked a few more paces around the curved corridor and then stopped. The laughing was now coming from in front of her.

Rachael drew a quick intake of breath and woke, eyes red, heart racing. Jumping out of bed, she went into the bathroom and splashed water on her face.

Staring at her reflection in the mirror, she watched as the water dripped down her face. She looked at the clock on the bench. It was almost six. She went to text Anna.

Forty minutes later, Rachael and Anna stood face to face, sweating. A few times a month they would find themselves there, locked in combat as they punched, kicked and wrestled each other.

They had met a few years before at a social group someone had set up for female detectives. The group turned out to be an excuse to drink wine and moan about work, but she and Anna had immediately hit it off. Anna was a member of the Mixed Martial Arts gym and had invited Rachael down one day.

The gym was large enough that they could stake a

claim on an area on a large mat in the corner and not be bothered by anyone. The younger people at the gym tended to come in later or at night, so it was generally fairly empty when they were there in the early mornings.

Rachael slid her way out of a hold and pushed Anna away. She immediately threw a jab with her right glove, and followed it with a left hook. Following through, she stepped quickly across her body with her left leg, turned away and spun her right leg back around and up. Rachael's foot cannoned into Anna's headgear, knocking her sideways. Rachael kept her hands up in a defensive pose and looked at her friend, who nodded back that she was okay. Now Anna came in on the attack. Rachael avoided her jabs. Rachael was the better boxer of the two, but Anna was lethal down on the mat.

Rachael's phone beeped to signal the end of the third five-minute round, and they broke away from each other, sucking in deep breaths.

'You going okay?' asked Anna.

'Yeah, just having trouble sleeping. I've started a new case and I'm still working out what's what.'

'Any nightmares?' asked Anna.

'Nothing too bad,' lied Rachael, looking away. 'How's things with you?'

'I'm good. Locking up white-collar crims is always fun. Just work on cornering them and when they know they're caught, they generally want to make a deal. Guilty pleas make life easier. How's the new job going?'

'All good. It's a bit different at Cold Case as we work cases solo, and only pull in help when things are warming up. We get through twice as many cases, and there's no one looking over my shoulder unless I ask them to.'

'And no one to slow you down either,' said Anna.

Rachael laughed. 'Something like that.' She tapped her phone to start the next round.

'Good morning,' Rachael said, smiling as she passed the uniformed officer at the front desk of the Crime Command Complex in Spencer Street.

'Morning, Rachael,' he said, smiling.

I need to start learning these people's names.

Rachael was first into the Cold Case Unit office; she turned on the coffee machine, then went to her cubicle.

She had transferred around a few times over the years. After the academy, she had been in uniform for six years before getting the opportunity to train as a detective, and she was at Bendigo CIU for a few years working on general criminal cases. She was then transferred to the Armed Crime Squad for four years, before joining the Homicide Squad for five years.

Then she got the call a month back that she was being transferred to the Cold Case Unit. *Burned another bridge*, she had thought at the time. In a performance review once, she remembered being told that she was *overly direct*. Rachael knew it was meant as a criticism, but she couldn't help smiling. It might make her a difficult person to work with, but it also made her good at her job. She could live with that.

She sat down at her desk. The four Detective Senior Constable's desks were pushed together with partitions separating them, Rachael and Jess Brown on one side, and David Murphy and Paul O'Connor on the other side. Jess had transferred in from the Drug Squad six months before

Rachael, and was still in the honeymoon period, thrilled to be no longer policing dealers and users. David and Paul had been with the unit for a number of years. They had become close friends based on their shared ancestry, and devoted a couple of evenings a week to drinking irish whiskey together. Every now and then, a touch of practised twang would enter into their Australian accents, as if to test if it would fit. All of the crew put the job first, though, and Rachael liked them because of it.

Detective Inspector Kate West came up to her desk. 'How are you settling in, Rachael?'

'Very well, thank you, Detective Inspector.'

'You can call me Kate when it's just us,' she said, smiling.

'Thanks, Kate. I've just started on a new case. Couple of women killed in a collision up near Bendigo in 2007.'

'Much there so far?' asked Kate, leaning against the desk.

'Maybe. I was going over the case notes on the weekend and there seem to be a couple of holes. Some things don't look like they were chased very hard, so I'm going to check them all out again.'

'Sounds good. If something is there I am sure you'll find it. That's why I requested your transfer here in the first place.'

Rachael looked up at Kate. 'You *requested* my transfer? I thought I'd pissed off someone at Homicide.'

Kate laughed. 'Well, yes and no. Sure, you did piss some people off there, but that's exactly why I wanted you here. You think for yourself and you're comfortable swimming against the current. I don't take anyone's rejects. Some of these cold cases are cold because the detectives who investigated them the first time possibly didn't think about things from every angle. I want people who will.'

'Thanks, Kate, that means a lot.'

'You know, there's a big difference between the work we do here and what you were doing in Homicide. Homicide is about the immediate, the need to apprehend offenders fast. That comes with enormous pressures, obviously, but the thing about working homicides is that sometimes luck plays in your favour. A witness may come forward. An offender may not be able to handle the guilt and might walk in the door and confess. With cold cases, this rarely happens. Witness memories are fading fast. Offenders have learned to live with what guilt they felt in the first place. Then you have the victims and their family and friends who are trapped in pain. Look, solving cold cases is important. It is important for the victims and their loved ones, and it is really important as a message to the community—that we are still out there searching for perpetrators. We do not forget. This is why I need only the top detectives here.'

Rachael looked at Kate and nodded. 'I'll do my best.'

Kate smiled. 'I know you will. If you need anything, just knock on my door.'

'Will do. Thanks.' Rachael smiled, watching Kate as she walked off towards the kitchen area.

Rachael checked the phone listing and called the Bendigo CIU.

'Good morning, it's Rachael Schlank from the Cold Case Unit. I'm looking to speak to Mark Cullen.'

'Morning, Rachael. Bit early for Mark. It's Dave Boucher here; I'm his partner nowadays. I heard you got shifted across to Cold Case.'

Rachael bristled, but let it go. Dave was always decent to her when she worked out of Bendigo, though she hadn't seen him since.

'Hi, Dave. I didn't realise that you were partnered up with Mark nowadays.'

'Yep, I won the lottery.' Dave laughed sarcastically. 'Can I help with something?'

'Probably not. I'm looking at a collision from 2007 that Mark and his former partner worked on. I just wanted to ask him some background questions. Can you get him to give me a call?'

'Yep, no worries. Will do. Congrats on the new job, by the way. I hear Kate West's a great boss. You may have struck gold there.'

Rachael gave Dave her phone number and thanked him, before hanging up. She put Dave Boucher on the good side in her mental ledger of colleagues—he didn't have to congratulate her like that, and he'd sounded genuine.

Rachael went to the kitchen to get her morning coffee. Her detective sergeant, Amit Pandit, was standing in front of the coffee maker, staring absent-mindedly at the cupboard. He was about fifty, with a friendly smile and kind eyes. Rachael thought he had the bearing of a school counsellor, patient and wise. Someone crooks might like to confess to, Rachael had thought at first, though she knew now he toughened up and could be intimidating when interviewing suspects.

'Hey, Amit, how are you?'

'Oh, hi, Rachael. Just going over an interview from Friday. You know how sometimes the words don't match the body language and expressions? How's things?'

'Yeah, good. I'm starting on a new case today. Double fatality in a collision from 2007, up near my old stomping ground around Bendigo.'

'Yes, I saw that one was coming up. It's the first review, isn't it? Call out if you need a hand.'

'No worries. Will do. How did Dev's footy game go on the weekend?'

Amit smiled broadly. 'He did well. He kicked a couple of goals. They won.'

'Always makes the weekend a bit nicer, eh?'

'You're not wrong. Happy kid, happy house,' he said.

Rachael poured a coffee and went back to her desk, leaving Amit staring at the cupboard. She liked him. He didn't put on a macho front. Some might have seen Amit as a dreamy ponderer, but she liked that he would think things through until he found an answer.

An hour later, Rachael felt her phone vibrate in her pocket.

'Rachael Schlank,' she said.

'Cullen here. I believe you called.'

'Thanks for the call back. I have caught a double fatality collision from April 2007 that was originally yours and I wanted to ask a few questions and get some background.'

'Well, okay,' said Mark. 'That was a long while ago now. I'd have to go over my notes and get up to date again. When do you want to talk?'

'Soon as possible,' said Rachael. 'We've got a big backlog here, so I can't sit on it too long. How are you placed tomorrow if I drive up to Bendigo?'

'Yeah, sure. Make it after eleven am and I'll have had a chance to refresh my memory.'

'Okay, let's say eleven-thirty up there. Can you book us a room?'

'Sure, see you then,' said Mark, before hanging up.

Rachael reviewed her list of questions for Mark.

According to the file, no mobile phones had been located. This would be odd for anyone out on the back roads at night, especially two people from the city, but it was even more unusual that the absence of phones hadn't been discussed in detail in the report.

Another possibly significant oversight, given both women's outfits and activism, was the lack of a search for, or mention of, video or photographic equipment. They must have been looking for evidence of animal cruelty—why else be so far from home in the middle of the night? The video footage from mobile phones was not advanced back then, so proper video equipment would have been required. Yet there was nothing in the report about missing video cameras, or anyone thinking to search for them.

The statements given by family and friends made no mention of why the women were out there that night, so far from home. Even the Animal Action people had said they had no exact idea, which seemed odd to Rachael. She knew these types of groups had a fair bit of success collecting footage over the years, and it would be odd if this could occur without a good degree of planning.

Rachael sat back in her chair. *Something is definitely off here.*

6

The media were all set up in the large conference room at the Bendigo Police Station. All the national TV networks were there, along with the local regional TV station, the metropolitan and local newspapers and radio stations.

'Thank you for coming. Are we all set to go?' Detective Senior Sergeant Rob Morello asked, scanning the room. He saw those with cameras nod in his direction. Mark Cullen and Dave Boucher stood at the back of the room, waiting to see the Homicide team in action. Rob Morello had been a Homicide detective for as long as anyone could remember. He had a reputation with police as a smart leader who worked hard as part of his crew, not just as a figurehead. He was well known publicly too, since being outed two years before by a social media campaign started by the wife of an art dealer he had put away for murder. It hadn't been his choice to come out that way, but now he was glad. Life was simpler.

'At seven-twenty am yesterday at Frogmore Swamp, approximately fifty kilometres south west of Bendigo, a forty-eight-year-old married father of three named Steve

Lawrence was shot and killed. Initially, it was believed the shooting was the result of an accidental weapon discharge among the duck hunters, but once Mr Lawrence was examined post-mortem at Bendigo Hospital, it became apparent he had been shot once through the stomach with a high-powered rifle, using a soft-point bullet. Bullets of this type collapse and fragment on impact, which is often called mushrooming, and create a large exit wound. This is why it was initially thought that the wound had been caused by a shotgun blast at close range to the back. Police divers recovered the .308 Winchester bullet from the water this morning and the forensics team from Major Crime Scene were then able to determine the location from which the victim was shot. The only evidence we recovered from the shooter's location was shoe imprints. We believe the shooter was wearing a pair of Magnum work boots, size eleven. We are looking for anyone who has any information whatsoever to call Crime Stoppers on one eight hundred, triple three, triple zero.'

'Detective, was Mr Lawrence known to police?' asked a reporter from Channel Nine.

'No, the victim was not known to Victoria Police.'

'Do you have any suspects?' asked someone from Channel Seven.

'As yet, no. We are looking at all possibilities at this stage. No one is being ruled in or ruled out. As I said, anyone who has information, no matter how minor they may think it is, should contact us as soon as possible.'

His partner, Detective Senior Constable Julie Wang, then lifted a large photo of Steve Lawrence, printed on thick board, and held it up on the table.

'Police Media will send out copies of this

photograph to all the media outlets. This is all the information we are at liberty to release at present. Thank you for coming.'

Rob and Julie got up and left the room as reporters called out questions. Rob had not mentioned the note that the shooter had left behind at the scene. It contained one word. *Humane*. Above the note was taped a single feather. Initially they assumed it was a duck feather, but forensics had come back to inform them it was from a chicken, which was baffling them both. No fingerprints or DNA traces were found on the note or the tape used to secure the feather to it.

Rob decided that they needed to get a grip on what the note meant before releasing information about it to a frenzied press conference. There would have been a list of questions a mile long from the media, for which he would have had no answers.

After the note and feather were discovered, Rob and Julie had gone back to Frogmore Swamp and met the uniformed police officers who had been on duty at the swamp when the shooting occurred. The videographer from the Major Crime Scene team taped everything as the police walked the scene with Rob and Julie. One of the uniformed officers had brought a pair of rubber waders with him so he could go into the water and show where Steve Lawrence had been standing when he was shot. They went to the small rise where the shooter had been lying and the videographer took footage from the shooter's viewpoint. Rob and Julie had seen the Magnum boot prints, still visible in the dirt. Now that they were back at the station, Rob was still thinking about them.

'How did you go organising surveillance for next

weekend?' asked Rob, once they were out of earshot of the reporters.

'Should be fine. We'll have undercover officers disguised as duck hunters on scene at the main duck-shooting reserves. In addition, I'm looking to get some drones deployed with thermal imaging equipment to do fly overs. If he goes back for another shot next weekend and is hiding under bushes with a rifle, we'll be able to see him from the air and pick him up,' said Julie. She had worked with Rob for a number of years and they fed well off each other.

'We just have to make sure the drones are flown out of range of the shooters. They wouldn't be able to resist taking a shot,' Julie added.

Rob nodded, leaning against the wall in the corridor. 'Okay, so our best-case scenario is that this is a targeted killing. Some nice, easy, stupid motive. Money or sex. Our worst-case scenario is a random killing by someone unknown to the victim. There was nothing found at the scene. No DNA. Very clean, very professional. So I am thinking it is a targeted shooting. We'll start with the family and move outwards from there. I'll start with the victim's wife. That DS, Cullen, from up here interviewed her yesterday, but I want to see her myself. You go and see Gavin Smyth, the dead hunter's mate, and see whether the chicken feather rings any bells for him. See if he knows anyone connected to the victim involved in chicken farming.'

'Will do.'

'In the meantime hopefully we will get some calls from the public, once the press conference gets on the TV tonight.'

7

Rachael stopped her car on the dirt road. She had found the collision site easily. She had the exact longitude and latitude coordinates from the report, and the shrine on the side of the road confirmed she was in the right place. She got out of the car. All around her were paddocks, in the process of being transformed from gold back to green by the autumn rains. She could see a dozen cows on one side of the road, and some sheep on the other, all watching her intently. There were no houses in sight. It was silent, except for the occasional mournful cry of a crow, and the muffled sound of the wind passing by her ears.

The shrine had been there a long time, with laminated photographs and cards in both English and Vietnamese from family and friends. Some of the cards were crumbling away in the roadside grass, weathered and torn by the elements, but others were more recent. Usually the local council would come along and clean away shrines like these after a few months, but out on this back road, maybe no one took much notice. Looking at the messages reinforced Rachael's belief in her mission.

She opened the folder containing the collision scene photographs and concentrated on the ones that showed the whole area, including the road and the crashed vehicle, with its front wrapped around a gum tree. She looked at the photo and then at the tree, and then back at the photo, like some sort of deadly before and after. The dirt road was still as narrow as it had been, with banks of trees right along the edges. Rachael looked down at the rough surface of the road. It was a disaster waiting to happen, but as it was rarely used, no one would ever think of spending money to make it safer.

The car had crashed on a straight flat stretch where it widened a little, enough for another car to overtake. The photos showed it had not been graded in a long time when the women died there, with a lot of loose dirt sitting on the road surface. This allowed the Major Collision investigators to clearly photograph and take imprints of the tracks and the skid marks. It was clear to them that the second car had overtaken and swerved violently in front of the victims' car. The car had then hit the tree at high speed and the women's deaths were ruled to have been instantaneous.

Coming to the site on her own gave Rachael the space to focus on the crime scene without distraction. Given the violence of the crash, the silence of the place was both unsettling and appropriate.

She looked around, taking it all in. She would remember this place. The sight, the smell and the silence. She would use it as fuel to drive her forwards. Store it away with all the others.

In every case, she collected up the ghosts and places and took them with her. Even after each case was closed, the victims often stayed in the back of her mind. She didn't like the idea of them just fading away like they didn't matter or never existed. Someone in Homicide had once called her *The Collector of Lost Souls*. They had been right.

She stood at the shrine and shut her eyes to pray for the victims, and she made the same promise she always made.

8

The main police station in Bendigo, on the town's southern edge, was a modern building, all steel angles and glass. When Rachael had worked at the Bendigo Crime Investigation Unit years before, the station had been in a dark, cramped old building located in the middle of town. This was far better.

She parked her car and walked into the station. 'Hi, Rachael Schlank from the Cold Case Unit here to see Mark Cullen,' she said, holding out her badge. The officer at the front desk nodded and called Mark's extension. It rang for almost thirty seconds before it was answered.

'Hi, I've got a Rachael Schlank here to see Mark…oh, okay, I'll tell her.' The officer put down the phone.

'He's not at his desk at the moment. His partner is coming down,' she said. 'Did he know you were coming?'

'Yes, we have an appointment for eleven-thirty.' Rachael checked her watch.

The elevator doors chimed and Dave Boucher strode out towards her. 'Hi, Rachael. Sorry, Mark is around here somewhere. Come on up and we'll get you sorted,' he said, turning to walk back to the elevator.

Rachael caught up with him. 'How are you going, Dave? Long time, no see.' Before she had transferred out of Bendigo years before, Dave had been the kind of cop Rachael liked working with. She remembered him as a straight shooter, thorough and uncomplicated.

'Yes, all good. Sarah has just had another baby, so the nights are chaotic. And the days are a bit the same right now. Did you hear about our shooting?' The elevator doors opened and they stepped in.

'Yes. Couldn't miss it. Homicide snatched it from you yet?' Rachael asked.

'Yes, and Mark isn't too pleased. With the new baby though, I couldn't be happier. I needed the case like I need a third armpit.'

She smiled. Rachael had forgotten about Dave's quirky expressions.

'And how's it working with Mark?' she asked as neutrally as she could.

'Oh, you know. Mark grew up in the station, and used to come to work with his dad every chance he got. He's been all over Bendigo CIU since he was five years old, so he walks around nowadays like a prince in a palace,' said Dave. 'But, shit, he has the best clearance rate in the squad, so I guess I'll pick up all the positive qualities and just survive the, ah, moods.'

Rachael nodded as the elevator doors opened. Dave used his swipe card to let them in to the CIU squad room and led Rachel to a small windowless meeting room.

'I'll go and try to find the great man,' said Dave, wandering off down a corridor.

After about fifteen minutes, Mark appeared at the

doorway, his hawkish eyes looking her over. She remembered the look. He reminded her of an old priest, looking down his nose at her. 'Sorry, it's been really busy around here.'

'No problem. Do you remember me?' asked Rachael.

'Not really. Dave said you worked up here years ago.'

Rachael smiled at him. He stared back at her, pokerfaced, but the narrowing of his eyes gave him away. *You remember.*

She opened her folder. 'As I said on the phone, I'm reviewing a cold case involving a collision which killed two young women in April 2007. Have you had a chance to review your notes?'

Mark had his head tilted back. 'Yeah, I had a look this morning. Nothing new to report though.'

'I just wanted to check a few facts against your memory. There were no mobile phones found in the car or the surrounding area. I thought that was strange. Did you find out why this was? It's not highlighted in the file.'

Mark shifted in his seat. 'It was not established why the victims didn't have phones with them.'

'But they both owned mobile phones, didn't they?'

'Yeah, but they weren't located at the scene. We tried calling the phone numbers on and off that week, but they were off the whole time. So the phone issue went into the unknown pile.'

'Okay. What do you think happened to the phones, Mark?'

Rachael saw his eyes narrow when she used his first name.

'I have no frickin idea, detective. If I knew, so would you. It would be in the report.'

Rachael ignored his tone. 'Do you think someone from the second vehicle took them?'

'I wouldn't know.'

'What about cameras or video equipment?'

'What about them?'

'Well, it would seem that the women were animal rights activists a long way from home in the middle of the night. My impression is they would have been up this way shooting footage for one of those exposés that end up on the news or a current affairs show. You know, where the pork farm has pigs living up to their necks in shit, that sort of thing.'

Mark looked at her hard for a moment. 'No cameras or video equipment were located at the scene.'

'Okay, on the search for the mysterious Commodore, what was the scope around the search? How many cars were checked out?'

Mark looked at the wall behind Rachael. 'We checked out one hundred and four Commodore VZ owners in the local area. The road is pretty remote, so we figured it was probably someone relatively local. We looked at the owners within a seventy-five-kilometre radius, if I remember correctly. That includes Bendigo. That said, although the tread pattern matched the factory-fitted tyres from Commodore VZ models built in the two years prior to the crash, it may well have been a different make of car that had them fitted as replacements. All the Commodore VZ owners came up squeaky clean, as best as we could find out, as did owners of cars with similar wheelbases who'd had a set of those particular tyres fitted in the previous two years. Alibis were a bit hard to confirm as the crash was at about two in the morning—they either had a partner to vouch for them or no one.'

Rachael nodded, her mind ticking off the boxes of all her questions. 'Okay, thanks for your help on this one. I'll give you a call if I need anything else cleared up.'

'No worries. Good luck with it. I always thought it was road rage. Somebody was chasing them and they ended up choosing a shitty road to drive down to get away. They've got your bright new mind on the case now, so who knows, it might just get solved,' said Mark, a tight wry smile pulling up the right side of his mouth.

Rachael didn't take the bait, but got up, smiled, and shook Mark's hand firmly. On the way out, she stopped at Dave's desk to say goodbye and give him a look that said *good luck*.

9

The fog was burning off quickly in the early morning sunshine as Joab watched the truck pull into one of the two entrances to the property. The driveway was wide and ran in a horseshoe shape, straightening as it went past the front of the house, and curving again before it exited back onto the road. The house was a Spanish-style villa with arches all along its wide front. Behind the house was a row of stables. Three horses stood nearby, tied to a fence.

The road was long and wound through mostly unoccupied land dominated by rolling hills and native trees. The only thing that had stopped the area being urbanised by the Melbourne sprawl was the airport, just down the road. Jets boomed overhead every few minutes.

The truck stopped as it was straightening up near the house. From where Joab stood across the road, among the conifer trees, the truck was side on. Perfectly positioned.

The walls of the old Bedford truck were battered, having been kicked thousands of times from the inside. There was no roof on the back and four horses already on board strained their necks to try and see where they'd ended up.

The driver applied the handbrake and jumped down from the cabin. A man waited for him near the house.

'Morning, Jim. What you got for me today?' asked the driver.

'Couple of fillies and a gelding. No bloody good, any of them. Fillies were dead slow and the gelding just wanted to canter the whole way, looking at the scenery. You know, I warned them, you're winners or you're dog dinners. They obviously weren't listening.' Jim Camella laughed. The driver nodded, but shrugged as the other man turned away.

Joab watched as the driver lowered the ramp at the back and Jim led a chestnut filly towards the truck. Jim walked sideways, holding the lead in his left hand and a large stiff whip in his right. As the filly approached the ramp she hesitated and began to step backwards, lifting her head. Jim yanked sharply down on the lead and quickly smacked the horse twice across her shoulder with the whip. Joab saw the driver wince and turn away. The filly danced a little in panic, before she finally relented and stepped forwards, up on to the truck.

Jim came back down the ramp, his thumb clicking the clip at the end of the lead. 'Dumb as fuck,' he said loudly to the driver.

From the trees, Joab whistled. Two toned, high then low. Jim stopped and looked across the road at the tree line. He turned his head slightly, as if trying to get a better trace on the direction of the sound.

Joab breathed out. Jim cocked his head just as Joab let the arrow go from his bow.

The driver was also looking across the road and was

about to say something when Jim suddenly dropped the whip and the lead and put his hand up to the right side of his neck. It was then that the driver saw the blood, pulsing through Jim's fingers.

Joab quickly shot arrows into the truck's front and back tyres on its right side. He then packed away the compound bow.

10

The car's GPS read that the drive to Bulla should have taken thirty-three minutes, but Julie Wang got them there in twenty-five, flying up the Tullamarine Freeway, siren wailing, splitting through the traffic heading to the airport.

Rob used the time as a passenger to run the bad feelings he had about the case through his mind. The first victim, Steve Lawrence, was clean. No police record. They had been interviewing all his family, friends and colleagues over the past few days and had nothing. He had no gambling debts. His drug use went only as far as the occasional joint and it didn't appear he'd had extra-marital partners. His wife did not support any suspicions around domestic violence, even now he was dead, so they had nothing to go on.

No one associated with the victim had any idea how the word *Humane* was relevant, apart from the fact that he had used it when being interviewed by a TV reporter the day before he was killed; that interview had first aired that night, and was now being replayed during most of Channel Nine's updates.

The chicken feather attached to the note drew a blank as well. One of the victim's friends kept chickens at home, but they were exotic breeds, not the common Isa Brown, from which the feather had come.

There was no useful evidence that ballistics could get from the .308 Winchester soft-point bullet. The type of bullet was a common one used for hunting and was fired by many kinds of rifle. Based on the damage done to the victim's body, though, they were presuming that in this case it had been fired from a high-powered sniper rifle. Forensics had sifted through the area where the shooter had been hidden without success. Apart from the note he'd left, it had all the markings of a professional hit, but no one connected to Steve had the means to put out a contract to someone who was that good at hiding their tracks.

Now there was another death just five days later.

On the way to the scene, Rob had looked up the new victim's details on his laptop. Jim Camella was well known to the police. He had been to court a month back for shooting a deer twice through the top of its back leg with hunting arrows and leaving the animal to suffer. Over several days, several people who saw the distressed deer near roads had reported it to police, but it had taken them a week to locate and euthanise the animal; the wounds by then had been heavily infected. Jim Camella was identified through an anonymous tip and admitted his guilt by bragging about it to an undercover officer soon after. He went before the court, charged with animal cruelty and firearms offences. The prosecutor had wanted him jailed based on his record, which was extensive, with dozens of animal abuse charges over more than twenty years, but the magistrate fined him and gave him a community correction order. Rob remembered seeing Camella on the news leaving court, smiling and giving the thumbs-up sign to the television cameras. They may as well have put a medal on his chest, Rob had thought at the time.

Julie parked the car near the driveway entrance where most of the activity seemed to be. There was blue and white police tape tied across both of the driveway entrances, with uniformed police officers on guard at each. As Rob and Julie walked up they looked beyond the tape and could see two horses tied up to a fence and five horses on the back of the truck. A body lay on the ground near the ramp at the rear of the vehicle, a large pool of blood pooled around the head.

Rob and Julie gave their names and badge numbers to the uniformed officer guarding the entrance to the driveway. She noted it on a clipboard as they lifted the tape and ducked under it. A Qantas A380 roared overhead as it climbed into the sky.

'Crikey,' said Julie, 'I didn't realise how close we are to the airport.'

Rob just nodded and walked forwards. 'Rob Morello and Julie Wang from Homicide,' he said to the sergeant.

'Good morning. Tom Green from Sunbury,' the sergeant said, shaking their hands. 'Your victim's Jim Camella, fifty-eight years old, horse trainer, divorced, no kids. He was loading up for the glue factory when he was shot through the neck with an arrow. Witness is Henry Jarvis, truck driver. He's on the other side of the truck,' he said, nodding in that direction. 'Arrow went into the side of the victim's neck, hitting a vein or artery I'd say, given the amount of blood. Came from that direction,' he said, pointing down the driveway and across the road. Rob and Julie looked down and saw the arrow sticking out of the victim's neck.

'Thanks. We've got it from here.'

'All yours. Good luck,' said Green.

They approached a member of the Major Crime Scene team, hunched down next to the body, the word *Forensic* in bold white lettering across his blue jumpsuit. 'The arrow cut the carotid artery on the side of the neck,' said Damien Harris, in his crisp English accent, without looking up at them. 'He bled out quickly. It looks like a carbon fibre hunting arrow. I suspect that when they get it out of him the tip of the arrow will have blades.'

'We got anything else at this stage?' asked Rob.

'Yes, my partner is across the road in behind those trees,' he said, pointing. 'She's found another note and boot prints in the dirt. The imprint from the boot says *Magnum*. Size looks about right for a match with the duck hunter killing from last weekend. Just one word on the note again. This time it says *Pests*. Same font used as the other note, but this note also has a logo printed on it for a company called PK Farm.'

Julie grabbed her phone to search for the company.

'Egg farm. A big one by the look of it. Near Bendigo,' she said after a moment, looking at her screen.

'The chicken feather,' said Rob.

Julie nodded.

'It's not my field of expertise,' said Damien, 'but I'd say he was using a high-quality compound bow, to shoot from across the road and have the velocity required to cut through the carotid artery.'

'Thanks, Damien. Let us know if you find anything else.'

'Will do.'

Rob and Julie walked around to the side of the truck.

'Well, our killer is efficient with language, I'll give him that,' said Rob, as they walked. 'Two notes, two words.'

As they came around the side of the truck, they saw the witness sitting on the ground, leaning against a tyre.

'Hello; Detectives Rob Morello and Julie Wang from Homicide. What's your name?'

'Henry Jarvis.'

'So, what happened, Henry?'

Henry lifted his head, but kept his eyes on his shoes. 'Jim had led the first horse on. He came down the ramp for the second one and stopped. There was a whistling sound from down the driveway and Jim was standing there staring. It was like someone was trying to get his attention. Then he dropped the whip and the lead. Took me a second to see the arrow sticking out, and the blood. He just stood there for a sec and then he fell to the ground. I called triple zero with one hand and tried to stop the bleeding with the other.' Henry stared down at his hand, dried blood in the folds of his knuckles and around his fingernails.

'Did the whistling sound like it was from a person or something else?'

'Sounded like a person whistling, definitely. Not like a wolf whistle though. More controlled. High pitched, then low.'

'Did you see anything?'

'No, nothing, except for those things taking off every few minutes,' said Henry, pointing up at a jet cutting into the low clouds. 'But it was dead quiet when it happened—I would have heard something if there was something to hear.'

'Was there anything strange going on in the lead-up?' Rob asked.

'What do you mean by strange?'

'You know, anything out of the ordinary.'

'Not really. Jim was trying to load a filly onto the truck and she was playing up, so he was hitting her with the whip. Had a temper, that Jimmy. Never liked the way he treated the animals—almost like he wanted them to play up so he could bash them around.'

'So, where were the horses headed?' Julie asked.

'Knackery up near Shepparton,' Henry said.

'That happen much? I thought racehorses were worth a fortune.'

'It happens enough to keep me and plenty of others employed full time. People think horse racing is all fancy hats and champagne, but lots of the slower ones end up sold for seven or eight hundred bucks a piece for pet food,' Jarvis said, his voice trailing off.

Rob and Julie stared silently at Henry Jarvis. A constable came around the corner and stood off to the side, waiting to catch their eye. Rob and Julie looked up at her.

'Detectives, the tyres on the other side are both flat,' she said. Rob and Julie walked around the truck and looked closely at the flat tyres. There was a small hole in the sidewall of each. Rob turned and looked across the road at the trees where Damien's forensics partner was working.

Rob nodded. 'Let the forensics tech know. There'll be an arrow buried inside each of those tyres or under the truck somewhere,' he said to the constable, who nodded, heading off to find Damien.

Rob and Julie walked back around to Jarvis. 'We're going to need your help getting those horses off the truck and into the stables. Two of your tyres are flat.'

Jarvis nodded, a vague expression on his face. 'I'll check which stables are free,' he said, pushing himself up off the ground. He brushed the grit off his hands on his jeans and wandered off.

'I'll go with him and see how many horses we already have here in total,' said Julie.

'Why's that?'

'We'll need the RSPCA or someone to come out. The victim was single, so there's no one here to give them food and water.'

'Right, good thinking,' said Rob, pulling out his phone. He liked working with Julie. She thought broadly and was proactive. Two traits it was hard to teach. He dialled Detective Inspector Tom Parker's phone number.

'So, is it our guy?' asked the DI as soon as he answered.

'Yes: we've got a Magnum boot print from where the arrow was fired. That will probably come back as a size eleven. Plus another printed note. This time it says *Pests*, but there is a logo of a company called PK Farm printed on it as well.' Rob could hear Tom typing in the background as he spoke.

'Got it,' said Tom. 'Major egg producer, south of Bendigo. Consistent with the chicken feather found at the first scene.'

'Still doesn't tell us much yet, though a visit there might move things along.'

'What about the victim there?'

'Victim is Jim Camella, multiple animal cruelty charges, latest of which was shooting a deer twice through the leg with hunting arrows and leaving it to die. He was on the news laughing it up after they let him off with a fine.'

'Psychopath.'

'He's not laughing any more. The forensics guy—it's Harris—reckons the arrow would have been fired from a high-quality compound bow, the kind hunters use,' said Rob.

'You thinking what I'm thinking?' Parker asked.

'Yeah, as long as you're thinking it's a vigilante.'

Parker sighed into the phone. 'The fact this guy is proficient with that level of weaponry makes this even more concerning.'

'Hopefully he's getting sloppy and there's some evidence left out there in the trees where he fired from. I'll let you know if they find anything.'

Rob ended the call and strode towards the contingent of media starting to gather near the entrance to the driveway.

'I'll be able to give you a quick presser in twenty minutes.' They all nodded and quickly picked up their phones to call their newsrooms with the update.

Rob walked back down the driveway, deciding what information to give and what to hold back in the press conference.

Julie was walking up the driveway to meet him, her limp a little more pronounced than usual. 'Twelve horses in there, plus the ones on the truck. I've called the RSPCA to get some help,' she said. 'Told them there was a lot of press here. Should get them here faster.'

'Good. Your leg giving you trouble?'

'No, I'm good,' she said.

11

Rachael woke with a start. It was still dark outside. She looked at the clock. Five am. *Shit.*

She sat up in bed and grabbed her laptop from the bedside table. She may as well work—too much adrenaline in her to sleep any more. She typed *factory farm Bendigo region* into Google and scrolled through the results. According to the map, the one closest to the crash site was a business called PK Farm; otherwise there was another chicken farm about fifty kilometres away, on the other side of Bendigo, and two piggeries a bit closer, but still a good twenty minutes' drive away.

PK Farm was only a kilometre or so from the crash site, and described as a major supplier of eggs. The website was sparse and contained little information, apart from the fact that the business had been established in 1996 by Paul and Dianne King and that it produced over ten million eggs per year. The website stated it went above and beyond in terms of animal care and was endorsed by leading animal welfare bodies. There were images of chickens running through fields and banners proclaiming the eggs were free-range. The contact details gave Paul King as the owner and manager, and listed the business address and phone number.

She then went onto the Animal Action website to look at information about egg production. She looked at various campaigns around chicken farms, pig production, dairy calves and other animals. Some of the imagery made even Rachael, who'd spent five years in Homicide, queasy.

She got out of bed and made herself a coffee. She decided she would go and visit the people from Animal Action first.

It was mid-morning when Rachael pulled up at a modest suburban house in the bayside suburbs. Nowadays the neighbourhood was wealthy, a short walk to the beach, but the house looked like it probably had when it was built in the late 1930s. There was no sign to indicate this was the headquarters of Animal Action, and Rachael double-checked the number on the letterbox to make sure she was in the right place. She opened the gate and walked down the path to the front door, which was on the side of the house. Through a gap in the backyard fence she saw a sheep staring at her, casually chewing some hay. Rachael smiled instinctively. *Not something you see every day in the suburbs.*

She rang the front door bell and a neatly dressed woman answered the door.

'Hello.'

'Hello, Ms Jennings. I'm Rachael Schlank. I called earlier.'

'Yes, come in. Call me Emma.'

Rachael walked into a neatly furnished living room.

'Have a seat, Rachael. Or should I call you

detective?'

'Rachael's fine.'

'Cup of tea?' asked Emma Jennings. She reminded Rachael of a loving aunt she'd once had: open hearted and friendly.

'Sure, sounds great. Just white please.'

'I've got soy milk or almond milk. Which do you prefer?'

Rachael took a guess. 'Soy milk, thanks.'

Emma smiled and went to the kitchen. Rachael stood up and looked around the room at photographs of animals that Animal Action had liberated over the years. Every animal looked healthy and happy, though she wasn't sure whether they were actually smiling or just looked that way. Rachael turned to find Emma smiling at her as she came back into the room.

'Some of our successes,' she said, setting the tray down on the coffee table. 'It's the eyes.'

'What is?'

'I'm guessing you were thinking they looked happy.'

'Yes, you're right.'

'Everyone thinks that. It's the eyes that give it away.'

'Lovely photos. A lot different from what's on the website,' said Rachael, sitting down.

'Yes, I see enough grief already. This room is more of a happy zone.'

Emma went on to explain she had set up the organisation around forty years previously and that they had made a significant impact on many people, getting them to change their attitudes towards animals and the way they are treated.

Rachael took a sip of her tea. *This actually tastes okay.*

Emma saw her staring at her tea. 'There is a bit of a taste adjustment when you first try it. It usually takes around two weeks for your brain to recalibrate, but it grows on you quickly. Especially if you know what happens in dairies.' She smiled. 'But you didn't come to learn about milk.'

'No; as I said on the phone, I'm with the Cold Case Unit and we're looking again at Grace and Helen's car crash, reviewing the evidence, re-interviewing people connected to the victims.'

Rachael saw a cloud of emotion pass across Emma's face. The older woman paused for a second, collecting herself. 'What do you need to know?'

Rachael opened her notebook. 'What do you think Grace and Helen were doing that night, so far away from home?'

'Reconnaissance, I would say. I was actually on holiday up in Sydney—the first holiday I'd taken in three years. Helen was staying here looking after things for me. She and Grace were young and keen. Really passionate people, looking to make a mark on the world. The girls had been on a number of raids with me and the rest of the team previously, so they knew our protocols, but I think they made a spur of the moment decision. It's the kind of thing you do when you're young and brave.' Tears filled her eyes, but she continued anyway. 'We presumed they'd got a phone tip and just decided they could take a quick look to make sure it was legit.'

Emma paused, remembering. 'Anyway, I got a call

the next day telling me what had happened and came back immediately. I gave all this information to the first detective who came to interview me back then—what was his name?'

'Mark Cullen.'

'That's it. Big man, grumpy. He came and spoke to me in the week after the crash. He didn't have much time for people like us. He kept slipping into contempt and ridicule. To tell you the truth he didn't give me a feeling of being fully engaged in investigating the deaths of animal activists. I suppose he's retired nowadays?'

'No, he's still there. But he's not on this case any more. What about phones and video cameras? Neither were found at the crash site. Would they have possibly gone without their phones?'

Emma shook her head. 'No, your report must be inaccurate. I told the detective that they both had phones and they had the two Animal Action video cameras with them.'

Rachael's gaze shot up from her notepad. 'Sorry, what?'

'The detective, Cullen, told me that their phones and both of the video cameras must have been taken by whoever had been chasing them. He said they checked everywhere around the crash site, but found nothing at all. The detective told me they were disappointed because they were hoping it might help identify where the girls had been or even who was involved in their deaths.'

'Oh, okay. I must have misunderstood the case notes. Are you sure that's what he said?' Rachael asked, trying to keep outwardly composed. She knew there was no mention of any missing video cameras in the case file.

'Yes. I definitely remember. I couldn't believe that someone would have taken their stuff whilst they were lying there dead.' Emma shut her eyes and took a deep breath. Tears spilled down her cheeks.

Rachael waited as Emma wiped her tears away with a tissue.

'Sorry,' she said. 'I didn't want to upset you by dragging all this up again.'

Emma sucked in a deep breath. 'It's okay. I still get upset about it even without the questions. I want to help, really. Go on.'

'So did the detective say where he thought Grace and Helen had been that night?'

'I asked him that and he said he didn't know. I told him the most likely target would have been PK Farm, being the closest factory farm operation to the crash site. He told me they had looked at PK Farm the next day, as it was so close, but the owners were confirmed to have been interstate on holidays. He also said there was no one else staying at the house there that night and that no employees were on site after hours. There was no one from that place to chase them. The whole thing is just one big mystery.'

'I see. Have you had other tips on animal cruelty in that area since then?'

Emma thought about this for a second. 'No, I mean we get a lot of tips and some of them have been in that general vicinity, but that road where it happened is in the middle of nowhere, way off the beaten track, so to speak. If they weren't at PK Farm, I don't know where they were.'

Rachael put away her notebook. 'Thank you for your help. I may need to be back in touch at some point if other questions come up.'

Emma gave the smile that reminded Rachael of her aunt. 'That would be no trouble at all. It's nice to have a visit from the police that doesn't result in me getting arrested for once.'

Rachael frowned. 'Sorry, what do you mean?'

'The raids we do. Usually the farm owners want us charged for trespass or criminal damage. My police file is long. According to the law, farm animals are property. The farmers can basically do whatever they want to them. It's the people with compassion who are the criminals. Hence I have a big file on your database.' Emma got up and then stopped mid-thought. 'I remember thinking at one stage that maybe the crash had something to do with Grace being about to finish her law degree at Melbourne Uni.'

Rachael took out her notebook again. 'How do you mean?'

'Well, if she was convicted of trespassing or something that might have stalled her admission as a lawyer the next year. And maybe that was why she was trying so hard to get away at that speed. I don't know, can't know really. Poor girls: so much potential. There are so few people who care enough as it is.'

Rachael pulled out her business card and handed it to Emma. 'If you think of anything else, anything at all, please give me a call.'

'Thank you.' Emma stood up from the couch. 'Just a thought: there is an animal activist event happening tomorrow at the Melbourne Town Hall. You'd be more than welcome to attend. It might help you understand Helen and Grace a bit better.'

Emma saw Rachael hesitate for a moment. 'Up to

you, of course, but it might be of interest.'

Rachael smiled. 'Thanks, I might just come along.'

'That would be great. Probably best you don't announce you're a cop though. Victoria Police are always trying to infiltrate us with undercover police. They used to be called the Security Intelligence Group — you know them?'

'Yes, I've heard of them. They're called the Intelligence and Covert Support Command nowadays.'

'That's them. They try to plant an undercover officer once or twice a year or so to see what we're planning. It's usually the person who suddenly starts volunteering and wants to take the notes at meetings. So people may be wary of you if you say you're with the police.'

'No worries. I might see you then.'

Rachael and Emma shook hands and said goodbye. As Rachael walked down the path, her mind was racing. *Why was there nothing in the case file about the missing video cameras?*

12

Rob Morello looked across the conference room table at Julie Wang. The interviews they had conducted with friends, families and associates had given them no leads to follow. They had gone to PK Farm and interviewed the owner, as well as interviewing employees and ex-employees. It was a large-scale egg producer, without debts or enemies. No one they spoke to seemed to have any idea why the business was being linked to the crimes.

Rob and Julie were frustrated. Two linked killings with no leads or suspects was a Homicide detective's worst nightmare.

'So, what are the similarities and the differences? Let's get them up on the board.'

Julie stood up and went to the whiteboard. Taking a black marker, she drew a vertical line, splitting the board into two halves.

'Okay, similarities?'

'Victims were both hunters,' said Rob.

Julie wrote the word *Hunters* on the left-hand side. 'Both ambushed,' added Julie, writing that as well.

'No DNA at the scene,' said Rob.

'The notes left at each scene,' Julie said, writing it down, adding the words *Humane* and *Pests*. 'Both intimate a link to PK Farm, through the chicken feather and the logo.'

'Magnum boot prints, size eleven,' said Rob. Julie noted this on the left hand side.

'What else?' said Julie. They both just stared at the board for thirty seconds.

Rob sighed. 'Okay, differences?'

'Different weapons,' said Julie, writing it down on the board.

'No apparent link between victims,' said Rob, as Julie wrote it down. 'Anything else?'

Silence.

Rob took a deep breath. 'So what we may have is a random killer executing hunters, using similar methods to what the victims used themselves in the past. The perpetrator is an expert with weapons and knows how to cover his tracks. We currently have no connection between the victims and no suspects. To sum this up as a case, it is a pile of crap.'

'Time to bring the DI in on this?' Julie asked reluctantly.

Rob looked at his watch. It was five minutes to six. 'Yes, I think so. He won't be too thrilled to be getting this news on a Friday evening.'

Rob picked up the phone and dialled Tom Parker's extension.

'Morello here. Do you have a sec for a quick briefing with Julie and me on the two homicides?…Okay, we're coming over.'

Julie got up wearily. Asking for help was something

they preferred not to do. They plodded their way to the detective inspector's office and gave him the rundown on what they knew.

Tom Parker leaned forwards in his chair and rubbed his eyes with his hands. Tom had been at Homicide since he was thirty years old and was now sixty-two. The lines etched on his face and the distant look in his eyes showed the toll the job took. Everyone in Homicide had their limit on the amount of misery they could take. For some, a couple of years was enough to empty their tank. Tom was a stayer, but that still came at a cost.

'Well, here are our choices. We can just sit around on our hands, waiting for this guy to kill someone else and possibly make a mistake. Which seems unlikely, based on how clean the first two scenes were. Or we get a taskforce together and stick significantly more weight behind it. And hope for a break.'

Rob and Julie nodded, not saying anything.

Tom continued, looking at his watch. 'I'll get on the phone to the assistant commissioner now and get things started. We are as busy as a one-armed person swimming laps at the moment, so we'll have to get outside help.'

Rob and Julie gave each other a look, which Tom noticed. 'Don't worry. You'll get an experienced crew. This case is too high-profile for bag carriers. May take a couple of days to pull together. Rob, you will head the taskforce up. Between the two of you, get an operational order together to get everyone briefed and up to speed.'

Rob nodded and stood up to leave. 'Okay. Thanks boss.' Julie followed him out of the office.

'I'll start getting the information in order for the op order,' she said.

'Thanks. It shouldn't take long as we don't have too much. In the meantime I'll contact the Federal Police and the other state police forces directly to see if there are other cases like ours elsewhere,' Rob said. 'Our guy may have moved here from interstate.'

'Good thinking.' Julie headed off towards her desk.

13

Rachael escaped into the sunshine outside the Melbourne Town Hall, taking a deep breath. At the entrance, a grey haired man in a three-piece suit and his equally elegant wife were engaged in friendly conversation with a young woman with dreadlocks, whose T-shirt exposed colourfully tattooed arms. *Eclectic bunch.*

She sat on an empty bench seat, shut her eyes, and tilted her face up towards the sunshine. Trams passed in front of her along Swanston Street every minute, their drivers frantically sounding their bells, trying to catch the attention of pedestrians, who wandered across the road staring at their phones, oblivious to the danger.

From her handbag, Rachael pulled out a postcard she had picked up inside. There was a photograph of a pig crammed inside a tiny metal stall. Next to the pig was written, *Slavery was legal, the Holocaust was legal, women not being able to vote was legal, and apartheid was legal. Using legality as a gauge is a very poor measure for what is right or wrong.* Rachael stared into the pig's tormented eyes.

'Rachael, I thought I saw you in there,' said Emma Jennings as she approached in her black Animal Action T-shirt.

'Hi, Emma; yes, I just needed some air.'

Emma looked at her for a second, as if appraising her mood. 'I'm glad you could make it. Can I sit with you?'

'Yes, of course,' said Rachael, as she shifted along the bench a little.

Emma sat down and watched the trams for a few moments. 'It's fairly confronting, isn't it?'

'That's an understatement. I was sitting in a session hearing about what happens in dairies to bobby calves and thinking, how I can be thirty-eight years old and not know this stuff? Is it hidden or are people deliberately kept in the dark?'

Emma gave her a sympathetic smile. 'It's a bit of both. It is a kind of informal contract between consumers and the meat and dairy industries. *You don't ask and we won't tell*. It's the way it's worked for a long time.'

'I was thinking in there that it's a bit like when you discover as a kid that Santa isn't real and the Tooth Fairy is your mum—but I'm not a kid any more. I should know what goes on.'

'Even pet owners, who understand what it is to love an animal, and see the pet as having feelings, will often argue the animals they eat *don't* have feelings. And if that's the case, why worry about how they're treated? Society has somehow decided that some animals are to be loved and cared for, and others are to be treated poorly and eaten,' said Emma.

Rachael nodded silently.

'Did you get to have a look at the other organisations that were in there?'

'Yes, I had a walk around. I saw the ones advocating against jumps racing, live cattle export, vivisection and puppy farms. I went to your stall. Thought about Grace and Helen standing there with the volunteers, playing videos for people.' Rachael looked at Emma, who was staring at her feet. 'I'm sorry, I shouldn't have said that. I didn't mean to be insensitive.'

Emma smiled again. 'It's okay. I'm sure they would have been here today, chipping away. I'm glad they have you investigating their case. If it's possible to solve it, I think you'll be the one who'll do it.'

'I'll do my best,' said Rachael, swallowing hard as she felt the weight of Emma's expectations.

'They would have liked you. Grace and Helen were spirited and driven people, just like you.'

Rachael half smiled and looked away, embarrassed by Emma's compliments.

A woman approached them, a broad smile across her face. 'Hi, Emma.'

'Yvette. Hello. Yvette, this is Rachael.'

Yvette smiled warmly as she shook Rachael's hand.

Emma continued, 'Rachael is a cold case detective investigating Grace and Helen's crash.'

Rachael saw the sharp burst of sadness in Yvette's eyes.

'I'm glad someone's still trying,' Yvette said. 'They were brave. The best of us.'

Emma took a breath. 'I'd better go back in,' she said, standing up and turning to Rachael. 'Let me know if I can help any more on the case. Anything at all.' She touched Rachael's arm and smiled at Yvette as she was leaving. 'I'll catch you inside, Yvette.'

Rachael and Yvette watched Emma walk back towards the entrance to the town hall.

'She thinks of those girls every day. She's still upset, all these years later. Do you have any new information?'

'Early stages. I'm reviewing everything right now.'

'Good luck with it. I hope you get whoever did this. What brings you here today?' asked Yvette.

'Emma thought it would be good for me to understand the issues Grace and Helen were passionate about. It has been eye opening. I had no idea.'

'Yes, when you understand industrialised animal abuse for the first time, it can mess you up. Initially you hit denial, which is where most people stop. They just tell themselves it isn't real or that it wouldn't happen here in Australia. For whoever is still thinking about it, they then move on to anger, which in itself isn't all that constructive. After that you soon get to action, which is where Grace and Helen were at when they died.'

'Were you were close to them?'

'Yes, I was studying law with Grace at Melbourne University. She was the person who opened my eyes to all this.'

'Are you a lawyer now?'

'Yes, but I'm in a different place from where I was headed ten years ago. I have a small practice in Woodend, up in the Macedon Ranges. One of Grace's dreams was to buy a place in the country and start a farm animal sanctuary. It was something that always stuck with me, so I decided I'd do it.'

'That sounds lovely.'

'You're welcome to come on up and visit if you want. I can introduce you to the animals.'

'That'd be great.'

'You free tomorrow?' said Yvette, smiling, as if daring her.

'Sure.'

Grabbing a pen and some paper from her bag, Yvette wrote down her address and gave it to Rachael. 'Say around eleven am?'

'Sounds good. See you then.'

'Wear old shoes,' Yvette said. 'Older the better.'

14

Rachael drove up the long driveway and parked outside Yvette's house. As she opened the car door, a Golden Retriever greeted her, his face a broad smile, tail whooshing in the air.

'Hello there,' said Rachael to the dog, running her hand over his head.

'Hi,' said Yvette, walking around behind the car. 'Jasper, let her out of the car, please.'

Jasper continued to wag his tail excitedly, retreating just a couple of steps to let Rachael get past him.

Rachael smiled. 'Beautiful place you have,' she said, looking out over the nearby mountain range. She could feel the chill in the air against her face and was glad she had decided to put on a jacket before leaving home.

'Yes, it's heaven up here. Do you want to have a coffee first or meet some animals?'

'Meeting some animals would be good, thanks.'

'No worries, let's go.'

Rachael noticed Yvette smiling as she inspected her shoes. 'Oldest ones I have,' said Rachael. She thought

Yvette looked a picture of contentment in her gum boots, old jeans and T-shirt.

They walked into a paddock and towards a clump of trees. A sheep popped its head around from behind a tree and then came running over, followed by four others. Yvette kneeled down as the largest male sheep sniffed around her face. 'Hey, Billy, I've brought you a new friend to meet.'

'Is he sniffing you or kissing you?' asked Rachael, watching from above.

'A bit of both.'

Yvette gestured to Rachael to bend down. Billy stepped across and snuffled Rachael's face. She started rubbing him affectionately as he moved his head around under her hand.

'He's adorable,' said Rachael. 'I don't think I have ever been this close to a sheep before.'

'Yes, he's a beautiful little man. He was hand raised so he's not scared of us at all. Same goes for Banjo over there,' said Yvette, pointing to a smaller sheep nearby. 'Banjo was born on a truck on its way to the slaughterhouse. He fell out of the side of the truck, umbilical cord still attached. Someone driving past saw something move on the side of the road and thankfully stopped to check. He spent the first three months of his life being bottle fed, living with a family and their three dogs. They would even take him for walks on a lead. It took him a while after he came here to understand he was a sheep and not a dog. Our other three sheep are girls. They were found wandering the streets in the outer northern suburbs of Melbourne. They probably escaped from some sort of backyard butcher.'

'They're lucky to have ended up here,' Rachael said.

'Yes, you have a much better chance of winning the lottery than these ones had of being saved.'

Billy stared up at Rachael, all the while chewing on some grass. 'You are just gorgeous,' said Rachael, cupping his head in her hands.

'He loves humans, that boy.'

Rachael nodded and then breathed in deeply. 'I forget how fresh the air is out here.'

'Yeah, I can really tell the difference when I go into Melbourne nowadays. Let's go and find some cows,' said Yvette.

They wandered over to where four cows sat near a tree. As they approached, one cow after another slowly stood up.

'They were all born on a dairy farm and were rescued an hour before they were to be put on the truck bound for the slaughterhouse,' said Yvette. 'They're by-products of the dairy industry. They were just a couple of days old and were only about this tall when they arrived here.' Yvette bent over and placed her hand at her knee.

'They're huge now. How old are they?'

'Just over two. There are three boys and a girl.'

'Why is there a girl here? I thought they said yesterday dairies kept the girls in those tiny pens on powdered milk so they can become dairy cows too.'

'Apparently she was too small to be commercially viable as a dairy cow, so she was put with the boys to be sent to slaughter to become veal.'

The cows were curious about the new visitor and came over slowly to greet them.

'Just put your hand out still and they'll give it a

smell to check you out,' said Yvette.

'A bit like a dog.'

'Exactly the same.'

One by one, the cows came up and stood in front of Rachael and Yvette, sniffing and licking their hands with their tongues.

'Their tongues are all rough, like cat's tongues,' said Rachael.

'Yes, it helps them grip the grass or the hay when they're eating,' said Yvette.

Rachael rubbed the side of Jessie's head as she would to a horse. 'I thought just the bulls had horns. Her horns are huge.'

'Some breeds of cows have them, some don't. It's nothing to do with gender. Those horns will continue to grow as the cows grow.' Yvette leaned forwards and a jet-black steer instantly licked her on the face. 'Cheapest exfoliation in town,' she said laughing.

Yvette rubbed the steer behind his ears and under the chin. After a while, all the cows went back to eating grass.

'They really trust you,' said Rachael.

'They'll trust anyone if they're treated well. These ones have only known love since they were a few days old, so they're very comfortable with humans. Cows are very social animals. Every evening they head down to the back paddock to visit the cows from next door, over the fence.'

Yvette and Rachael walked back towards the house, shutting the gate behind them, and then entered a large chicken enclosure. They sat down on some logs. A group of chickens ran out from behind their coop and stopped short when they saw Rachael. They immediately started chirping to each other and looking her up and down. A couple of the chickens ran around behind Rachael, chirping back their reports.

'They're talking about you,' said Yvette.

'I'm getting that feeling,' said Rachael, laughing.

'I can't interpret chicken speak, but I'd say they're determining whether you're friend or foe.'

'I come in peace,' said Rachael, spreading her arms with her palms open. The chickens chirped some more.

One of the chickens came running across and flew quickly up onto Yvette's knee. Then the other chickens came over and began to check Rachael out more closely. Yvette gently stroked the chicken standing on her knee. 'This is Katie. She loves a cuddle.' As Yvette stroked her front, Katie sat down slowly on her leg.

'She obviously enjoys that,' Rachael said.

'Do you want to hold her?'

'Sure,' she said.

Yvette gently handed Katie across.

'These girls came from an egg farm. They called it free-range, but in reality there were ten thousand birds crammed together in a shed, living in their own faeces. When they got here they were all bald and didn't really know how to be chickens. They were kind of catatonic. It took a day to scrape off the shit that was caked onto Katie's feet. The feathers grew back over time and they slowly learned what it was to be free. Then their personalities came out.'

Rachael was staring down at Katie, who was gently chirping away, looking up at her. 'I have to say I've had an eye-opening week. A lot of animal agriculture seems to be a nightmare, whichever way you look at it,' said

Rachael.

'People who eat animals will say it's their personal choice,' said Yvette 'but they're forgetting that there are innocent victims involved who have no choice. And those victims are also voiceless.'

Rachael nodded, gently stroking the feathers on Katie's neck. The chicken slowly closed her eyes, crouched down and started cooing softly.

15

Rachael pulled the case file over and looked at the list of Commodore owners interviewed. Mark Cullen had requisitioned details of all Commodore VZ owners within a seventy-five kilometre radius of the crash site. Rachael scanned the list again. It contained one hundred and four names.

When she got a third of the way down the page, she stopped. The name *King, Paul* was listed. She picked up the file with the original statements from the Commodore VZ owners. They were in alphabetical order, and Mark and his then partner, Johannes Petra, had divided up taking the statements. She soon found the one belonging to the owner of PK Farm.

The statement was short. It said Paul and Dianne King were on holiday, towing a caravan, and were in Tumut in the Snowy Mountains, about five hundred kilometres away, on the night of the crash. It also stated there were no staff on site after six pm that night and that no one was staying at their house. This was the same as what Emma Jennings said Mark told her all those years ago: no one had been at PK Farm that night.

Rachael noticed the statement was not signed by Paul or Dianne King—it was a telephone interview taken by Mark.

In the kitchen area getting a coffee, she was grabbing her new soy milk when she noticed someone had finally turned the page on the calendar on the fridge over to the current month. *Fuck*.

Rachael walked quickly back to her desk and grabbed the pile of statements from Commodore owners. She pulled the King couple's out and looked at the date. Thursday, 12 April, 2007.

She opened her diary and picked up her phone to call Emma Jennings at Animal Action.

After three rings, she answered. 'Hello?'

'Hello, Emma, it's Rachael Schlank from Cold Case.'

'Hi, Rachael.'

'I have a quick question. Do you have a sec?'

'Yes, sure. What is it?'

'Do you remember what day Detective Cullen came and saw you after the crash, once you had returned from holiday?'

'Yes, it was the Monday. I got the call about the crash on the Friday before and was back home on the Saturday. He called on the Sunday and asked to see me on the Monday morning.'

'Are you sure about the day?'

'Yes, absolutely. I've kept a journal since I was a kid, and I had another look after your visit last Friday. Plus I remember it was Monday because it's bin day and he arrived as I was wheeling the bins in and he didn't offer to help.'

'Did he come to see you another time or call you to discuss the case?'

'No, I just spoke to him the one time.'

'Okay, thank you.'

'I can't see how it's relevant though,' said Emma.

'I'm just getting my timeline sorted. All a normal part of the review process.'

'Oh, okay. Anything else I can help with?'

'No, that's all—oh, by the way, I visited Yvette's place yesterday. Thanks for the introducing us.'

'Oh, that's great. There's nothing like meeting animals up close and personal. Did Billy try and kiss you?'

'Sure did,' said Rachael, laughing at the thought. 'What a friendly sheep he is. Anyway, thanks again.'

They said goodbye and Rachael put down the phone. She opened the file and came to Mark's notes from his discussion with Emma. They were dated Monday 9 April 2007, which lined up with what Emma remembered as well. Rachael looked through the notes. There was no mention of PK Farm. There was also no mention of the mobile phones or the video cameras.

Rachael searched methodically through the case file for any reference to Mark having contacted Paul King or anyone from PK Farm the day after the crash. There was nothing there.

She sat back in her chair and thought about what her next move should be. She had two big issues. One was Mark telling Emma on the Monday that the people from PK Farm were away on holidays *before* he took their statement the following Thursday. The other was the missing Animal Action video cameras that he had neglected to mention in his report.

Usually Rachael would go straight to Johannes Petra to cross-check the known facts of the case, as he had been Mark's partner at the time. But Johannes was now at Professional Standards Command, and something was telling her this whole investigation was something that might end up being reviewed by PSC in the future. Rachael felt the tension building in her neck. She knew she had to tread carefully, whatever she did.

She had never liked Mark, but she had always thought he was professional regarding casework, whatever his other failings might have been. Not that she'd worked that closely with him, of course.

Rachael needed some advice. Amit was out with Jess interviewing suspects, so Rachael walked across to the DI's office. She knocked on the door and Kate West looked up from her keyboard.

'Do you have a sec?' Rachael asked.

'Sure, come in. What's up?'

Rachael took her boss through her review of the case so far. Kate listened intently, poker faced until the end.

'What day was it again that Cullen took the statement from the PK Farm people?'

Rachael opened the file to double-check. 'It was the Thursday, the twelfth, three days after he spoke to Emma Jennings.'

Kate sighed. 'Shit. So he's told Emma that the PK Farm people have been cleared before he's officially spoken to them.'

'Yes. The other thing I can't get my head around is why Mark made no note in the case file about the missing video cameras once he saw Emma. He seems to have just ignored it.'

They sat in silence for a moment, thinking it through.

'Also,' said Rachael, 'why didn't they go hard at the animal activism angle in the first place? I mean, two activists from the city, clad from head to toe in black, being run off the road at two in the morning, in the middle of nowhere. Why wouldn't this be the direction the investigation would take?'

Now Kate was nodding. 'You're right. Let's just say you need to tread somewhat carefully until you get on firm ground here, especially seeing as Cullen's ex-partner is now at PSC. But you know that and that's why you're here. Usually I would inform Professional Standards immediately, but it doesn't seem prudent just yet. You do need to speak to Johannes Petra to get background, but do it subtly. Get Amit involved on the case right away as well. Go and see this Paul King to test out this alibi first, then go see Petra. After that, the picture will be clearer.'

'Thanks, boss. Appreciate the advice.'

'Any time. Keep me up to date,' said Kate.

Rachael walked back to her desk as the unit DS came in the door.

'Hi, Amit. My case is heating up and I need to you to jump on board for a while. Is that going to work?'

Amit nodded. 'Let's grab a meeting room and you can bring me up to speed.'

16

Rachael drove over the Bolte Bridge with Amit in the passenger seat, the case file in his lap. To their right, Melbourne's skyline loomed large. A new glass-clad tower seemed to appear every few months, replacing smaller grey versions and open space. The Melbourne Star turned slowly near the bridge.

'Ever been?' Amit said, nodding towards the giant Ferris wheel.

Rachael was silent, deep in thought. 'Sorry, what's that?' she asked after a few seconds.

'The Melbourne Star... have you ever been on it?'

'No, you?'

'No, it's more for the tourists. Looks good at night though, with all the patterns of coloured lights,' said Amit. 'My kids love it all lit up. You seemed like you were miles away just then. Everything okay?'

'Yeah, I was just thinking about a case from a few years back. A homicide near the base of this bridge. A nasty one.'

Amit nodded. 'It's sometimes hard to let them go.'

'Crime scenes change—buildings are knocked down and rebuilt, overgrown creeks turn into pristine parks, but whenever I pass them, I wonder, do people remember what happened there, or is it just me? Years later I can still feel the echo of those cases when I'm nearby.'

'Yeah, I know what you're saying,' said Amit, looking across at her. 'So, how do we want to play this one with Paul King?'

His question brought Rachael back to the present. 'We are backgrounding at the moment, so we'll just play it as it comes. The fact is that the victims were animal rights activists and Paul King owns a large factory farm operation close by. The only one nearby. So he is definitely a person of interest to us. I want to hear about the trip he was on at the time, his alibi. See how he acts and reacts to questions. That's why I didn't call ahead to say we were coming.'

'No worries,' said Amit. 'I'll sit back and jump in only if you need me to.'

Rachael nodded. She liked that Amit let his team run their cases themselves and acted as a mentor, only interjecting directly if required. Rachael was used to working with senior detectives who ran the cases themselves, with the junior detectives supporting them.

Amit read through the case file most of the way up the Calder Freeway. As she drove, Rachael noticed the colours changing, from the remains of summer gold in the paddocks to the now autumn green of the ranges, revealed in stages as they rose higher over each ridge towards Mount Macedon.

As they passed the turn off to Kyneton, Amit put down the file and turned to Rachael.

'This business about the missing video cameras is weird. Why wouldn't Mark have put it in the report after he spoke to the Animal Action woman?'

'No idea.'

'So what's he like? Mark, I mean.'

Rachael paused for a moment. It wasn't her habit to speak about people negatively behind their backs—she preferred to be upfront—but Amit needed to know. 'I worked with him when I was in uniform and also when I was starting out as a detective. He has the best rate of clearing cases of anyone in Bendigo CIU, always has had. He is old-fashioned—learned his behaviours young from his dad, who was also a detective in Bendigo. Mark doesn't like women too much unless they are submissive and silent, so he hated me when I was up there.'

'Got it. I know the type.' Amit picked up the file again and kept reading.

About ten kilometres before reaching the outskirts of Bendigo, Rachael turned off the freeway. Twenty-five minutes later they pulled up at the gate to PK Farm.

'The crash site is down that way,' Rachael said, pointing down the road. 'Four hundred metres along there is a turn-off and it happened another six hundred metres down a dirt road. I am guessing the women were trying to lose their pursuers by taking the dirt road.'

Rachael lowered her window and pushed the intercom button.

'Yes?' said a female voice from a box mounted on the pole next to the driveway.

'Hello. Detectives Schlank and Pandit from Victoria Police to see Paul King.'

There was silence on the other end. After a moment, the gates started to automatically swing open. Rachael drove up the long driveway bordered with clipped hedges towards a large house a few hundred metres away. Behind the house, about three hundred metres further back in the distance, were six industrial-sized sheds. The wide crushed-granite driveway wound its way back to them. Rachael turned off at a fork in the driveway towards the house. Outside was a sign that read *Office*.

The gardens in front of the house were perfectly maintained and a new platinum-coloured Range Rover was parked outside the garage.

'The egg business is obviously good,' said Amit, as they walked to the front door.

Rachael knocked on the door and a manicured woman, mid-fifties, slim, with shining blond hair cut short came to the door. She wore a tailored dress and a large diamond ring dominated her left hand.

'Mrs King?' asked Rachael.

'Yes,' she said plainly, as if police dropping by unexpectedly was an everyday event. Rachael was used to people looking slightly panicked when she appeared at their door.

'I am Detective Senior Constable Schlank and this is Detective Sergeant Pandit from the Cold Case Unit. We are investigating a case from 2007, a car crash down the road. We were hoping to speak with you and your husband.'

Rachael saw a tiny quiver cross Mrs King's eyelid.

'You'd better come in,' she said, opening the door.

She led them through to a living room decorated in a French provincial style. They sat down and got comfortable.

'Now, how can I help?'

'Is your husband here today?'

Mrs King looked down. 'My husband passed away

late last year.'

'Oh my… I am very sorry,' said Rachael, now off-guard.

Mrs King waited a moment, took a deep breath and composed herself. 'Thank you, Detective. Paul committed suicide last November. It was unexpected,' she said, the last part an almost vacant whisper.

Rachael let a moment go by before speaking. 'Mrs King…'

'Call me Dianne, please,' she said, smiling faintly.

'Dianne, as I said, in 2007, there was a twin fatality not far from here and we're interested in what you know about it.'

Dianne jolted her head back slightly. 'What do you mean, what do I know about it? I know nothing about it.'

'Are you saying you don't know about the crash?'

'Oh, no, I misunderstood. Yes, I *heard* about it, but no, I don't *know* anything about it.'

'So, where were you when it happened, Dianne?' Rachael asked.

Dianne hesitated, looking away as she thought. 'I don't know—I mean it was a long time ago, how would I remember now?'

'As it was only a kilometre away and the first responders would have been going past your front door the next morning with their sirens blaring, it seems the sort of thing you would remember. Might you have been away overseas at the time?' asked Rachael, gesturing towards a large book on the coffee table titled *The Musee D'Orsay*.

'No, I don't think so.'

Rachael waited a few seconds before asking her next question. 'Dianne, do you know a Detective Sergeant

Cullen from Bendigo CIU?'

Dianne smiled. 'Oh, yes, Mark. I've known Mark since I was a child. Paul did as well. They went to school together at Marist Brothers College in Bendigo. Do you know him?'

'Yes, I do. Are you still friends with him?'

'Yes, why? How is that relevant?' Dianne was looking confused.

'Have you ever been to Tumut?' asked Rachael. Her instinct said to try to keep Dianne off balance.

'No. Tumut, where's that?'

'It's a small town in the Snowy Mountains. Are you sure you've never been?'

'Yes, I am sure I haven't been there. Why?'

'Maybe you took a holiday and passed through the town?'

'No, I've never heard of the place,' Dianne said.

'You're sure?' asked Rachael.

'Yes, I'm positive,' said Dianne, impatiently. 'What are you talking about?'

Rachael gave a faintest of smiles. 'Because after the accident your husband apparently told Detective Sergeant Cullen that you were on a caravanning holiday and that you were both staying in Tumut on the night of the accident.'

Dianne looked confused. 'If that's the case, why were you asking whether I was here that night?'

'We are re-looking at everything about that night, looking at any errors made or inaccurate statements. Everything.' Rachael let that last word hang in the air for a second. 'So if you weren't on a caravanning holiday in Tumut and you weren't here, where were you that night?'

'Look, maybe we were in that place. A lot of those towns are the same. I must have forgotten we were there.' Dianne made a move to get up from the couch to put the conversation to an end. Rachael and Amit stayed seated, looking up at her.

Dianne sat slowly back down.

'Do you have a diary or journal that could help confirm it for us?' asked Amit.

'No, I don't. I don't know why you'd be digging around all this time later. Aren't there crimes happening now that you could be investigating?'

'Justice matters, Mrs King,' said Amit. 'It has no expiry date.'

Amit and Rachael stared at Dianne, who nodded, looking chastised.

'So tell me about your business here,' asked Amit.

'We produce free-range eggs.'

'Is that what the sheds are for?' he asked.

'Yes.'

'Don't free-range chickens live outside, running around in paddocks?' asked Rachael, feigning naïveté. She had seen videos of free-range chicken sheds on the Animal Action website, with thousands of chickens crowded together, living in their own filth.

Dianne laughed, shaking her head. 'That's just what people want to see in their television ads. Happy chooks running around. The only way to make that commercially viable would be to sell eggs in the shops for fifty dollars a dozen, and nobody's buying that. But they are out of battery cages in those sheds, so they are free-range.' Dianne sounded defiant, as if she had been defending the company's ethics for many years.

'Have you ever had any issues with animal rights people?'

'Oh, every now and again. But those people only care about the animals—they never worry about the poor families trying to make money. Every once in a while we would get people trying to break in and take pictures or release the chickens. Just common criminals, one and all. Meanwhile we're the ones paying our taxes and being law-abiding citizens.'

'What would happen when these people were on the property?'

'Back in the day, Paul would chase them off.' Dianne hesitated for a moment. 'Off the property, I mean.'

'Did you ever tell the police about this trespassing?'

'Yes, we used to tell Mark, because he's the only policeman we know. Sometimes Paul would call Mark if he heard them and Mark would drive out and let them know to leave and not return.'

'Did Mark, Detective Sergeant Cullen, ever arrest anyone out here?'

'No, we thought that if we did that there would be court appearances. We didn't want to breed more trespassers through the publicity court cases would have attracted.'

'So no paperwork then?'

'Not that I know of. Mark got results the old-school way, none of this *pat them on the head* policing. Mark's dad was like that too when we were growing up.'

'So did Mark come out on the night of the accident?'

'What do you mean?'

Rachael replied quickly. 'Did you or your husband call Mark out that night?'

'No, neither of us did.'

'So, you were here that night?'

'No, no, I didn't say that. I can't remember where I was. I already said that.'

'But you're sure that Detective Sergeant Cullen wasn't here that night?'

'Yes, as far as I remember.'

'But you said you didn't remember being here either. Isn't that right?' Rachael knew she was starting to badger Dianne.

'I just can't remember, Detective. Sorry I can't be a better help.'

Rachael wasn't sure whether Dianne was being evasive or actually couldn't remember. She did know she was getting nowhere with her line of questioning. She would need to find more information and come at Dianne another day.

'Do you mind if we have a look at the sheds?' asked Rachael, switching gears.

Dianne hesitated. 'What? No, you can't. You're a potential bio-hazard,' she said.

Rachael smiled at her. Dianne looked confused at the out-of-context smile. Rachael wanted to leave her off balance.

'Okay, if you think of anything else, please give us a call.' Rachael pulled out a business card and placed it on the table as she and Amit stood up. 'Thanks for your time.'

They walked out the door with Dianne King looking far less self-assured than when they had arrived. As they drove away, Rachael shook her head. 'Based on her reactions, that alibi of theirs is highly suspect. Glad we didn't call ahead, else she would've got her story straight beforehand. But Mark took the statement from the husband, and now he's dead. I would love to have a trace on her phone right now. I'd bet she's calling Mark as we speak.'

'We need to see Johannes Petra,' said Amit. 'We'll need to tread very carefully until we know where he sits in all this. If this all blows up, shrapnel will fly in all directions. Including back at us.'

17

Professional Standards Command was located at the Victoria Police Centre on Flinders Street in Melbourne's central business district. Rachael and Amit parked in the car park and made their way to the lobby.

'Detectives Schlank and Pandit from Cold Case Unit to see Johannes Petra,' Rachael said as they showed their badges. The police officer at reception wrote their names and badge numbers in a book and gave them visitor passes hanging from plain black lanyards.

'If you wait over there, someone will come for you shortly.' The officer picked up the phone, all the time eyeing them both suspiciously.

Rachael and Amit rolled their eyes at each other as they wandered over to the chairs in the reception area. 'Guess she thinks we're here to be investigated, rather than investigating,' said Amit laughing, holding the visitor badge and examining it.

The elevator dinged and a tall blond man strode out towards them. His shirtsleeves were partly rolled up and he wasn't wearing a tie. He gave them both a friendly smile and put his hand out to shake hands.

'Hi, Johannes Petra.'

'Hi Johannes. Rachael Schlank and Amit Pandit from Cold Case.' They shook hands.

'Yes, I thought I recognised your name when you called, Rachael. You were up at Bendigo years ago, weren't you?'

'Yes, that was me.'

'Yeah, I remember now,' he said, smiling warmly.

'Somewhere we can chat?' she asked.

'Coffee shop chat or interview room chat?'

'Coffee shop should be okay,' Rachael said.

'Great, let's head across the road. Let me take those,' Johannes said, pointing at their visitor badges.

Rachael and Amit handed back the badges, which Johannes dropped back on the reception desk before meeting them at the door.

'It's just across and down the road a bit,' he said, leading the way.

They walked into the café, deserted after the lunchtime rush. The waiter came over for their order.

'Flat white with soy milk for me, thanks,' said Johannes.

'Caffe latte with soy milk for me,' said Rachael.

Amit laughed. 'Regular flat white, thanks.'

Rachael nodded then turned to Johannes. 'As I said on the phone, we're looking at a cold case from 2007 that you and Mark caught, the twin fatal car crash up near Bendigo.'

'Yes, I remember the one, and I reviewed my notes after you called. I'm afraid we didn't get too far with it. No witnesses to the crash, no third-party DNA, no prints, no paint transfer. We got the confirmation from Major Collision telling us the make and model of the tyre the week after the crash. They also told us the most probable vehicle we were looking for was a Commodore VZ built within the previous two years. Then we got on to VicRoads to get a list of relevant car registrations so we could start checking. We got nowhere with that, or with locals who had the tyres as replacements, unfortunately.'

'So who organised to get the list from VicRoads, you or Mark?' asked Rachael.

'Mark did. It was weird he didn't ask me to do it, actually. His usual way was to get the junior partner to do all of the grunt work. I remember thinking he was beginning to treat me like a proper partner for once, but it was short lived.'

'So, how did you divvy up the list?'

The coffees arrived and they all stopped talking for a moment. Rachael noticed that Johannes' sleeve had ridden up: a tattoo was visible on the lower half of his arm. It was a downward facing dagger with Latin written across it. *Foras Admonitio.*

As the waiter walked away, Petra continued. 'Mark just gave me a list of names a day later when they came through from VicRoads. He gave me about half of them and said to get started going out to interview everyone. There were just over a hundred names in total so it took a while to speak to them all. Everyone checked out or, at least, no one I interviewed stuck out as a suspect. They were all pretty relaxed under questioning.'

'You've got a great memory. This was all a long time ago.'

Johannes smiled. 'Not really. I keep personal notes

of all my cases, in addition to the official diaries, which are in the archives. Just in case.'

'In case of what?' asked Amit.

'Who knows. Someone from Cold Case might drop by,' he said, smiling at them. 'Or perhaps a journo. And I've just always had a thing about accountability, you know. Guess it's why I've ended up at Professional Standards Command.'

'Fair enough,' said Rachael. 'Do you have your notes handy?'

'Very.' Johannes pulled a diary from his back pocket and opened it where the ribbon sat. It was long and thin, with Monday to Wednesday on the left hand page, Thursday to Sunday on the right. The pages were filled with tiny writing, covering the entire surface, with only the dates unmarked. *Obsessive compulsive?* thought Rachael.

'I've got the main activities that I did on the case listed here,' he said, 'although any notes I took are in the official diary, which will still be stored up at Bendigo CIU.'

'So, what date did Mark get the records from VicRoads that you divided up?' asked Rachael.

Johannes ran his fingertip down the pages. 'Okay, the crash happened early on Friday 6 April and we got the report from the Major Collision Unit on the following Wednesday 11 April. Mark immediately requested the data on Commodore VZs from VicRoads and we got it next day, the twelfth, a Thursday. The rest of that week and the next were spent interviewing the owners of the cars.'

'How was the list split between you both?'

Petra looked back at his diary. 'My first call was to a Fred Langer.' He flipped over to the next page. 'Yes, I had L through to Z. Mark took A through to K. I started at the top of my list and went from there. As I said, we had nothing to allow us to prioritise any one person over another, so I started at the top and went through it alphabetically.'

'Going back to the crash scene. No phones were found. Did you think that was strange?'

Johannes sat back in his chair. 'Yes, we sure did. I mean reception is patchy out there, but surely women like that would have had phones anyway. They both owned mobile phones, but we found none, despite a good search. Anyway, the phone issue went into the list of unknowns. We tried calling their phones that day and the next, but they were turned off, or out of battery, so that was that.'

'So why do you think Grace and Helen were out there that night?' Rachael asked before taking another sip of her coffee.

'I think they were out there on some sort of animal cruelty mission. I mean, they were dressed for it: all in black, even down to their socks and sneakers. But there was nothing reported to police anywhere nearby. The closest factory farm to the scene, PK Farm, was vacant that night. Mark spoke to the owners the day after the crash and they were away on holidays. Caravanning, I believe.'

Rachael noticed Amit's quick glance up. Johannes had just confirmed the information Emma Jennings had told Rachael: that Mark had received Paul King's alibi the day after the crash, not a week later.

Johannes continued, 'Those factory farms usually

have high-grade security and they would get on the phone if there was any trespassing or break and enters. Plus, they usually have weapons and they're more than happy to pull them out, legally or not.' Johannes paused. 'But the strange thing was that we found no video cameras or even digital cameras in the wreck. We were sure we'd find some tech, seeing as the victims were animal rights people, and then we could have viewed the footage and progressed the case, but there were no cameras found.'

Rachael and Amit shared a quick look. She wanted to ask about Emma telling Mark that the Animal Action video cameras were missing, but decided to hold off on that for the moment. Amit instinctively understood what she was thinking.

'So how did you find the attitude of the Animal Action people?' asked Rachael.

'You'd have to ask Mark about that one. He left me up there interviewing Commodore owners and came on his own down to Melbourne to interview the people connected to Animal Action and the victims' families. I remember him saying that it sounded like the two women had broken protocol if they were on a mission on their own.'

'Thanks, Johannes, that's very helpful. By the way, how did you get along with Mark?'

'Okay, I guess,' Johannes started cautiously. 'He was my partner, but he liked having authority over people. You know what he's like from when you were stationed up there. Why?'

'Just wondering. His nose was a bit put out when we went to see him. Are you still friends with him?'

Johannes laughed. 'No; he is okay to work with I

suppose, but I wouldn't socialise with him through choice. Plus, I am with Professional Standards Command now, and you know what the rank and file officers think of us.'

'Got it. Thanks for your time, Johannes. We may need to speak again. By the way, what does the writing on the tattoo mean?' Rachael asked, pointing at his arm.

'Ah, that's from my army days. Means *Without Warning*. I was a corporal in the Fourth Battalion, Royal Australian Regiment. Called Second Commando Regiment now. Did three tours in Afghanistan before I joined the police force.'

'Must have been a big change.'

'Yes, fewer people trying to kill you makes a big difference,' Johannes said, smiling.

'Thanks for seeing us today. We really appreciate it.'

They got up to leave. Rachael took a twenty-dollar note from her pocket and gave it to the waiter, waving Johannes' hand away when he reached for his wallet.

'Thanks,' he said. 'Next time I'll buy the coffees.'

Rachael received her change and receipt. They walked back across the road together, shook hands with Johannes and said goodbye.

Amit waited until Johannes was well out of earshot before he spoke. 'What do you make of all that?'

'Well, Johannes is certain that Mark told him he spoke to the owner of PK Farm the day after the crash, which gels with what Emma Jennings told me. But if Mark had actually taken a statement from the King couple the day after the crash, he wouldn't have taken another one a week later.'

'Right, why take two statements a week apart

confirming the same thing?'

'So I'm thinking this statement Mark allegedly took the day after the crash never actually happened.' Rachel paused. It was a big allegation to make against a serving police officer, even just in a casual conversation like this on the side of the road. 'The other thing is the video cameras. Emma Jennings is adamant she told Mark that the video cameras were missing, yet Mark has completely ignored this in the case file. No mention at all.'

Amit shut his eyes for a moment. 'I get the feeling this case is about to blow up on us. I can't see any way it isn't ending up in a Professional Standards Command investigation.'

'I agree, but I don't think now is the right time to let PSC know. For one thing, Johannes Petra works there now and I think we have to get a better handle on whatever the truth is before we let them know.'

'And we don't know what Johannes really knows about the inconsistencies in the case,' said Amit. 'I mean, he seemed perfectly cooperative, but who knows.

'Exactly. Plus, any PSC investigation is always massive and would completely overshadow our review. Once we get clarity on what we've got here, then we can let PSC in on the action.'

Amit nodded. 'Okay, but be careful, and make sure your notes are perfect.'

18

Rachael walked through the paddock, looking around the trees for Billy. She could hear him baaing in the distance. Eventually she spotted him behind a tree, standing nonchalantly, chewing some grass. He lifted his nose in recognition and started to walk towards her. Suddenly he stopped, as Rachael heard footsteps coming up behind her. A group of people pushed past her, knocking her shoulder as they went by. Billy was staring at them, motionless. Rachael saw the knives in the hands of the crowd. The mass of people surrounded Billy and he was gone from view.

She ran, trying to yell for them to stop, but no sound came from her mouth. She hit and slapped at their backs, trying to pry a wedge in to get to the sheep, but the people formed a solid mass. Rachael felt warmth at her feet and looked down. She stopped and saw a line of blood trailing behind the mob of people as they continued to move away.

Rachael woke with a start, gasping for air, her eyes wet with tears. She sat up and quickly looked around the darkened room, as she slowly realised it had been a dream.

She slid down the side of the bed to the carpet. Hugging her knees to her chest, Rachael silently watched the lights of the city absently, her mind a blur.

Five hours later Rachael stifled a yawn as she sat at her desk, the report into Paul King's death opened in front of her.

The report stated that the body of Paul King was found at seven am on Monday 7 November, 2016, by one of his employees arriving for work. He was found lying beside the garage adjoining his house. He was fifty-five years old, five foot ten and morbidly obese. When he was discovered, he was wearing expensive designer glasses, jeans and a white shirt.

He had died from a self-inflicted gunshot wound to the head from a Beretta 92, a semi-automatic pistol, which was found next to his body. One bullet was missing from the gun's magazine. The serial number on the gun had been destroyed. How the gun came to be in his possession was never discovered.

The report stated that the King family had no significant debts and, by the account of Dianne King, they had a good marriage.

The toxicology analysis stated there were no traces of drugs or alcohol in his system. Gunpowder residue was found on the victim's hands.

Dianne was on holiday in Paris when her husband's body was discovered. She returned to Australia immediately on receiving the news.

Paul King had left no note. It was determined that he had been dead approximately six hours when he was found, meaning he had died around one am.

Rachael looked at the photographs of the body and a head and shoulders photograph of Paul King that had been supplied by his wife. It was a photograph taken for the business, maybe for the website or a conference. The photo showed a chubby-faced man smiling coldly at the camera.

She went back to the start of the report to check who had been assigned to investigate the suicide. Mark Cullen and Johannes Petra. Rachael sat back in her chair. 'You've got to be kidding me,' she said aloud.

Amit Pandit rolled his chair back from his desk so he could see her. 'What's up?'

'Paul King's suicide. I'll give you two guesses which detectives investigated.'

'By the look on your face, I only need one,' said Amit.

'I know Bendigo isn't that big a place, so them catching the case isn't a huge surprise, but still...'

'I would have thought Mark would have not taken the call to go out there, seeing as it was his friend,' said Amit.

'Agreed,' said Rachael. 'I would have got them to send someone else when I heard the address.'

Rachael looked up and noticed Kate West walking towards her.

'Hi there. Sounds like you're making headway into your case, but I've got some news. I spoke to the DI at Homicide, Tom Parker. You've been requested to join a taskforce for the next couple of weeks. It's those killings in the country—the duck hunter and the horse trainer. They're worried they might be witnessing the start of a serial killer's career.'

'Okay,' said Rachael, stunned by the news.

'The Taskforce is being led by Rob Morello. They need you upstairs at eleven this morning for a briefing. Any questions?'

'No,' said Rachael, her shoulders dropping slightly.

Kate looked at her. 'Don't worry. You're coming back here. I'm not in the habit of losing talent.'

Rachael smiled, relieved. 'Thanks, boss. See you in a few weeks then.'

'No worries; just get the cold case filed away so you can pick it up running when you get back.'

Kate turned and walked away.

'Well, I guess that's that for now,' Rachael said.

Amit shrugged. 'Good luck.'

19

Rachael entered the conference room. Rob Morello saw her; broke away from a group of people gathered around a whiteboard and walked over, his hand outstretched. 'Rachael, good to see you again,' he said, shaking hers.

'Good to see you too, Rob,' said Rachael.

'Let's introduce you to the crew. Excuse me,' said Rob, addressing the people standing together. They stopped talking and turned.

'This is Detective Senior Constable Rachael Schlank from Cold Case. Rachael, you know Detective Inspector Tom Parker and Julie Wang from when you were working here.' Rachael smiled and nodded at Tom and Julie, who nodded back. 'I'm not sure if you know Mark Cullen and Dave Boucher from Bendigo CIU?'

'Yes, I do. I was based in Bendigo years ago.' Rachael gave a nod to Dave first and then to Mark.

'Great to see you again, Rachael,' said Mark enthusiastically, a broad smile across his face. Rachael saw Dave give Mark a confused sideways glance. She gave Mark a subdued smile back. *Okay, that's new.*

They sat around the table, DI Parker at the head. Dave sat next to Rachael, while Rob, Julie and Mark sat on the opposite side.

Rachael had been relieved when she had heard Rob and Julie were on the crew from Homicide. Although she had not worked on any cases with them directly, they had a good reputation as a team that got the job done. Her stomach had tightened though when she learned Mark was on board. *Small world*, she thought when she had heard.

Two whiteboards were set up against the corridor windows. At the top of each of them was one of the victims' names, with crime scene photographs and headshots for each from when they were alive. On Steve Lawrence's board was a photograph of the soft-point .308 Winchester bullet, mangled and deformed. Alongside it was a photograph of an un-fired version, a long copper-coloured round with a flat dull grey tip. On Jim Camella's board was a photograph of the arrow that killed him, three angled blades at its point.

Tom sat back in his chair and addressed the room. 'Okay, welcome to Operation Torchlight. Since three of you are from outside Homicide, this is the way things will run. Rob Morello is running the Taskforce. His word is final. He and I will have regular meetings to bring me up to speed and discuss developments. You'll meet here every morning to coordinate your activities. Now Mark and Dave are here from Bendigo CIU because they caught the case originally with the duck hunter and they have local knowledge of people and geography. Rachael, we asked you to come back because you are highly skilled and have experience working in Homicide, plus you've spent time out there too. Rob, can you bring us up to date on the cases?'

Rob opened his folder. Over the next twenty minutes, he and Julie outlined everything they knew about the two killings. The new members of the Taskforce took notes as they spoke.

Julie was wrapping up her summary of the second killing, '…again, the scene was clear of evidence apart from the Magnum boot prints and another note. Just one word. *Pests*. This time there was a logo printed on the note as well, from a company called PK Farm.'

Rachael looked up sharply at Rob, who was passing the photograph of the second note to Julie. She slid it on it on quickly to Mark. Rachael looked across at Mark, who was staring hard at the photograph of the note in his hands. Slowly he slid it across the table to Dave.

'What does PK Farm do?' asked Dave.

'They are a large scale egg producer, just south of Bendigo,' said Julie. 'Big contracts with the major supermarket chains.'

'Hence the chicken feather taped to the first crime scene's note,' said Dave, nodding.

'Correct,' said Rob, 'except we don't really know what it means. We've spoken to the owner of PK Farm and she claims to know nothing about it. Same with employees and ex-employees.'

'So, there is definitely a link,' said Julie, 'but what that is, is currently unknown.'

'Based on these two cases, what we appear to have is a vigilante going eye-for-an-eye against hunters,' said Rob. 'I've checked with the other police forces in the country, including the Federal Police. No crimes like this have been reported anywhere else.'

'Rob, there is one thing you all need to know,' said Rachael. 'Before coming across to the Taskforce I was working a cold case and PK Farm was being looked at as part of the investigation.'

'How do you mean?'

Rachael ignored Mark's gaze from across the table.

'There was a twin fatality car crash in 2007 involving animal rights activists,' said Rachael. 'They hit a tree at high speed while being chased by an unknown second vehicle. PK Farm is the closest factory farm to the crash site and therefore the most obvious place that these women may have been before they died. I was just there yesterday conducting an interview and checking alibis.'

'Where's that at?' Rob asked.

'Still early days, but this all seems weirdly coincidental, seeing that the cold case in 2007 involved animal activists and these homicides appear to be about animal cruelty *and* are being linked by the killer back to PK Farm.'

'Any suspects?'

'No, not yet. Just a lot of questions without answers at present,' said Rachael, turning her head towards Mark and meeting his stare. *Why isn't Mark saying that he originally investigated the crash?*

'Okay,' said Rob, 'we'll keep it in mind. It may be relevant, but it is more probably coincidental.'

Rachael nodded. 'The other thing I was thinking was that the second victim's court case could've piqued our killer's interest in this guy.'

Across the table Mark sat smiling, shaking his head. 'Sure. Except that our first victim, the duck hunter, hadn't been to court for animal cruelty, so how does that fit your theory?'

Sitting beside Mark, Julie interjected, 'The day before Steve Lawrence died was the opening day of the duck hunting season and he was interviewed on the TV news, talking about how duck hunting was all about conservation and how humane it is. Humane, just like the note says. All our killer needed to do was watch the TV news to find his targets.'

Mark kept his eyes on Rachael and continued to shake his head slowly. She held his stare.

'Doesn't shooting ducks classify as animal cruelty?' asked Rachael.

'Well, it is legal, isn't it?' said Mark.

'Duck hunting. Sure, it is legal. But there's plenty of animal cruelty that's legal. Circuses, hunting, rodeos, marine parks. What's legal isn't always the best gauge of what's ethical,' said Rachael, remembering the postcard she'd picked up at the animal rights event. 'And this guy doesn't seem to be using legality to gauge what's right and wrong, at least in his own mind.'

'Ah, for fuck's sake—' Mark was still shaking his head.

'Okay, enough of that,' Rob said firmly. 'We need to go at this from every angle at the same time. First up, we are going to look for a personal link between the victims. Go right back. They may have crossed paths before. Mark and Dave, go and see if Steve Lawrence's family and friends have heard of Jim Camella. Julie, you do the same with Jim Camella's family and friends. See if they know of Steve Lawrence. Rachael, in the case of our killer being unknown to either victim, I need you to go upstairs and see Detective Senior Sergeant Debbie Flint. She's a profiler and we need her input to get an idea of the kind of person we could be looking at here.'

'Yes, got it,' said Rachael.

'I want everyone to review all of the evidence from the first two crime scenes. We have the walk-through video taken at both scenes and the sketch artist maps detailing the sites and all known facts. I need everyone across this information by lunchtime today. Okay, let's get to it,' said Rob, flipping his folder shut and standing up. Everyone took this as a cue and stood up as well. Mark was the last to rise. They all walked out of the conference room and headed in different directions.

Rachael's mind was racing. As soon as she had mentioned the possible link between her cold case and PK Farm, Mark should have told Rob he originally worked the case. She knew that there was something very wrong with the original investigation of her cold case, but she couldn't progress that case whilst she was on the Taskforce. If she spoke up now, without necessary proof, she would be seen to be throwing allegations around against a senior detective. The cold case would be pulled from her in a heartbeat. It would also be career suicide.

Walking back to her temporary desk Rachael could feel heavy footsteps behind her, keeping at the same speed. *Mark*.

She reached up to her lapel and clicked the button, switching on the digital recorder.

'Fucking bitch,' he whispered under his breath.

Rachael spun around quickly, causing Mark to flinch backwards.

'What did you say to me?' she asked.

'I think you heard. What right have you got to take over this investigation?'

'What are you talking about, Mark? That meeting is for sharing information and ideas. What do you think it's for? Do you still think I should be there just to smile sweetly, agree with everything you say and take notes like in your idea of the good old days?'

Mark just stared at her, fuming, but silent.

Rachael pointed a finger at his chest and looked him directly in the eye. 'You may think I am a bitch, but I am not your bitch. Got it?'

She turned again and continued walking towards her desk. *Fuckstick.*

20

Rachael had taken Detective Senior Sergeant Debbie Flint, a forensic psychologist, through everything they had so far. They sat in her office poring over the files and the crime scene photographs. Although there was a lot of material on the table in front of them, Rachael realised how little substantial information was actually there.

'A smart guy,' said Debbie.

'Why's that?'

'Two separate killings and no real evidence, that's why. No fingerprints, no bullet casing left behind at the swamp, no prints on the arrows from the horse trainer's property, no DNA, no leads. Only one real witness at each scene and both saw nothing except the victims falling. Most people who get caught give themselves away. Or tell someone what they're doing. Not this guy. He's going to be hard to catch because he's not going to help us too much. He's too careful. Everything we currently know is information he is purposefully telling us. The link to PK Farm is obviously the biggest clue at the moment.'

Rachael nodded. 'I was telling the team downstairs that I've just been working on a cold case involving the deaths of two women, both animal activists, in a crash. They were run off the road and into a tree not far away from PK Farm. The owner, Paul King, had the right vehicle to have been the chaser, but was alibied as being interstate that night. Trouble is, the owner is now dead. Suicided last November.'

'Whoever is leaving the notes might be incorrectly assuming a link between your cold case and PK Farm, and must not know about the alibi,' said Debbie.

'That's the other thing. Based on my cold case investigation, that alibi now looks highly suspect.'

'Okay, well that changes things.'

'It sure does. And because you will be presenting your profile to us, you should know that the detective sergeant who took the original alibi is now on the Taskforce with me. He caught the original shooting, the duck hunter, and he and his partner were drafted in as they know the area and understand the culture up there.'

'Messy,' said Debbie.

'In a word, yes.'

'Thanks for the heads up.'

'No worries,' said Rachael.

'I'll be able to give you a picture of what the offender would typically be like, but there are always outliers who slip through. Hopefully your guy is typical for all our sakes.'

Rachael felt her phone vibrate in her pocket. She took it out and saw a text message from a number she didn't recognise. *Coffee? – Wang.*

An hour later Rachael was sitting in a café two hundred metres from the Homicide office. Julie Wang walked in, her limp less obvious than it had been that morning. She noticed Rachael looking at her leg as she came closer to the table.

'I needed to take my leg for a walk,' said Julie smiling. 'It works better the more I walk on it. That's why I didn't suggest the café downstairs. Coffee?'

'Yes, flat white with soy milk, thanks.'

Julie went up to the counter and ordered, before sitting down again.

Rachael smiled. 'Sorry, I didn't mean to be staring when you came in.'

'Don't sweat it. It doesn't hurt, just kind of goes to sleep if I spend too long cooped up behind a desk. It actually keeps me active as I need to exercise it to keep it working properly. I never know when I'll need to start sprinting after a crook.'

'I prefer it when they just put their hands behind them to be cuffed, like the ladies and gentlemen they could have been if they'd tried a little harder,' said Rachael. They both laughed.

'The other good thing about this café is that no one else at Homicide will go this far for a coffee, so we can chat in peace,' said Julie. 'Hey, look, what's the story with Mark? I overheard some of your conversation in the hallway after the meeting this morning. You two don't seem to be any sort of love connection.'

'No. Mark was at Bendigo CIU when I was starting out. He gave me a hard time and there was not a lot I could do. Eventually I got offered a transfer to Armed Crime, and I walked in on Mark giving the office a graphic description about how I supposedly got the job. All very sexual. I let him have it right there in front of most of the squad. Once I'd been at Armed Crime for a few months I found out someone had been feeding rumours into the department about me having been transferred from Bendigo because I had some sort of dodgy relationship with a suspect. Very vague and complete bullshit. It was Mark's parting gift to me. Made it hard to settle in at the new squad with that hanging over me.'

Julie shook her head.

Rachael looked up. Julie's eyes were full of pity.

'Hey,' said Rachael, 'I survived. No need to look so sad.'

'No, it's not that. I just remembered that when you first transferred to Homicide a few years ago there was a persistent rumour that you were an informant for Professional Standards Command. That was why people were stand-offish with you at first. Probably why I didn't reach out either, I am sorry to say.'

The waiter arrived with the coffees as Rachael let Julie's words sink in. 'Well, that might also have been Mark's work,' she said after a few seconds. Rachael shook her head. *Would he still be doing it after all this time? I left Bendigo CIU nine years ago.*

'Fuck, this is awful,' said Julie. 'Do you want me to have a chat with Rob and get Mark tossed off the Taskforce?'

Rachael took a breath. 'No, I'm tough enough to deal with him. I just need to not engage in his games—it will infuriate him—and then I'll win. So, it's my turn to ask some questions. What's Rob like?'

'Rob is great. You know he got outed on social media a while back, don't you?'

'Yes, could hardly miss it.'

'Well, the gossip around Homicide about him was running hot for a few days, but he just got on with the job and ignored the whole thing. Soon enough everyone just forgot about it. The good thing that came out of it was that our relationship as partners really improved. I always had the impression that he was holding back on me, but once he was out he relaxed and let me under his guard. Since then we've become much closer. He's a lot happier now as well. He told me he loves being able to go out with his boyfriend without having to worry about running into colleagues. And the best thing about Rob is that he will always back you up. Always. I trust him like family.'

'Sounds good. So, what's your story?' asked Rachael.

'Well, I was in uniform when I got shot and it took me a while to finish rehab and get back to work. There had been a lot of press when the shooting happened, seeing as for a while there they thought that I might lose the leg. The media loved it—some big diversity success story— the Chinese-Australian police officer kills the drug dealer who shot her. Magazines kept hounding me for makeover stories, can you believe it? So when I did start work again it was hard. I couldn't do foot patrol or public events because people recognised me and wanted to take selfies all day. It was easy to spot the tall, limping Asian police officer when I was in uniform. Eventually I got offered the chance to train as a detective and I was then based in the suburbs doing general casework for a few years. I became the go-to detective for any cases involving Chinese people. One day there was a homicide in a Chinese family and I got sent over to help work it with Rob and his partner. We wrapped up the case quickly and I went back to normal duties. A year later the partner got sick of dealing with murder every day and transferred out, and Rob gave me a call. I've been there ever since.'

Looks like you fell on your feet in the end,' said Rachael, finishing her coffee.

'As soon as I recovered from being knocked on my arse by that bullet. Yeah, you could say so.' They both smiled as they stood to go.

'Coffees are on me,' said Rachael, waving Julie away as she reached into her bag.

'Thanks, next time we'll make it wine. My treat,' said Julie.

'Sounds like a fine plan.'

21

Detective Senior Sergeant Debbie Flint stood in the conference room at the Homicide offices. The five members of the Operation Torchlight Taskforce sat in front of her.

'Thanks for coming in this morning, Debbie. We really appreciate it,' said Rob Morello.

'No worries. Rachael has taken me through everything you have and I've put together a profile of our potential suspect. Let's get started.'

Debbie looked down the table. 'The killer is most likely a white male between thirty and fifty years of age. His age is an estimate based on two factors, the first being the care taken removing evidence from the crime scene. This requires a degree of maturity and good impulse control. The second factor is that he would need to be fit enough to get in and out of environments quickly while carrying a large weapon. He is a smart person, IQ most probably over one hundred and thirty, resourceful and organised. It is most likely that the killer is working solo.

'I believe he is most probably living between Melbourne and Bendigo, within an hour by car either side of the Calder Freeway joining the two places. He would be operating within his comfort zone, and have well-planned escape routes, should he require them.

'He is a functional individual, probably in steady employment, but in a job where he has a large amount of flexibility and is able to manage his commitments and movements without supervision. He could be a business owner, a tradesman, or be in some job not tied to a desk. He is an organised killer, which means that he is likely in a relationship, and this relationship may appear normal or even mundane. If he were a disorganised killer he would most likely be single.'

Mark tapped his pen on the table. 'And if he was disorganised, we'd probably have caught him by now,' he said, half-smiling.

'Go on, Debbie,' said Rob, eyeing Mark.

'He most likely lives in a house with a garage attached, where he can maintain and transfer his weapons in and out of the car in private.'

'The killer has, since childhood, been driven by a deeply held sense of personal justice, but not necessarily justice in the traditional law and order sense. He lives by a moral code he has developed over many years, possibly influenced or taught to him by a mentor of some sort, maybe a parent or sibling, or somebody he worked with.

'He is obviously going eye-for-an-eye in the way he kills his victims, but I would not say he is necessarily a religious type of person, although he may have been as a child. I'd say it's more likely than not that he is an atheist who believes people should be held accountable for their actions here on earth, rather than in some potential afterlife.

'The notes are unusual in that they are so short. Just the one word on each. Also, the words are not consistent. *Pests* is a negative word and *Humane* is positive. It may be that these words are somehow connected to things that the victims have said to people before, possibly even directly to the killer, to justify their hunting activities. I know the first victim used the word *Humane* when he was interviewed on the TV news the night before he was killed, but to me that seems a bit too close to the time of the shooting. He would be organising this with more than twelve hours' planning. This guy is not that impulsive. I would say that the duck hunting victim has used the word *Humane* before that TV interview and that your killer has picked up on that. Through the notes he is building a message for you, one word at a time.'

Julie half-raised her hand. 'We have checked their entries on social media—Facebook and such—there is no mention of the words there.'

'If that's the case then I would say it is more likely that the killer has been in direct contact with both victims,' said Debbie. 'The chicken feather attached to the first note and the PK Farm logo on the second are significant. He is giving us the best clue so far that his motivation for the killings is directly linked to that business in some way.'

Debbie glanced quickly at Rachael. Mark noticed and shot Rachael a look across the table.

'The Magnum boot prints are also a message. He has not covered his tracks at all there. They seem to have been left like a signature to link the crimes. He wants you to know that the crimes are being committed by a single person and not a group.'

Dave lifted his pen off the table. 'Do you think that

the size eleven boots could be misdirection? Maybe the killer is a size ten or ten and a half and is stuffing his shoes with newspaper or wearing thick socks?'

'That's certainly a possibility,' said Debbie, 'but based on everything I have seen so far, including the notes he is leaving, I don't think this guy is worrying too much about being caught. The fact he is so organised has him feeling confident.'

Dave nodded.

Debbie continued, 'The shooter sees himself as different from the general community, removed somehow. He is not a psychopathic killer, as he is showing empathy for the animals. True psychopaths cannot feel real empathy for anyone or anything. They mimic it to fit in with people, but it isn't real. Psychopaths only ever do things for themselves, not for any third parties. This guy is doing it for the animals. There is nothing in it for him.

'As he empathises with the pain animals feel, killing people would not be an entirely comfortable experience for him, but something he feels he has to do. He would probably feel he is on a quest of sorts. He is also sending a message to the community that he is out there and to think twice before hunting. He would feel he can trust animals, but not humans. He would literally see the killing of an animal on the same level as the murder of a human.

'He is obviously very comfortable with weapons. It is quite possible he has had military or law enforcement training some time in the past, or is a target shooter or a competitive archer. He may have grown up in a rural region where guns and compound bows are easier to access and use. It is likely he would be drawn to a military or police career, as he would see this as a way to right wrongs in an active way. Careers like this would not have worked out for him long term though, as he is an independent thinker who would not respond well to any orders he disagrees with, or which go against his own ethics.

'Membership of an animal rights group is a possibility, but unlikely in my estimation. Animal rights activists are generally ultra-compassionate and off the charts on sensitivity and empathy measures, so they're not people who would naturally be inclined to kill. They are also fairly social and this guy would prefer to do things solo.'

'Would you say this guy is acting like a typical serial killer?' asked Dave.

'He certainly is showing a number of signs,' said Debbie, 'although the empathy he is demonstrating about animals is very rare. The other thing is that the short time between the crimes indicates to me that he might be a spree killer, rather than a serial killer.'

'What's the difference?' asked Julie.

'Spree killers kill multiple times over a short period of time. There are usually three or more victims. They then might stop, whereas serial killers may kill over a longer period, with more time in between the murders, and it is more rare for them to stop. Both are hard to catch, but a spree killer can just stop one day and disappear altogether.'

Everyone sat mute, absorbing that news. If the killings were to stop suddenly, with so few clues and no leads, they would have a hard time making an arrest. The alternative was more deaths. Neither option looked good to any of the people in the room.

'The last thing is that assassin-type killers like this often tend to be paranoid and do not like making eye contact. That's basically it. If he was leaving other evidence along the way we would be able to surmise a whole lot more and be more specific, but that's as far as I can reach right now.'

'Okay: thanks, Debbie. That's a lot to digest,' said Rob. 'I want to get us working on people fitting the description who may have flunked out of the police or the defence forces over the past ten years. We need to speak to the Human Resources departments of all state and territory police forces, the federal police, plus the army, navy and air force. That's plenty of departments to cover. People discharged for refusing orders or operating outside the chain of command. We're most interested in those living in the region between Bendigo and Melbourne, or thereabouts. If anyone else looks good for this, flag them as well. And remember to cross match against the shoe size.'

Rob went to the whiteboard at the back of the room and wrote down the names of each agency. He wrote Rachael's name alongside Victoria Police, Dave's name with the New South Wales Police and Australian Capital Territory Police, and Mark against the Australian Defence Forces. Rob took on the South Australian, Queensland, Northern Territory and West Australian Police Forces. Julie got the Australian Federal Police, Tasmania Police and all the local archery and target shooting clubs. Rachael noted that Rob took on the biggest workload of the group himself, despite being the head of the taskforce.

Everyone got up to get to work.

22

Rachael sat down at her desk back in the Cold Case Unit. Amit rolled his chair back to see her. 'How goes it stranger? You back?'

'Hey Amit. Not yet. I just came downstairs to check messages before a meeting with human resources about the Taskforce case.'

'What's HR got to do with it?'

'Our profiler said that the perp may have been with the police or the military and could have been booted out because he didn't like to follow orders he doesn't agree with. So, we are data mining everywhere to try and find some potential persons of interest. I scored Victoria Police.'

'How are you going working with Mark?'

'You heard he was on the Taskforce, eh?'

'Yes, news travels fast,' said Amit.

'They pulled him and his partner, Dave Boucher, in from Bendigo. Mark is still being a prick, but that's just a normal day for him,' said Rachael.

'Did you want to come back down for lunch?' asked Amit. 'It's Tiffin Wednesday.'

Rachael smiled. One of the traditions Amit had brought to Cold Case was a traditional Indian lunch every Wednesday. A selection of curries was delivered to the office in tiffins, an old Indian custom, and it brought the team together.

'Thanks, but I might have to give it a miss this week.'

'No worries, more Mumbai Magic for me,' he said, smiling.

'Hey, quick question,' said Rachael. 'When I first was transferred here, did you hear any negative rumours about me?'

Amit pursed his lips and looked at her thoughtfully for a moment. 'There was talk you'd been kicked out of Homicide because you'd botched a case. I told the crew that it sounded like crap and to ignore it. Sorry, maybe I should have said something.'

Rachael was torn between her anger at Mark and her gratitude towards Amit for having her back. 'No, it's okay. It sounds like Mark has been spreading rumours about me to whichever department I was transferred to for the past nine years.'

Amit breathed out heavily. 'Fucker.'

'Yes, exactly,' said Rachael, barely suppressing a smile. She had never heard Amit swear before. She got up. 'Time to head off to HR. See you later.'

'See if you can arrange a pay rise for me while you're there.'

'Will do. And some extra sick days,' said Rachael, smiling as she walked.

23

Rachael packed away the files on her desk and picked up her bag, ready to leave for the day.

Julie looked up at her. 'Wine o'clock?'

Rachael thought for a moment. 'Sure, why not.'

'Excellent, there's a new bar nearby I've been wanting to try.'

Julie grabbed her bag and they walked towards Rob's office. 'We're heading out for a drink,' said Julie at his door. 'You want to join us?'

'Thanks, but Eddie is at home making dinner. It's our anniversary. Have fun though.'

'Congrats. We'll have a drink to you both,' said Julie.

'Keep yourselves tidy, ladies.'

'Always,' said Rachael, smiling.

'Or at least, usually,' laughed Julie.

They took the lift to the ground floor. As they walked out the door, a man passed them with his head down, walking in. Julie turned.

'Zachy, long time no see. How are you?'

The man turned back and stopped, his face suddenly

breaking into an easy smile.

'Jules, crikey, it's been ages.'

Rachael looked at the man as he hugged Julie. He had closely cropped hair and wore a black T-shirt and jeans. The only thing that told Rachael he was a police officer was the Victoria Police lanyard hanging around his neck, holding his ID.

He looked across at Rachael. She felt like her whole body was blushing.

'Oh, sorry,' said Julie. 'Zach, this is Rachael.'

Zach shook Rachael's hand, staring into her eyes. 'Good to meet you,' he said. Rachael's chest suddenly felt tight. *Stop it.*

'What are you doing here?' asked Julie.

'I was just heading back in to get my car from downstairs.'

'Come out and have a drink with us. There's a new place around the corner.'

Zach hesitated for a moment. 'Sure, can't stay long though.'

Julie strolled through the after-work crowd at the bar, her confidence seeming to create a path in front of her. Rachael and Zach followed behind in her wake.

The bar was the size of a large barn, with booths around the edges and tables scattered throughout. It was full of bespoke-suited finance workers, each trying to talk over one another, their collective noise creating a loud hum that bounced off the polished concrete floors. The repetitive beat of a pop song was battling unsuccessfully to break through.

'Noisy,' said Zach over Julie's shoulder. 'Let's find

a spot at the back.'

'Sure,' Julie said, correcting her course towards an empty booth.

'What are you drinking?' he asked them both as they arrived.

'Cold beer, dealer's choice,' said Julie. 'Thanks.'

'Same, thank you,' said Rachael.

'Too easy,' said Zach, as he turned and walked back towards the bar.

'So, what do you think?' asked Julie.

'About what?'

'About Zach.'

Rachael felt herself blush again, suddenly feeling thirteen. 'What…? I don't know. I just met him.'

'Listen, he's a great guy. We worked together for a couple of years. He's a straight up and down gentleman and it's obvious you're interested. I saw you blushing.'

Rachael shut her eyes. She hated this type of thing, but she knew Julie was right. She had been instantly drawn to Zach as soon as she saw him; she looked across to him waiting at the bar. 'Just be cool about it. You don't even know whether he's single,' said Rachael.

'No worries. I can do cool, you just watch,' said Julie.

I should have just gone straight home.

Rachael could see Zach from the corner of her eye walking back towards them with three beers.

'Three handcrafted beers from somewhere or another,' he said smiling, putting the beers down on the table. 'If you want all the details, the bartender can tell you what type of soil the hops were grown in. Sorry, I tuned out and just nodded.'

'Cheers,' said Julie and Rachael almost simultaneously, lifting their glasses.

'Cheers. So, how goes Homicide?'

'It's going okay,' said Julie. 'We're on that Taskforce chasing the guy who is killing hunters.'

'Yeah, I'm familiar with it—must be exciting,' said Zach.

'Not at present,' said Julie. 'More like frustrating. We're chasing a clever one—really we're waiting for him to slip up. How about you? You still with the spooks?'

'Yeah, it's been about three years now.' Zach looked across at Rachael, who looked confused. 'Sorry, spooks is Julie's term for Intelligence and Covert Support Command.'

Rachael nodded. *Undercover.*

'We don't hear much about you guys,' said Rachael.

'No, we try and stay off the radar. Working undercover is okay, but you can get to feeling like you have two heads sometimes.'

'What have you been working on?'

'I spent my first year embedded in a political hacking group. They were ultra-paranoid types, suspicious of everyone and everything, so it was hard work. They spent half the time doing surveillance on new recruits, me included, so I had to be *on* all the time. For the last couple of years I've been embedded with a few animal rights groups.'

Julie and Rachael quickly looked up at each other.

'What?' asked Zach.

Julie leaned forwards, lowering her voice slightly. 'The profiler working with us doesn't think it's likely that our killer might be a member of an animal rights group.

What do you think?'

Zach laughed. 'Seriously? I think they're right.'

'Are you saying that there's no one who could possibly do something like this?' asked Julie.

'I'd never say never, but—'

'What is it?' asked Julie after a moment.

'Let me have a think about it. In terms of activities they are doing around animals, they are relatively open with each other about what's going on. Makes it easy to keep track on things. I'll need to look at them through a different lens and see if anyone stands out for your case. There might be one or two. Not sure.'

'That would be great,' said Rachael. 'Thanks.'

'What are the groups like?' asked Julie.

'They're fairly open to new people and friendly. Compared to the political hacking group, they're a joy. The animal rights groups are more outwardly focused, trying to get people to see what they see. So they're easier to blend in with.'

'Aren't those groups worried about being infiltrated by the police?' asked Rachael, remembering her conversation with Emma Jennings from Animal Action.

'Yes, they're always on the lookout for people like me, but they haven't shown any sign of noticing me yet. One of the groups has kind of put me in charge of looking out for infiltrators. Ironic, eh?'

Zach gave Rachael a broad smile. They both laughed.

Rachael looked across at Julie, who was beaming back at her. *Very pleased with herself*, Rachael thought.

They all chatted like old friends for the next half hour. Rachael smiled; it felt good to be socialising.

'Another round?' asked Julie.

'Sure,' said Rachael.

'Just water for me; I'm driving,' said Zach.

'Cheap round then,' said Julie, wandering off to the bar.

'You're lucky to be teamed up with Jules,' he said to Rachael, when Julie was out of earshot.

Rachael smiled at Zach. 'Yes, she's been great.'

'Did you know she saved my life once?' asked Zach.

Rachael looked up sharply. 'What? No, I didn't.'

'It was when she got shot. We thought we'd cleared the house of suspects and were searching the rooms for drugs or drug paraphernalia. Then I heard the shot and went flying off in her direction—came around the corner into a bedroom and she was on the ground, bleeding badly from a leg wound. The window was open and my split second thought was that the offender had jumped out. I was focused on her and then suddenly the crim stepped out from behind a closet, his pistol pointed at me. She put two shots into him before I could even raise my gun. She was cool as a cucumber. She'll always have your back.'

Rachael realised that she had stopped breathing listening to the story. She took a sharp intake of breath.

At that moment, Julie arrived back at the table with a beer and a water. 'Bad news, I've just got a text. Got to bolt off. Sorry.'

Rachael smiled at her. *Subtle, real subtle.*

'What?' asked Julie, trying her best to look incredulous.

'No, nothing,' said Rachael. 'Can we help with your emergency?'

'No, I've got it covered. Rachael, I'll see you

tomorrow,' she said. 'Zach, you be good. I'll call you tomorrow to talk about any suspects you can ID for us.' She leaned across and kissed Zach on the cheek.

'No worries,' said Zach.

Julie walked triumphantly towards the door, and Rachael caught a glimpse of her smile reflected in the mirror behind the bar.

24

The morning light streamed into the conference room. Rachael walked in with a coffee, stopping short when she saw Julie sitting with Zach, files spread in front of them.

'Good morning,' she said.

'Hey Rach. Zach had some thoughts about our case after we spoke last night and texted me. We've just gone over the profile.'

Zach smiled at Rachael.

'That's good.' She smiled quickly back, before looking away and sitting down. *Be cool, Rachael.*

The other members of the Taskforce walked in and Julie introduced Zach to them all.

'Zach, Jules said she's taken you through the profile that Debbie Flint prepared. Do you have any thoughts based on what's in there?'

'Yes, we had a good read through it. The profile makes sense to me, and I'd agree it's unlikely that your guy is an animal rights activist. As Debbie noted, most animal rights people are sensitive types. Bloodshed horrifies them. I've been embedded undercover with these groups for a couple of years now and there are very few people I would classify as being remotely capable of this.'

'But there are some though, right?' asked Rob.

'Yes, there are two guys. One is Andrew Davies, thirty-four years old, works as a welder, from Melton. He is a passionate sort of bloke who gets fired up after a few beers.'

'And what does *fired up* sound like with this guy?' asked Rachael.

'He goes on a rant about wanting to take direct action against animal abusers. When you ask him what that means, he says these people should be taken out, permanently. If you ask him again after he's sobered up, he'll just shrug it off and say it was the beers talking. I don't think he's your guy, but it's better to be safe than sorry.'

'Any weapons experience?' asked Rob.

'Not that I'm aware of. I vetted him fairly rigorously regarding weapons after he talked about direct action. Told him I wanted to try target shooting for fun. He didn't seem to have any idea about weapons or where to get them. I think he's just a talker with beer bravado. He doesn't have a military or police background.'

'What about the other guy?'

'He is Martin Jamieson, twenty-eight-year-old computer programmer, single, lives in a share house in the northern suburbs, in Coburg. Works for a company in William Street here in the city. He's a quiet guy, but I see he's got a lot of pent-up aggression. He tends to disappear from the scene every now and then. People say he takes time out from the animal activist campaigns to chill out. When he comes back he's always calmer for a day or two, but then he gets angry at the world all over again.'

'What gets him so angry?' asked Dave.

'He sees the evidence of animal abuse and just can't stand the fact that the general public just doesn't care about it like he does. I've never heard him make threats of violence, but there is definite aggro in his eyes.'

'Any intel on his access to weapons?' asked Rachael.

'No, no deep intelligence on that,' said Zach. 'I checked this morning and he has nothing registered in his name. I doubt he would know how to shoot a gun or fire a crossbow, except on a video game. That's why I don't think he'll end up being your guy. He just wouldn't have the skills.'

'Thanks for that,' said Rob, 'but we're going after them both all the same.'

'Of course. I've got a copy of both of their files here. Photos included.' Zach opened his folder and pulled out two files, which he dropped on the table. 'They'll both be at work today. All the relevant details are in there, including addresses. Just be careful using any of the specific intelligence in there when you speak to them. I don't need my cover and two years of work destroyed by one interview.'

'We've got this,' said Julie, her tone reassuring.

Zach nodded. 'As I said, I wouldn't get your hopes up, as I think your guy is going to come from outside these groups.'

'Understood,' said Rob. 'We may need to get your help down the track, as things progress.'

'No worries, happy to help. If you don't need me for anything else, I should get back to it.'

'I think we're all good. We'll be in touch.'

Zach picked up his folder. 'Good luck with this one.' Rachael noticed him give Julie a wink as he was leaving.

'Any joy in linking our two victims?' asked Rob.

'No, we checked with Steve Lawrence's family and friends. They'd never heard of Jim Camella,' said Mark.

'Same story in the opposite direction,' said Julie. 'None of Jim's nearest and dearest knew of Steve Lawrence.'

'That sounds like a dead end,' said Rob. 'Okay, Mark and Dave, take a drive and go and question this Andrew Davies at Melton. Rachael and Julie, you head over to William Street and chat to Martin Jamieson, the computer programmer. If either of them looks remotely likely, pull them in for a chat.'

Rachael stood up and picked up the two files where Zach had left them. She dropped one of the files on the table in front of Mark as she and Julie left the room.

25

'Martin Jamieson, please.' Rachael held her badge out towards the woman sitting at the reception desk.

'Oh, okay. Um, can I ask what it is regarding?'

'No, you can't. Is he here?'

The receptionist looked immediately flustered. 'Ah, yes. Just a moment. I'll go and…' The woman pushed her chair back and walked out behind a wall separating the office from the lobby. Rachael and Julie could hear the humming noise of the open-plan office behind the wall. The clickety-clack of keyboards interspersed with a multitude of whispered conversations.

After a minute the receptionist returned. 'I can't seem to locate him.'

'What does that mean?'

'He's not at his desk.'

'Bathroom?'

'I didn't check the men's room.'

'Where is it?'

'I'm not sure you can just—'

'Listen, do you really want to be impeding the police?'

'No, er—'

'Where is it? Right now. Move.'

The woman took off, half-running in her high heels, Rachael and Julie following quickly behind her. They made their way through the large, open-plan office, a hundred sets of eyes following them.

Halfway across, the woman pointed at three bathroom doors at the back of the room.

'Thanks.' Rachael and Julie sprinted ahead towards the men's bathroom door. Rachael slammed the door open and she and Julie entered. A young man stood at the urinal, simultaneously jumping and turning his body away quickly when he saw it was two women entering.

'Hey—what the fuck?' he protested. Rachael and Julie looked at him. It wasn't Martin. They went along the stalls looking in: all empty.

They left the men's bathroom. Julie walked into the women's while Rachael checked the disabled toilet.

As Julie came back out shaking her head, Rachael turned to the receptionist, who was still standing there, mouth slightly ajar.

'Where's the other exit?'

'Over there.' She pointed at an exit sign in the far corner of the office.

'Where does it go?'

'Fire exit. Goes to the ground floor. All those doors lock from the other side. The only one that opens is at the ground floor.'

'What about the roof? Can you access the roof from the stairs?'

'I don't know. I've never been up there.'

Rachael and Julie ran towards the exit. All of the staff had now stopped working and were standing to watch.

Rachael opened the door and they went through. She nodded and Julie started running up. Rachael started fast down the stairs, taking three at a time, using the railing to keep her balance. Thirty seconds later she entered the ground floor near the lift and ran out the front door onto William Street, in the heart of Melbourne's legal district. She looked up and down through the sea of people, searching for Martin Jamieson's face based on the photograph from Zach's file. *If he isn't gone completely, he'll be close.*

Rachael scanned the other side of the street. As she did, she caught sight of him across the road. She continued to scan as if she hadn't noticed him.

A minute later, Julie came out of the building, puffing. 'That's my gym work done for the day. Any sign of him?'

'Yes. Don't look now, but he's across the street in a café staring at us. Just start shaking your head to let him think he's got away. Let's say our goodbyes and you stay here, checking your watch and looking impatient. I'll jump in a cab and come back to surprise him. He should still be focused on you, waiting for you to give up and leave.'

'Sounds good.'

Julie started to shake her head and Rachael walked to the curb. She shot out her arm to hail down a cab. One pulled over immediately and she got in the front.

'Don't start the meter,' said Rachael, showing the driver her badge as he pulled away from the kerb. 'Just head down the road for a block, do a U-turn and bring me back this way.' Rachael placed a ten-dollar note on the console between the seats.

The driver looked across at her for a moment, and then at the badge, before nodding. 'Okay, okay, no worries.'

A minute later, Rachael asked the driver to stop three doors down from the café. She thanked the driver and made her way towards Martin, walking close to the buildings so he wouldn't see her coming.

Martin was seated near the window in the empty café, staring straight across the road at Julie. He jumped in fright when Rachael placed a hand on his shoulder. He stood up, kicking back his chair, and tried to quickly push past her, but she hooked his ankle with her foot and he fell to the floor.

Rachael came down on top of him, one knee firmly in his back.

'Bad idea, Martin. You should always watch where you're walking,' she said, pulling out her handcuffs and securing his hands behind his back. Julie rushed in through the door.

'Are you hurt?'

'No, I'm all good. How about you, Martin? You okay?'

Martin said nothing. He stared at the floor, silently fuming.

'Shall we get a divvy van to take him to the station or should we walk him back? It's only two blocks away,' said Julie.

Rachael looked out through the café window to the other side of William Street. She could see the receptionist from Martin's company standing on the footpath, along with about fifty other people, all squinting and jostling to see.

'Let's walk him. We can all use the fresh air.' Rachael helped Martin to his feet and started to read him his rights.

Julie walked back to the counter and asked the gobsmacked owner, 'What does he owe you for the coffee?'

'Don't worry about it, it's fine.'

'Okay, thanks. We may have to come back and get a statement from you at some point,' she said, wandering back, leaving the man at the counter, still in shock.

26

The bottle of water sat untouched in front of Martin Jamieson where he sat alone in the interview room. Rachael and Julie stood with Rob watching his body language through the monitor. They knew the innocent usually sit, have a quick look around the room and then just wait, hands on the table or in their lap. The guilty often pace the room as if looking for another door that will lead them out again. When the guilty ones do sit, their legs will bounce around in a nervous jig. And they stare often at the cameras set up in the room.

Martin was sitting, right leg vibrating fast, with his head tilted, staring straight at the camera in the corner.

'He's looking like a junkie in need of a fix,' Rachael said.

'Sure does,' said Julie. 'Give me a minute or so and I'll get him sorted with his caution and rights again. I'll do my version of good cop and see how we go.'

Rachael and Rob nodded silently, keeping their eyes on the monitors. They watched as Julie came into view and started speaking to Martin.

'Any news from Mark and Dave on the other suspect?'

'Nothing as yet. I'd expect they're only just arriving there now. It's a bit of a hike to Melton.'

They concentrated on the monitor as Julie continued reading Martin his rights.

Once she had finished, Julie sat still, silently looking at Martin for ten seconds.

'Why did you bolt today when we came to see you, Martin?' she asked eventually.

'I didn't,' he said quickly. 'I was just getting a coffee from across the road.'

'Really. So if we go back and interview everyone in your office, no one will tell us that you jumped up when you heard us out the front asking for you, and took off out the back door. Is that what you're saying?'

Martin said nothing and stared down at the table.

'Come on, mate, let's be fair here. My colleague came up to you in that café and you jumped like a jack rabbit. I want to hear your side of the story; if not we can just work off the evidence we have already.'

'What evidence?'

Rachael opened the door to the interview room.

'Let the record show that Detective Senior Constable Rachael Schlank has entered the room,' said Julie.

'Hi, Martin,' said Rachael, her tone upbeat and breezy.

Martin squinted at her and shook his head slowly.

'I was just asking Martin to tell us his side of the story,' said Julie.

'Oh, good. I'm glad I arrived in time. Sorry to interrupt. Go ahead, Martin,' said Rachael, smiling.

Martin looked at Rachael and then Julie, and then back at Rachael. They were both now smiling at him. Then he shook his head again. 'Fucking Todd.'

Rachael and Julie shared a quick glance.

'What about Todd?' asked Julie.

'I can't believe he gave me up. Fucking arsehole.'

'Tell us about it, from your side,' said Julie.

Rachael was riveted, staring blankly at Martin. In her mind she was high-fiving Julie. *We're there*, she thought, relieved. She had an overwhelming desire to lean back on her chair and rest her feet on the table.

'What's to tell? We were going to get the rabbits out. Easy, do it, find the rabbits new homes, and move on.'

Shit.

'So can you confirm what the target was,' asked Julie.

'You know already.'

'For the tape, Martin,' said Julie. 'Co-operating gets you a long way around here.'

'The research labs in West Melbourne, where they keep the rabbits.'

'And when were you planning for this to happen?'

'Sunday. Around eleven at night.'

'So, what was the plan?' asked Rachael.

Martin sighed before speaking. 'We decided, Todd and I, that it would just be the two of us. Keep it simple. Thought if we involved too many people someone might talk and blow it.' Martin started to laugh, before catching himself and stopping. 'I can't believe he talked.'

'What about the other ones, Martin?' asked Julie.

'What other ones?'

'You know, that duck hunter and the horse trainer,'

said Rachael.

'What… what are you talking about?'

'We're talking about that duck hunter who was shot and the horse trainer who was killed with a cross bow. Those missions.'

'That had nothing to do with me.'

'Come on, we know all about it. What's your shoe size, Martin?' asked Julie.

'Ten and a half, why?'

'Got thick socks then, I presume?' asked Rachael.

'What the fuck are you talking about? Are you drunk?'

'No, no I'm not. But I think we might be celebrating tonight though,' said Rachael. 'What do you think, Julie?'

'Yep, I think there will be a few rounds bought.'

They then both sat silently, staring at Martin with deadpan expressions. Again he looked from one to the other, apparently confused.

'Why Steve Lawrence?' asked Rachael.

'Who?'

'The duck hunter. Was he a random victim or did he do something to provoke you?'

'I already said I had nothing to do with that. *Killing* someone? No way!'

'So where were you on Sunday 19 March, at around seven in the morning?' asked Julie.

'In bed at home, I'd say.'

'Anyone able to verify that?' asked Julie.

Martin looked at the table for a moment. 'No.'

'What about Jim Camella, the horse trainer, what was your issue with him?'

'Nothing, the first time I heard his name was on the

news.'

'Maybe Todd knows more. We probably should ask him. I'm sure he'd be happy to get out in front of the charges we have him on. Maybe he'll be more helpful.'

'I honestly don't know anything about what you're asking me. I told you about what we were planning for Sunday. I don't know anything about who killed those men.'

'But you know about the killings, don't you?'

'Sure, it's been all over the news.'

'And what do you think about it?' asked Julie.

'I think whoever is doing this is doing a great job. They are killing defenceless animals for fun. Fuck them. I hope they suffered. And if you're running around asking me about it, you must be fucking miles off catching the person responsible.'

'So, where were you on Thursday 23 March?'

'At work.'

'In the morning, before work, at around dawn.'

'I was at work. We had a big project that was overdue and all the programmers were doing fifteen and sixteen hour days to get it done. We were all at work by six in the morning all that week.'

'Okay, let's take a break while we check this with your work. By the way, what are Todd's details?'

'What? You've already spoken to him. You have his details.'

Julie smiled at Martin.

As it dawned on him, his face dropped. 'Fuck.'

'I'd suggest you cooperate,' said Julie. 'We haven't yet decided whether you will be charged with assaulting police when you tried to knock my colleague over earlier.'

Martin sighed. 'Okay, give me a pen.'

Rachael opened her folder and slid a pen over to Martin, who used it to write down Todd's details.

'Interview suspended at eleven forty-nine am. Stay put, Martin. We'll be back soon.' Rachael and Julie got up and left the room.

They walked into the monitoring room. Rob was sitting, still looking at the screens.

'Catch all that?' asked Julie.

'Yes,' said Rob. 'Let's get this alibi of his checked straight away. If it holds up, we'll pass him on to Melbourne CIU. They can deal with the conspiracy to commit break and enter charges for Martin and go and grab his mate, Todd. We need to stay focussed.'

Rob's phone rang. 'It's Dave,' he said, looking at the screen. He answered the phone.

'Dave, hold on a sec,' he said, putting the call on speaker. 'Go ahead, I've got Rachael and Julie here.'

'No worries. Andrew Davies went off like a frog in a sock when we started questioning him, all offended about feeling accused, but he has solid alibis for both killings. Was away with his family when the duck hunter bought it and was confirmed as working when the arrow went through Jim Camella's neck. We can cross him off the list.'

'Okay, thanks,' said Rob. 'See you guys back here.' He ended the call.

'I'll check with Martin's office to confirm his alibi,' said Julie.

Rachael nodded. 'And I'll get back onto the HR department to see how the mining of the police database is going. Hopefully there'll be better luck for us there.'

27

Rob turned his chair slightly to avoid the glare of the morning sun. 'Okay, what did we get from the data mining of the police and military databases?'

Rachael stood up and picked up the marker. She wrote the name *Jonathon Shimmer* on the whiteboard and taped a photograph of a man up next to the name.

'Who's Shimmer?' asked Rob.

'Jonathon Shimmer, thirty-eight years old, former constable with Victoria Police, based at the Ballarat station. Lives now in Ballan, married with two children. He is a weapons collector and wanted to go into special ops to become a sniper, but was let go eight years ago because he couldn't follow orders. He was allegedly a bit of a cowboy. Involved in unauthorised high-speed pursuits, getting too rough with suspects, that sort of thing. He was counselled a few times, but it just made him resentful. He wears size eleven shoes. Our human resources contact had six potential suspects for us but checking shoe sizes brought it back to one name. Three had size twelve feet and the other two were a nine and a nine and a half.'

'Understood,' said Rob.

'Shimmer has been working as a self-employed courier driver in recent years, so he has flexibility in his working life. No record of him caring about animals or being political—his full-time obsession seems to be how Victoria Police apparently screwed him over. Once we're done here I want to go and see him for a chat.'

'Yes, good work. Who else?'

Mark half raised his hand to Rob's question and stood up. He went to the whiteboard and grabbed the marker. He wrote the name *Robert Vassar* and an address, and taped up a photograph. 'Robert Vassar, forty-two years old. Was a sergeant in the army until two years ago. He developed post-traumatic stress disorder after his third tour in Afghanistan. Witnessed an improvised explosive device injure some of our guys. He was in the following vehicle and saw the whole thing. Apparently the explosives were hidden inside a dead German Shepherd that had been laid beside the road as if hit by a car. He was basically catatonic for a week and by the time he came good again he couldn't remember what had happened. Turns out his family had German Shepherds when he was growing up and that seized the wiring in his head. He was pensioned out. Before that he had a reputation as a tough operator. He's got a hobby farm near Castlemaine now with rescued donkeys and sheep. This guy fits the profile perfectly.'

Rob nodded. 'What about weapons? Any intel on what he has at home?'

'No record of anything licensed to him, but that doesn't mean much,' Mark said.

'Anyone else got any names?' asked Rob.

'No one likely came up in my searches of the AFP or Tasmania Police,' said Julie. 'Local shooting and archery clubs came up with nothing as well. I spoke to multiple people at each of the clubs and they knew of no one who'd be interested in doing harm to hunters. A lot of them are hunters themselves or who have mates who hunt.'

'Me neither,' said Dave. 'Most of the people who have been kicked out of New South Wales and ACT forces have headed north to the sunshine of Queensland or have stayed put.'

Rob tapped his pen on the desk. 'My search of the rest of the police forces came up with nothing as well. No one living in the area we're looking in, at least.'

'So, we've got two contenders,' said Julie.

'Okay,' said Rob, 'here's the plan. We're going after Mark's guy first. He seems like the more likely candidate, based on his history. We'll go after Rachael's guy after that.'

Rachael could see Mark smiling smugly in her peripheral vision.

'Mark and Dave, do you guys have contacts at Castlemaine station?'

They both nodded. 'Yes,' said Mark, 'we know almost everyone there.'

'Okay, call the sergeant up there and request that one of their more experienced officers do a discreet drive-by of Robert Vassar's place in an unmarked car. Emphasis on discreet. We want to see if it looks like he's home. I don't want to drag us all the way up to Castlemaine to find out he's on holidays somewhere.'

'You got it.' Mark pulled out his phone to make the call.

An hour later, they were back in the conference

room.

'Vassar is definitely home,' said Mark. 'He was spotted on the property fixing a water trough.'

'Okay, it's now just after nine-thirty,' said Rob, looking at his watch. 'Dave, get on to the Critical Incident Response Team and organise a team to get up there to back us up. Give them a briefing and let me know if they want to discuss it with me. Vassar's farm is south of Castlemaine, so get CIRT to rendezvous with us outside Kyneton Police Station at noon. We'll all drive up together to Vassar's place in convoy from there. Give them Vassar's address so they can check out the satellite map of the area beforehand.' Dave nodded and headed out of the room to call CIRT.

Rob continued, 'Mark, you and Dave will be going up to the door. Although this is probably going to be very routine, I want everyone in vests. I'm looking at the satellite image of the property now.' Rob looked down at his laptop as he spoke. 'It has trees around the fence line, with what looks like quite a bit of thick growth along the front boundary. That will give the CIRT team good cover. Looking at this map, the house is about seventy metres from the front boundary, which is well within the effective range of the CIRT team's weapons. If it all goes south, their team has a negotiator on board as well. Mark, call the Castlemaine Police Station again and tell them we'll need some uniformed officers to assist with road blocks at either end of the road.'

'Yep, you got it. Let's go,' Mark said, standing up and walking towards the door, as if dismissing the meeting. Rachael, Julie and Rob ignored him and stayed seated.

28

The unmarked Volkswagen Transporter van rolled slowly to a stop half a kilometre before Robert Vassar's farm. The side door slid back slowly and one of the members of the Critical Incident Response Team carefully exited the vehicle with his SIG Sauer machine gun, pushing the door silently closed behind him. Crouching in camouflage, he moved quickly into the trees along the roadside and started to make his way towards Vassar's farm. The van moved forwards, gaining speed quickly so it passed the farm at near the speed limit. Once it was well past the farm, the driver pulled her foot off the accelerator and it coasted again to a stop. The second member exited the van and got himself quickly into the tree line. He then made his way back towards the front of the farm.

A kilometre away, the Taskforce were gathered as the CIRT van returned from dropping the members off in the treeline.

'My guys are in position,' said Senior Sergeant Byron Tubb, head of the CIRT team. 'They have radioed in that a male matching your suspect's description just entered the house.' Alongside Tubb stood a serious-looking CIRT officer holding her machine gun pointed at the ground. The members of the Taskforce looked at it with some interest. It made their firearms look like toys.

Rob addressed the group. 'Okay, we'll get the roadblocks set up at both ends of the road. No one will be using that road but us. There's only five other farms on this road, but we'll leave the residents where they are— there's so much distance between houses there's no chance of people running into crossfire. Plus, we are in the country: we don't want a neighbour giving him a friendly phone call to warn him.'

Rob gave Julie a nod. She radioed for the two standby police cars to move into position and set up the roadblocks.

'Okay, Mark and Dave are heading in through the gate, the rest of us will be stopping two hundred metres back and coming up on foot. We'll fall in behind the CIRT van. Remember everyone, safety first.'

Mark and Dave both wore loose rain jackets with *Victoria Police* written on the front and back to disguise the fact they were wearing ballistic vests underneath. They got into their unmarked car and drove off slowly.

They passed the roadblock, the uniformed officers nodding as they went by. They turned in at the gate to Robert Vassar's farm. Dave got out and opened the gate, all the time watching the house for any movement, shutting it again once Mark had driven through.

Dave got back into the car. 'That chain is just hanging there through the gate in case we need to drive straight through it.'

Mark nodded. They drove the seventy metres up to the front of the house.

'Okay, let's do it,' Mark said, undoing his seatbelt.

They both got out of the car and started to walk towards the front door. A German Shepherd lay on a mat beside the door, impassive and unimpressed. Mark pulled the rain jacket up over the top of his holster on his hip so that his gun was exposed and easy to reach.

As they walked up the steps, a voice came from behind the screen door.

'What do you want?'

Mark and Dave stopped suddenly. They couldn't see anything through the thick mesh of the door and they suddenly felt completely exposed. 'We just want a chat, Mr Vassar,' Mark said, making his voice friendly.

'How do you know my name?'

'We just want to ask you a couple of questions.'

'What about?'

'An ongoing matter. Mr Vassar, can you please come outside?'

'Get your toy soldiers to stand down and I'll come out.'

'What do you mean?'

'There's two trigger-happy characters in the trees by my fence playing soldier with machine guns. I'll come out when they point them at the ground, instead of at my front door. Plus, I could hear multiple cars up along the road. More traffic in the last five minutes than we've had all week.'

Dave spoke up. 'They're just there for our protection. Can you come out so we can chat and they can stand down?'

'Get them to point those guns away first. I don't want any twitchy fingers out there. Then I'll come out. I don't see a warrant in your hands, so it's my property, my rules.'

'Okay, okay, just take it easy,' Mark said, bringing his portable radio up towards his mouth. 'Can we get everyone to point their guns at the ground while we chat with Mr Vassar?'

'Received,' came the reply.

'Okay, now that's done, can you come out for a chat? Nice and slowly, if you don't mind.'

There was silence behind the door.

'Mr Vassar?'

'Yeah, I'm coming.' The door opened and Robert Vassar walked out onto the front porch. Behind him, Mark saw high-powered binoculars on the hall table. The dog looked up at Vassar, and sat up at attention.

The man still had the look of an infantry sergeant. All muscle, shaved head. He walked to where Mark and Dave stood. His eyes looked them over, sizing them up, before staring past them to the tree line. Only his eyes moved as he surveyed the area, his head perfectly still. 'At least nine or ten of you here, right?' he asked, as he crossed his arms in front of him.

Mark ignored the question. 'Anyone else in the house?'

'No, just me. Let me know if you want me to give your guys some training on how to approach unseen.'

'Sure, will do,' said Mark. 'We want to chat with you about your movements on Sunday 19 March. Where were you that day?'

'Two weeks ago? Probably here. I tend not to go far unless I have to.'

Mark took a short step forwards, so that he was close

to Vassar's face. Vassar stared back, unimpressed. The German Shepherd cocked its head and stared at Mark.

'Ever been to Frogmore Swamp?'

'No.'

'You a duck hunter?'

'You're joking, right? Are you here about that duck hunter who got smoked?'

'Just answer the question.'

'No, I have never been there and I'm not a duck hunter. I don't have any desire to shoot little birds for fun. I have been in actual wars, where the enemy has guns as well. I don't need to play soldier like those pussies. I only ever shoot at humans who have guns pointed back at me, you understand. Not defenceless animals.' Vassar let his gaze fall down on Mark's shoulders and torso.

Mark felt his face flush. 'What about Thursday, the twenty-third?'

'No idea. I was probably here again.'

'Ever been to Bulla?'

'What, down near the airport? Sure, I've driven through it. I was there last year.'

'So you weren't down that way on the twenty-third?'

'That's right, I was not.'

'Did you hear about someone getting shot in the neck with a hunting arrow that day?'

'Nope, missed that. I don't bother too much with catching the news.'

Dave raised his pen and interjected. 'Mr Vassar, we are looking at two murders. One is the duck hunter at the swamp and the other is a horse trainer down at Bulla. If you're saying you had nothing to do with these crimes, would you be willing to give us access to do a quick search to help us eliminate you from the investigation?'

Robert Vassar pursed his lips and looked across at Dave. 'Okay, I will let you guys in, but I want to see everyone who enters the house or the shed. I don't want anyone planting anything in there. Call up your team. Let's get this over with.'

Mark's face got hot at taking directions from a potential suspect, but it was worth it to get into the house without a search warrant. He raised the portable radio to his mouth. 'We have Mr Vassar's permission to do a property search. Come on up.'

The serenity of the scene was broken by the sound of the vehicles starting their engines in the distance.

Two minutes later they were all lined up in front of Vassar's house. Rob and Rachael led the way up to the front door.

'Thank you for agreeing to do this, Mr Vassar. I am Detective Senior Sergeant Rob Morello. It's most appreciated.'

'I just want to make sure you guys don't take anything in with you. I want no evidence planted in there.'

'We are searching for a double murderer. No one is planting anything.'

'So, why me?'

'We had intelligence that led us here,' said Rob.

'Bullshit.'

'I'm not at liberty to say any more right now.'

Vassar pulled the screen door back and held it open. 'Right, let's get this done then.'

As Mark was about to go through the door he stopped. 'Any weapons on the premises?'

'Nope,' said Vassar.

An hour later the Taskforce members gathered near the cars, out of earshot of Robert Vassar.

'So nobody found anything?'

Around the group, everyone shook their heads.

Rachael spoke up. 'The place is clean, but this guy is clever enough not to store weapons here. Maybe we should consider some surveillance.'

'Hard work to follow someone out here without getting seen. Can't really hide in the crowd,' said Rob.

'True,' said Rachael. 'Let's try something else. Leave me here with a car when you all go and I'll keep an eye on him. There's a group of trees a hundred metres down the road to the south. I can park behind them to give me cover. If he's at all spooked by our visit he will more than likely make a move straight away and the road to civilisation goes to the north. If he moves he will probably head north to Castlemaine and I can follow him. If anything happens, I'll call Castlemaine Police Station for back up. They're only a few minutes away, coming at full speed.'

Mark interjected tersely. 'He will spot you. He saw the CIRT guys easily enough.'

'Maybe, maybe not,' said Rachael.

Rob studied her for a second before responding. 'Okay,' he said, 'but only with backup. Who's going to volunteer?'

'I'll do it,' said Dave.

'Okay, done. Rachael and Dave, head back into Castlemaine now and get some food for tonight. It will be a long one. We'll hang around here for half an hour until you're back, and then Julie and I will head back to Melbourne with Mark,' said Rob.

'Got it. Back shortly,' said Rachael, nodding to Dave.

29

It was dark. Rachael felt herself being shaken gently. She opened her eyes to see Dave Boucher with his hand on her shoulder, rocking her awake.

'Good morning, Rach. It's six.'

Rachael yawned, mouth wide open.

'Morning,' she said quietly. She had been dreaming she was at work. *She had seen Julie across the squad room, facing away towards a bench, a case file spread out in front of her. Rachael had called out, but Julie didn't respond, as if she hadn't heard her. Rachael walked over and tapped her on the shoulder. When she turned it was not Julie, but Helen Ng. Rachael had jumped backwards in surprise. At that moment, Grace Blackwood walked in the door and stood next to Helen. They both looked at Rachael, a look of deep sadness on their faces.* Then Dave had woken her.

'You okay?' asked Dave.

'Yes, was just in the middle of a dream. Any movement from Vassar?'

'No, not a peep,' said Dave, raising the thermal monocular back to his eye and pointing it towards Vassar's house. 'I've spent the past four hours watching the sheep and donkeys sleep through this.'

'It's a nice piece of gear, but I reckon the CIRT team are going to want it back,' said Rachael.

'Yep, back to regular old binoculars for us.'

Rachael went back to thinking about her dream. *What are my ghosts trying to tell me?*

Dave Boucher laid his head on top of his folded arms on the conference room table. Rachael stood at the whiteboard reviewing what they knew. For a while, she had thought she would see something new in the photographs and the words by just standing there, but then she realised that she was staring at the white spaces and was basically asleep standing up.

Rob Morello entered the room carrying two coffees. 'Hey you two. Compliments of Victoria Police.' He put the cups on the table in front of them.

'Thanks, boss,' Rachael said, smiling. Mark and Julie followed him in. Julie was carrying two cartons of milk.

Dave squinted as he woke up, confused to be at work. He looked at the coffee in front of him. 'Thanks for that,' he mumbled. Rachael gave Julie a smile to thank her for bringing in the soy milk.

'So, any movement from Vassar last night?'

'Nothing,' Rachael said. 'He fed the sheep and the donkeys at about five, then settled in for the night. We had a good line of sight on him through the trees most times. He cooked himself some food, had a beer and spent the night reading a book. As far as we could see he didn't make any phone calls, didn't use the computer, didn't watch TV. Went to bed around ten and was up around six-twenty as the sun was coming up. He fed the animals and checked the water troughs before going back inside. All very normal stuff. We packed up around seven.'

'Get any sleep?'

'Yeah, I did the ten till two watch and my sleepy buddy did the two to six watch. All good,' said Rachael, as Dave raised his right fist slowly into the air in mock triumph, before yawning.

Rob sat down at the head of the table. 'Just to catch you two up, when we got back to Melbourne yesterday, I asked Julie to chase up with PK Farm to see if they had ever heard of Vassar.' Rob turned to Julie. 'What did you find?'

'Nothing,' said Julie. 'I called Dianne King and she said she had never heard of Robert Vassar. I emailed her his photograph and she said she'd never seen him before either.'

'Okay, Vassar looks less likely now to be our guy. He wasn't acting like a suspect would, but we'll keep an open mind. Today we'll go and see Rachael's person of interest, what's his name?' asked Rob, looking up at the whiteboard.

'Shimmer, Jonathon Shimmer,' Rachael said, stifling a yawn. 'Thirty-eight years old, former Ballarat cop. Lives in Ballan. Has a wife and two children. He's a weapons collector, and has multiple weapons stored at home, so it will be simpler to pick him up at work. It will save us getting CIRT involved again. He's a courier working as a contractor for a big firm in Ballarat, Double Speed Couriers. I spoke to someone there yesterday morning, without mentioning his name, and was told they have real time GPS tracking on all their vehicles. They all work Saturdays as they specialise in deliveries for mechanics and garages. We should be able to sweet talk them into giving us his location.'

'Yes, maybe, or they could be obstructive and tip him off,' said Mark.

'True, but it's worth a shot,' Rob said, turning towards Rachael. 'You open to doing the sweet talking?'

'Yes, sure. Just give me an hour and I'll bolt home, have a quick shower and change clothes.'

An hour later Rachael and Rob set off for Double Speed Couriers in Ballarat, with Mark and Julie following. Dave had been ordered to bed to get some rest.

'How goes Homicide nowadays?' Rachael asked.

'Okay, I guess. Never ends, as you know. No chance of getting made redundant, that's for sure,' he said. 'How's Cold Case going?'

'Good team there, but we deal with fading memories and witnesses who have died or disappeared, so there's a lot of tail chasing.'

'Yeah, we all do our share of that. I've heard good things about you. Jules is a big fan. I like that you don't take crap from anyone.'

Rachael smiled and nodded. 'Yes, occasionally that works in my favour.'

Rob checked his watch. 'Could you turn the radio on to 3AW? Tom's being interviewed about our progress.'

'Sure.' Rachael turned on the radio and found the station. They heard the familiar sound of the detective inspector's voice.

'…we are leaving no stone unturned in our efforts to apprehend the offender,' said Tom.

'That is all well and good, Detective Inspector, but how close are you really?' asked the interviewer. 'We have had two killings within a week, two hunters killed using the very methods they used themselves in hunting animals. The truth is that your team doesn't have the first clue—'.

Rob turned off the radio. 'On second thoughts, I'd prefer not to hear that,' he said. 'The interviewer sounds like he fell out of bed this morning. I don't envy Tom's role at all. The talkback radio crowd want instant results, regardless of evidence. They'll be phoning into the station demanding Tom be sacked in a couple of minutes. And us too.'

Rachael nodded. 'I avoid all media during high-profile cases.'

Rob nodded. 'Sounds like a good strategy. None of the media are giving us a break on this case. It's like that all day and all night long.'

Rachael let out a long breath. They drove on in silence.

They pulled in to Double Speed Couriers just before lunchtime. Rachael checked her hair and teeth in the mirror. 'Good luck,' said Rob.

'Thanks,' she said as she swung the passenger door open. As she walked towards the office, she saw Mark and Julie pull up to the kerb. She hoped Jonathon Shimmer was not about to arrive in the car park. He would spot unmarked police cars from a mile away.

Rachael opened the front door and pulled out her badge as she went up to reception. 'Hi, I'm Detective Senior Constable Rachael Schlank. I'm looking to speak with Peter Sims.'

The receptionist looked startled for a moment, the way the perpetually innocent do. 'Yes, sure. Can I say what it is regarding?'

'Just tell him I'm following up on a chat we had yesterday. He'll know.'

'Okay,' the young woman said meekly, disappearing from sight behind a wall.

A minute later, a dark-haired man around forty-five appeared, smiling in her direction. 'Detective Schlank,' he said, extending his hand to shake hers. 'Good to meet you. How can I help?'

'Is there somewhere private we can chat?'

'Yes, sure. Britney, is the conference room free?' he said over his shoulder to the receptionist, who had returned to her desk.

'Yes, Mr Sims.'

He indicated to Rachael to follow him and they walked behind the wall into a sparsely furnished conference room and sat down.

'Mr Sims,' said Rachael.

'Call me Peter.'

'Sure. Peter, as we discussed on the phone yesterday, you've got real time tracking on your contracted drivers, yes?'

'Yes. Helps when we have customers wanting to know about deliveries.'

'Okay. We're interested in talking to one of your drivers. He's come up as matching a profile we have of a suspect and we need to speak to him to eliminate him from our enquiries. It's important you understand that it is likely that he is not the person we are looking for, but we need to speak to him to confirm that.' Rachael paused, looking at him to emphasise her point. He nodded that he understood. 'We're hoping we can do it discreetly, so as not to draw undue attention to him or your company,' she added, smiling.

Peter smiled back. 'Got it, I understand. Who's the guy?'

'Jonathon Shimmer.'

'Jonno. Seriously? The guy used to be a copper.'

'Yes, I am aware.'

'Okay, I'll help. What do you want me to do?'

30

Rachael sat in the passenger seat as Rob Morello drove at high speed down the Western Highway. Mark and Julie followed close behind.

The courier company had told them Jonathon Shimmer would be in Bacchus Marsh making a delivery at a garage in around twenty-five minutes. Going at the speed limit had them arriving there in thirty minutes, but they knew Shimmer was driving across from Gisborne and would not be using the highway, so both unmarked police cars turned on their flashing lights, leaving their sirens off for their own comfort, and made it in twenty.

They waited separately two hundred metres either side of the garage where the parts would be dropped off. Rachael called Peter Sims at Double Speed Couriers.

'How far out is he?' she asked.

'Based on what I see on the computer, he should be there in two minutes.'

'Thanks, Peter. We appreciate your help.'

'No problem. I'd appreciate it though if you left me out of it when talking to Jonathon.'

'You got it. We won't mention a thing. All the best.'

Rachael hung up. *I think he'll work it out for*

himself. She radioed the other car. 'Target is within two minutes. Let's wait until he's done the delivery and get him driving away.'

'Thanks, boss,' Mark said sarcastically into the radio.

Rob shook his head. 'You two really aren't close at all, eh?'

'You could say that. It's okay, though. I find if you ignore people who are trying to get under your skin, it tends to slowly drive them bonkers.'

A white van approached them from behind and passed by. Rachael read the licence plate. 'Confirming Shimmer has just gone past.'

'Got it,' replied Julie from the other car.

They watched as Jonathon Shimmer parked outside the garage, got out and picked up a box from the back of the van. He walked inside and came back out within a minute. Jumping into the van, he pulled out onto the street, heading towards Rachael and Rob. She got out of the car and Rob switched on the flashing lights. Rachael wandered in front of the police car and put up her hands, indicating for Shimmer to stop.

Shimmer's van slowed when he saw the police car and Rachael standing out in front of it. Rachael relaxed as she waved him down. *That's it, nice and easy.* When he was almost beside her, he suddenly accelerated and tore past them.

'Fucker,' she said, as she ran back to the car and jumped in.

Rob turned on the siren. The tyres screeched as he kicked the accelerator to the floor and spun the steering wheel. The car's back end slid as they did a tight U-turn.

Rachael struggled with the seatbelt while grabbing for the radio. 'Bacchus Marsh two-five-one. All available units in the Bacchus Marsh area. In pursuit of a white Ford Transit van, registration is Echo, Tango, Alpha, One, Three, Eight. Currently heading north on Graham Street towards Main.'

Rachael listened through the radio as the duty supervisor at Bacchus Marsh Police Station organised police to head to their vicinity. She leaned forwards and looked through the side mirror. Mark and Julie were right behind them.

After two hundred metres, the van turned left. 'Suspect headed west on Main Street,' Rachael said into the radio.

'I don't have a good feeling about this one,' said Rob.

'Me neither.'

Shimmer did not slow down approaching a roundabout and travelled straight through, causing other vehicles to brake sharply to avoid a collision. The two unmarked police cars in pursuit slowed down in order to navigate the roundabout without incident, then accelerated to try and catch up to the van, which had gained a hundred and fifty metres on them.

After half a kilometre they had almost caught up to the van as the radio came to life. 'Unit Four positioned on Halletts Way near the next roundabout. Do you want us to intercept?'

'Affirmative, stand by,' said Rachael. After another few seconds, Rachael got back on the radio. 'Unit Four, ready?'

'Affirmative, we're ready.'

'Unit Four, go, now.'

As the van approached, a police car rolled around the roundabout and stopped, blocking the van's path, its lights flashing and siren blaring. Shimmer partially mounted the kerb to try and avoid the police car. The van clipped the front of the police car. Shimmer over-corrected and the van flipped onto its side, sliding across the road, its tyres spinning wildly.

Rob drove over the kerb past the damaged police car and skidded to a halt beside the van. He and Rachael jumped out and pulled their guns as they moved quickly around the upturned van. Shimmer was inside, semi-conscious and bleeding from the head. Rachael glanced over towards Mark and Julie, who were helping the officers out of the damaged police car. 'Anyone need an ambulance over there?'

'No, we're good,' said Julie.

Rachael kept her gun trained on Shimmer as she raised her portable radio with her left hand. 'Bacchus Marsh two-five-one. We have a two-car Code Twelve and Sixteen at the intersection of Halletts Way and Main Street. Need one ambo and firies to assist. Also, this roundabout will be blocked for a while so we'll need some units to divert traffic.'

'Received. En route,' came the reply through the radio.

'Give us a boost up,' Rob called across to Mark.

Mark ran to stand beside the van, cupping his hands together near his knee. Rob got a boost onto the top of the toppled van, then opened the door upwards. Holding it open with one hand, he pushed the button that automatically lowered the window, and then let the door fall shut again. He lowered himself through the open window down into the vehicle. Rachael stood outside, watching through the windscreen, her weapon still drawn. Rob worked his way down through the cabin and turned off the ignition. He checked Shimmer's pulse and looked up at Rachael through the windscreen. 'His pulse is good and the bleeding isn't too bad. I'll leave him as is until the firies and ambo arrive.'

'Any weapons in there you can see?'

'No, nothing.' At that moment Rachael could hear two different types of sirens approaching in the distance.

Two minutes later an ambulance was on the scene along with two fire trucks.

31

'Remember me?'

Jonathon Shimmer stared at Rachael from his hospital bed. His head was bandaged, pushing his long hair away from his face, which was bruised on the left side. 'Yeah, what the fuck do you want?'

'What I want is for us all to go back in time and for you not to make a stupid mistake by driving off, that's what I want. How about you? What do you want?'

'Nothing from you.' Shimmer's handcuff rattled against the railing of the hospital bed.

'Why'd you do a runner when I tried to pull you over?'

'Dunno, it was kind of a spur of the moment-type decision.'

'Not a good decision though, was it? We found the bag of dope under the seat. Hardly worth setting off a police pursuit.'

'Guess not.'

'Well, we've got some questions for you, Jonathon. We can discuss the marijuana later. You know that you have been arrested for *Evade Police, Drive in a Manner Dangerous to the Public* and *Conduct Endangering Life*.

Our questions aren't about that. Our dash cam video tells that story quite nicely. What we want to know is where you were on 19 March.'

A sullen pause. 'I can't remember.'

'It was a Sunday. Do you usually work on Sunday?'

'No.'

'So what's a usual Sunday look like for you?'

'I dunno. I get up late on Sundays. Maybe watch the footy in the arvo. Normal stuff.'

'Okay, so think back two Sundays ago and tell us what you were doing.'

'I can't remember: nothing memorable. Probably did something with my family.'

Rob was standing at the back of the room, leaning on the wall with his hands in his pockets. 'Ever been to Frogmore Swamp?'

'No, where's that?'

'Up near Bendigo. Where you and your mates go duck hunting. Ring any bells now?' Rob was smiling at Jonathon across the room.

'Which mates of mine go duck hunting? What are you frickin talking about?'

Rachael interjected, hoping to keep Shimmer off an even keel. She knew if they gave him too much time to think, he'd ask for a lawyer. 'Ever shot a high-powered rifle?' she said.

'Sure.'

'At a target or in a hunting situation?'

'At a target. Why?'

'Is your rifle at home?'

'Yeah. I have plenty of rifles at home. I collect weapons.'

'Jonathon, do you know someone named Steve Lawrence?'

Shimmer sat quietly thinking for a moment, long enough for Rachael and Rob to share a glance. 'Hold on, isn't that the dude who got shot duck hunting? I read about it in the news. Is that what this is all about?'

Rachael jumped back in. 'Okay, where were you on the morning of Thursday, the twenty-third?'

'The twenty-third? I thought you were asking about the nineteenth?'

'I was. Now I'm asking about Thursday, the twenty-third.'

'I'd have been working if it was a Thursday.'

'No, you weren't. You called in sick.'

'Oh, yeah. I had a cold that day. I remember now.'

'Ever been to Bulla?'

'Sure.'

'Were you in Bulla on the twenty-third?'

'No, I was home sick, like I said.'

'Can anyone verify that?' asked Rachael.

'Yeah, my wife.'

'Was she home with you?'

'She was in the morning. She started work at six. Works in the café at the local hospital. She left me in bed, sick. The kids were on school holidays that week though. They were home with me.'

'How old are your kids?' asked Rachael.

'Oldest is fifteen. The younger one just turned thirteen.'

'So old enough to look after themselves if you popped out for a while, eh?' asked Rachael.

Shimmer said nothing, looking up at her.

'What about Jim Camella? You know him?' asked Rob.

'No. Who's that?'

Rob pushed himself away from the wall and walked towards Shimmer. 'Come on, Jonathon. We know all about it. Why don't you do yourself a favour?' He was now leaning over Shimmer in his bed.

'So, what did I do?' Shimmer said, staring up at Rob's face hovering above him.

'You killed the duck hunter and then you killed Jim Camella, didn't you?'

Shimmer pushed himself up in his bed, away from Rob. 'Who put these ideas in your head? Those pricks at internal affairs? Are they still trying to fuck me over?'

Rachael's eyes widened. 'What's Professional Standards Command got to do with this?'

'They're the ones who got me chucked out of the police force in the first place. Looks like they're still after me.' Shimmer laughed ruefully. 'I've had just about enough of this. I want a lawyer. Now. I was a copper, I know how this bullshit goes down.'

Rachael sat forwards in her chair. 'You sure about that, Jonathon? We can't help you once you engage a lawyer. You know that.'

'I don't think helping me is on your agenda. Lawyer, please.'

32

The smell hit him as soon as he jumped over the side fence. Joab could see the house and cages in the distance. A tall hedge ran along the front of the property and the custom-made gate, fifteen feet high, had metal bars shaped into spears at the top. *Security for the unimaginative*, he thought. Just walk a few metres across the paddock on the next property and jump the side fence. Simple.

Joab watched the house from the dark shadows of the overhanging elm trees. He knew the dogs would soon start barking for their dinner. That would allow him to move up close without drawing attention. Desperately hungry dogs barking for food sound similar enough to a dog going off at an intruder. He waited.

After twenty minutes, one dog started barking. Twenty seconds later, they had all started. Joab moved up through the shadows closer to the large wooden house. It was surrounded by oak trees on about five acres of land. The scene might have looked peaceful, a patch of green oasis surrounded by cow and sheep paddocks as far as the eye could see. Idyllic even, if not for the horseshoe-shaped arc of metal cages running off to the side of the house, turning it into a prison complex. Fifty cages.

A few minutes later Sally Kinnaird kicked the flywire door open and walked out into the yard, a large bag of dog food under her arm. 'All right, you fuckers, I'm coming.' She was a short woman with blonde hair, hanging flat on her head. She dragged her feet as she went, pouring a small amount through the mesh roof of each cage. It fell through, hitting the concrete floor, some of it bouncing out of the sides of the cages. The dogs became mute for a few seconds as they chased the pellets of food around the floor.

Once she had finished with the bag, she then walked along with a long hose, attached to the tap in the middle of the yard, splashing water at the steel bowl in each cage. Most of the water simply bounced out of the bowl and onto the concrete floor of the cage. Any dogs unwise enough to bark in her direction got a squirt in the face.

Sally turned off the hose and started to walk back towards the house.

Joab came up behind her silently and quickly applied a choke hold. In a couple of seconds she was unconscious. He dragged Sally towards the cages, his gag reflex kicking in as he got closer. Rotting shit and urine. Joab opened the first cage and a small dog just stood, staring up at him. Her fur was long and matted together in large clumps, her breed unknowable from looking at her. All Joab knew was that she was female. They all were.

'Come on, little one,' Joab said, holding out a hand as he shifted some of Sally's weight on to his knee. The dog moved slowly forwards and sniffed cautiously at his glove. She then staggered out of the cage. Joab ducked down and dragged Sally inside just as she was just coming to. He stepped out and bolted the gate of the cage. He pulled out a padlock that he had tucked into his sleeve and secured the bolt in place.

Joab looked down at her as she lay there, blinking up at him, shaking her head, trying to get her bearings.

'Yes, this is real,' he said, reading the question she was thinking.

'Hey, let me the fuck out of here. Who the fuck are you?'

'You can call me Joab.'

'Joab. What sort of fucking name is that?'

He smiled at Sally.

'What gives you the right to break in here and stick me in a cage? I am going to have you locked up, you motherfucker.'

'Quieten down or you'll add a week to your sentence.'

'What the fuck does that mean?'

'You know what that means. Look around you. You're in a locked cage, Sally.'

'How do you know my name? What the hell are you talking about?' She dragged herself closer to the mesh wall of the cage.

'Sit back and give it some thought. If I find a blanket in one of these cages I will give it to you,' he said, pointing towards the other cages.

Joab picked up the matted dog that had walked out of the cage a few moments before; she shook with fear. He guessed it was probably the first time she had been held since she was put in the cage. He gently stroked her under the chin and felt her body start to relax.

Joab went into the house and found Sally's keys.

Clicking the button on the key, he unlocked the large Renault van parked behind the cages. He pulled open the back door with his spare hand and found some cages and dog crates in the back. On the ground nearby there were many more crates. *She buys new crates to save her cleaning the used ones.* Joab put the matted dog in one of the cages. 'Back in a sec, little lady.' The dog looked up at him, bewildered.

After an hour, Joab had all the dogs loaded inside the van. A couple had litters of puppies. These he placed in large cardboard boxes with their lids open, jammed against the walls so they would not tip over. Luckily, the dog crates had solid bases so he could stack them in the back of the van.

Joab made sure the air vents in the back of the van were open and then walked back to Sally's cage. 'I couldn't find any blankets in any of the cages, so none for you.'

She just stared back at him, her mouth now a slashed sneer.

'Do you know what the term *sentience* means?'

Her jaw dropped. Clearly, whatever she'd been expecting, it wasn't a vocabulary test. 'Uh. Yeah, it's when you put words together to say something.'

'No, Sally, that's *sentence*. I said *sentience*.'

'No, I don't.'

'Look it up if you get out of there. It is a big part of the reason you are in the cage right now,' he said. 'So, now you are to serve your new punishment. The magistrate in your case gave you a ten thousand dollar fine, but I have decided that was grossly inadequate. Sally

182

Kinnaird, I have decided you deserve jail time for your crimes. I know what you said in court, about how well you treat your animals and how much you love them, so I would think you'd be happy to be treated the same way.'

Sally glared up at him.

'Sally, you don't know how lucky you are. I am letting you live. Maybe to learn.'

'Learn what?' Sally spat the words at him.

'To learn that making money through torturing animals is a morally bankrupt way to live. If I ever have to come out here again I will end you. Do you understand?'

'I'm not torturing no animals.'

'You think that sticking dogs in small cages to spend their whole lives on a concrete floor, in scorching heat and freezing, wet winters, while they make money for you by continuously breeding designer puppies is not torture? Is that what you're saying?'

Sally said nothing.

'As I said, if I need to come back here, you will die. That is a promise.' Joab pulled out his Glock pistol. 'Do you understand?'

Sally's eyes opened wide. 'Yes,' she said, her eyes fixed on the gun.

'You got enough water there?' he asked, pointing to the half-filled bowl.

'Yes.'

'The dogs will be properly cared for. I'll drop them off at a safe place tonight and call in their location to police.' He smiled at her. 'As I am sure you have them all properly registered and microchipped, the authorities will be able to track down your address and they will be here to let you out before dawn.'

Sally just stared at him. She already had the dejected look of a long-term prisoner.

'Goodbye, Sally.'

Joab walked over to the van. He put the folded note on the ground, and placed a rock on top of it. Then he got in the van and started the engine.

33

Rachael lay on the mat looking up at the ceiling of the gym. Sweat was running down the sides of her face and into her headgear. She took out her mouthguard and tucked it into her sports bra. She held her open-fingered gloves above her, clenching and unclenching her fists.

'How do they feel?' asked Anna.

'They're good. Lighter than my old pair.'

'I thought your punches seemed faster,' said Anna, smiling. 'You seem different. What's been happening?'

'I've met someone.'

Anna arched an eyebrow. 'And?'

'We were introduced a few days ago. He used to work with one of my colleagues and we ran into him at work. We went out for drinks that night and it was really good.'

'More details, please.'

'His name's Zach. He works undercover with the Intelligence and Covert Support Command. He's about my age, very cute and articulate. Intelligent too, and can actually hold a conversation that isn't all about himself. Haven't been able to find much wrong with him so far.'

'And how did the night end up?'

'He was a gentleman. He dropped me home and we arranged another date.'

'And?'

'And there was some kissing and it was spectacular.'

'Nice,' said Anna, smiling and nodding her head. 'That's what I like to hear. When's your next date?'

'Tonight,' said Rachael.

'Woohoo, nice work.'

Rachael laughed. She felt aglow just talking about it. It was energising her. She rolled over and pushed herself up off the mat, onto her feet.

'How are things going with the taskforce?' asked Anna.

'Okay, but we aren't much closer. We're dealing with a very clever crook.'

'Yeah, it's all over the news.'

'Yes, so I've heard. I've been avoiding all of the media coverage to be honest. Going home and hearing people's opinions about how hopeless a job we're doing doesn't really help motivate me,' said Rachael. 'How are things at your end?'

'Same old, same old. Sam is good; kids are good. No complaints,' said Anna.

'Your mum?'

'She's going okay. Recovering well from the surgery. Thanks for sending the card and the flowers—she *loved* them. It really cheered her up. She's been showing everyone who comes into her room.'

Rachael smiled, whilst stifling a yawn.

'You been sleeping okay?' asked Anna.

'Not great. I've just been having some really vivid

dreams. I was on a stakeout two nights ago in the middle of nowhere with a colleague and we were taking turns getting some sleep. He woke me at six yesterday morning while I was right in the middle of a dream about my cold case victims. One of them was standing in the Homicide office looking through files and then the other one walked in. They looked at me with the saddest expression. It has been puzzling me ever since.'

'What do you think that means?'

'Wish I knew.'

'Sounds like you need a break from it all,' said Anna.

'What do you think this is?' Rachael said, laughing.

'Yeah, some break. Come on then, let's get back to it,' said Anna, jumping to her feet. Rachael reset the timer on her phone for five minutes and put in her mouthguard. They squared up again to spar.

34

The rain was bouncing off the restaurant window next to their table.

'Glad we're in here,' said Zach, looking at the glass. 'It's pouring out there.'

'I like it. It feels cosier.' She smiled across at him.

'Hopefully it eases up before we leave, else you might have a different opinion.' They both laughed.

'How's your food?' he asked.

'Really good. How did you find out about this place?'

'It's got a great reputation in the animal rights community, so I'm here a fair bit. Everything on the menu is vegan and the food is great. It's been busy like this since the first day it opened.'

Rachael looked around. The restaurant was packed. Salsa music pumped through the air, as staff sashayed between tables, a sense of raw energy and passion filling the space.

'So, is this your usual choice of meal, or are you trying to impress me with how deep undercover you can go?' she asked, whispering the last part across the table.

'At the start I was immersing myself to make sure I would fit in, but soon I realised I actually liked the food and it became easy. The other thing is, working with animal rights groups exposes you to footage and information that gets into your head as well. I don't agree with all the ways the groups go about things, but once you've seen what happens in meat and dairy production, you don't forget it. It changed what I eat very quickly.'

'So, no meat ever?' asked Rachael.

'Not anymore, and no dairy either.'

'But where do you get your protein?'

Zach laughed. 'Same place as gorillas, rhinos, hippos and bulls. From plants. There is plenty of protein in plants and beans. How much protein do you reckon you need?'

'No idea.'

'Exactly. Almost no one knows. On average it is less than sixty grams a day. Too easy.'

'Sounds like they have turned you,' said Rachael, shaking her head and smiling.

'I wouldn't go that far, but it is hard to disagree with what they're saying. I just disagree with their methods.'

She wanted to tell him how easy it was to be in his company, but she knew it was way too early to be pouring her heart out. She'd made that mistake before. They'd been talking for hours, about their interests and hobbies, no awkward silences, no weirdness. She was glad they hadn't had to resort to talking about work. It was as if they had been a couple for a long time.

He looked across the table at her. 'It is so good to be here with you,' he said, as if reading her mind.

She smiled and gave a tiny shake of her head. 'I know what you mean. Tell me something. How are you possibly single?'

Zach laughed. 'That's easy. Shift work, being a cop, being an *undercover* cop, being very picky about who I date. How many reasons would you like?' he asked, smiling. 'I could ask you the same question.'

Rachael smiled back at him. 'Okay, makes sense.'

'The truth is I've had a few relationships over the years, but none of them have been right, for one reason or another. You find you're with the wrong person or they find you're wrong for them. Or the timing is wrong. Same reasons since the dawn of time probably. When I was younger it didn't matter so much, but nowadays I am wary of bad relationships. It isn't worth the hassle, or the heartache, depending on which shoe you're wearing. If it doesn't feel right to start with, I steer well clear.'

Rachael nodded. She knew exactly what he was saying. The logical part of her brain was telling her to stay cool, but her heart was telling her to reach across the table, grab him by the head and kiss him with everything she had. She made a compromise with herself and let her fingers brush against his hand. The touch made her shiver with pleasure. Their hands began to dance gently together, fingers intertwining.

'It's too bad you live so far around the bay,' she said.

'Yes, it feels like a long way in peak-hour traffic, but I try and avoid that as much as possible. The house was my family home growing up. When my parents died, there was just me left—I felt sort of obliged to look after it.' Zach fell silent for a moment.

'Your parents must have been young when they died.'

'Mum was forty-five when she got breast cancer. By

the time they caught it, it was too late. They had less screening in those days. After that, my dad kind of gave up. He couldn't cope without Mum and died a year later. He needed sleeping pills to be able to sleep. The death certificate says drug overdose, but the real cause was a broken heart.'

Zach looked down at the table. Rachael enveloped his hand in hers.

'We're both a couple of orphans, I suppose.'

He looked into her eyes. 'What happened to your parents?'

She looked away for a minute, not wanting to look too closely at the pictures in her head. 'They had a fine art gallery in Brighton and both worked there, just the two of them. They were really happy; we laughed a lot when I was a kid. One day they'd just locked up and a group of men picked the lock to the back door and got inside. They had semi-automatic pistols and wore hats and bandannas to cover their faces. They tied my parents up and started emptying the safe and taking all the artwork. They had pulled a truck up to the back entrance of the gallery. They took their time. My parents had installed security screens on the front window and doors after previous robberies, and Dad had pulled them down when he was locking up, so no one could see in from the street. When they finished, one of the men walked up and shot my mother in the head. Then he did the same to my father.'

'Fuck, that's awful. How old were you?'

'I'd just turned eighteen. I was about to start university—law—but everything changed that day. After feeling sorry for myself for a year, I pulled myself together enough and joined the police. I guess I wanted to go and solve the case.'

'Was it ever solved?'

'No, the perpetrators vanished. The police told me that they were hopeful of an early arrest, based on the fact that there was only a few grand in the safe and that the people would be looking to sell off the art fairly quickly, but there were basically no leads from day one. Not that I've seen it, but there is plenty of security camera footage showing the whole thing from multiple angles. Didn't help in the end.'

'God, Rachael.'

'Yeah. I went looking for them and panicked when I saw the back door had a swastika spray-painted on it and that it was slightly open—and I don't actually remember anything after that. Apparently I called the police from inside the gallery, but it's all a blank. It took me a long time to come out of it.'

They sat silently for a few minutes. Zach's hand was now wrapped around hers.

'Do you ever wonder about what you would do if you found the people responsible?' he asked.

'Sometimes,' she said, 'but for me that's a dark place to go. I like to think I'd arrest them and do it by the book, but who knows? If the people who killed my parents suffered, I certainly wouldn't lose any sleep.'

Zach nodded. 'Yes, I can understand that.'

He leaned down and kissed her hand. Looking down at him, she smiled as the waiter came by with the bill.

Rachael stood by the full-length windows in her living room, looking out over the blackness of Port Phillip

Bay, a couple of fishing boats being the only points of light in a wide arc of darkness. The lights inside were off and she knew no one could see into the tinted windows of the apartment. To her right stood Melbourne's office towers, lights blazing away, illuminating her.

She sensed him come up behind her. Zach's hands landed gently on her hips and she felt a sudden warmth as he leaned forwards and kissed the top of her shoulder. He then kissed his way across, towards the base of her neck.

She turned back to him and looked into his eyes. 'Do you feel it?'

He nodded.

It was unlike anything she had ever known. They were like two dancers, familiar and trusting with each other.

Rachael pulled his shirt up and over his head. She threw the shirt on the sofa and placed her hands on his chest. He gently tugged her shirt up too, teasing it off. Rachael put her arms up and he pulled it carefully off. They kissed as he tried to undo her bra, without success.

'It does up at the front,' she whispered, smiling, into his ear. She pulled back and unclasped the front. She let her arms drop to her sides and the black bra fell to the ground behind her. Rachael unbuttoned her jeans and pushed them down her legs and pulled them off.

Zach was standing back, watching her.

'Your turn,' she said as she peeled off her underwear. Zach tore off his jeans as if they were suddenly on fire.

They stood facing each other, naked, aroused, delicately touching each other's bodies, each suddenly fragile. She kissed Zach passionately. He started to move down her front, until he was on his knees in front of her. Rachael moaned with pleasure as she held his head in her hands.

Eventually she pulled him back up towards her, kissing him again. She slowly turned away, towards the bay. Zach grabbed her by the waist and Rachael bent to place her hands against the window frame. Zach stood still, as Rachael pushed slowly back onto him, shuddering quickly with pleasure.

35

The two helicopters circled the property, their side doors slid back so news cameras could be pointed down at the house. On the ground below, ten police cars were scattered, spraying the trees with red and blue light in the gloom of the autumn evening. For the local police, bored with the banality of arresting the same ten criminals over and over again, this was exciting news. They would be asked about this case for the next month.

An ambulance was inside the gates, back doors flung open.

The property was remote, on a dirt road going nowhere in particular. People lived out there on the flat plains for one reason. Anonymity. Even Australia Post didn't deliver out here.

A tip off had come in, with the caller saying a woman was being held in a cage at a puppy farm for *crimes against animals*. The caller, who sounded like a teenage boy, gave an address for a property about twenty kilometres south of Bacchus Marsh, fifty kilometres to the west of Melbourne. He had said he had been given twenty dollars and a note telling him what to say, before quickly hanging up. The police traced the call to a public phone in the city, but the caller had vanished before they arrived.

The first officers entered the property fifteen minutes after the call and found the woman lying down in the cage. The first responders had gagged at the smell. They had given her water, pouring it through the cage with a hose. They then had to step back to a point where they could control their gag reflex. They radioed in that the report was accurate and to send an ambulance and a pair of bolt cutters. At that point, every police officer within ten kilometres descended on the property, eager to have a look at the woman in the cage.

When Rob had heard the woman was alive, he asked Julie to call Zach to attend the crime scene with the rest of the Taskforce. With a live victim, he knew her verbal description of the offender could prompt Zach's thinking on possible suspects within the animal rights community.

Rob arrived first, with Rachael and Julie in the car. Behind them, Mark and Dave pulled up. The forensics team from Major Crime Scene were already at work.

They got out of the cars and looked at the front of the property. It was guarded by a tall thick hedge and a custom-made gate. The gate was wide open, with crime scene tape strung across the space. They gave their name and badge numbers to the uniformed officer guarding the perimeter. As they were doing it, Zach arrived.

'Thanks for coming,' said Rob.

'No worries,' he said, looking around and nodding greetings to the rest of the taskforce crew. Zach gave his name and badge number to the officer guarding the site, who tilted her head and flashed him a smile. Rachael felt a pang of jealousy. They all walked down the driveway towards the paramedics, who were placing an intravenous saline drip into Sally Kinnaird's arm.

The team stood by impatiently, waiting to speak to the victim.

Dave was looking back down the driveway at the high hedge along the front boundary and the huge gates. He turned back and saw that the other members of the taskforce were all watching him. 'I was just thinking that, with all the hedges, giant gates and barbed wires around these parts, this region's slogan should be *Mind your own fucking business*,' said Dave, flatly.

Rachael gave the start of a laugh, before stifling it and looking down at her folder.

'You've got five minutes,' said one of the paramedics. 'Then we need to get her to the hospital.'

'Okay, thanks,' said Rob.

He and Julie took the lead and went over to the woman. Dave and Mark stood off behind the gurney, upwind, to try and avoid the smell. Rachael and Zach stood behind Rob and Julie, who were crouched down in front of the victim. They all tried to breathe through their mouths to dampen the impact of the smell of rotting shit in the air.

'Sally, I am Detective Senior Sergeant Rob Morello and this is Detective Senior Constable Julie Wang. Can you tell us what happened?'

'As I told those two,' she said, pointing at the two uniformed police officers standing nearby, 'I was walking back in from feeding the dogs around six o'clock two nights ago and the next thing I knew I was in here. Said he was stealing my dogs, the bastard. There were fifty here, plus about twenty pups.'

'How'd he take all the dogs? Did he have a truck or something?' asked Rob.

'No, he took my van,' Sally said, pointing at the van nearby.

Rob and Julie looked over at the van and then back at Sally.

'If he stole the van, what's it doing sitting there?'

'He brought it back after he took the dogs somewhere,' said Sally.

Rob and Julie gave each other a look. 'So, he stole your dogs in your van, and then he brought the vehicle back. Is that right?' asked Rob.

'Yep.'

'And how long was he gone?'

'Dunno. Probably an hour, hour and a half maybe.'

'Okay, so what did he look like?' asked Rob.

'About five ten to six foot. Hard to tell, as I was on the ground. Muscular, but not fat.'

'Hair colour?'

'Dunno.'

'Why is that?'

Sally looked at Rob and Julie, and then up at Rachael and Zach. 'Don't you idiots talk to each other? Like I told those other two coppers, the guy was wearing a Lycra suit, with a hood, so I couldn't see his hair.'

Julie looked at Sally. 'You mean like cyclists wear?'

'Yeah, the suit was a cycling suit, I'd reckon. Except this guy's suit didn't have writing on it, or colours. It was jet black. The hood was more like what you see scuba divers wearing. Looked like it was made from wetsuit material.'

'So, how old do you think he was?' asked Rob.

'Hard to say; about thirty, I reckon.'

'What about his race. Was he light skinned, dark skinned, Asian?

'Yeah, I know what race means. Fuck me. He was white.'

'Any accent?'

'No, he was an Aussie.'

'Did he sound posh, working class, anything like that?'

'No, just normal like you sound. Except he was a thief who steals dogs.'

'Had you ever seen him before? Was he familiar?'

'Nah, never seen him before. But he knew my name. I asked him who he was and he said his name was Joab.'

Rachael looked up from her folder. 'Can you say the name again?'

'Joab.'

Rachael stared at Sally as she wrote the name down in her folder. 'What about the fact that you were found guilty in court for animal cruelty last year? They found lots of emaciated dogs here when they raided you, didn't they? You think that's got anything to do with this?'

'How do you know about that?' said Sally, looking up at Rachael.

'We know about it because you've got a criminal record.'

'I paid my fine. That's all you need to worry about. When am I getting my dogs back? I've got orders to fill.'

'Sally, the story about your "stolen" dogs has been big news in the media for the past two days, about whose they were, why they'd been moved, how they could have ended up in such a neglected and emaciated condition.

They were left in the backyard of an unoccupied hobby farm, near Hoppers Crossing, and the guy who took them from you called it in that night to the Werribee Police Station. The premier came out yesterday and said they are not going back to wherever it was they came from, under any circumstances. So the dogs are safe, but they're not your dogs any more. The Lost Dogs' Home people are working to rehome them. '

'Fucking pricks. I loved those dogs.'

'The smell around these cages says otherwise. It looks like he was in here to rescue the dogs, not steal them, seeing as he delivered them to a safe environment and called it in straight away, wouldn't you say?'

'I would say that he stole my property, but it sounds like you are making me out to be the criminal here. You should be out there chasing that prick and putting him in jail. He was the one waving a gun around.'

They all looked at Sally.

'What gun?' asked Rob. 'Was it a pistol or a rifle?'

'It was a pistol. A black Glock. My son was a gun nut as a teenager. This one had the Glock logo engraved into the side of it, and the number *33*—definitely one of them,' she said.

The detectives shared a glance while Sally Kinnaird lay back for a moment and breathed heavily. She rallied to add, 'He also talked about my court case. Seemed like he knew a lot about it.'

'Anything else?' asked Julie.

'Yeah—he was a real smart arse. He asked me if I knew what the word *sentience* meant. Told me to look it up because that's why he locked me in the cage.'

'We'll have a look into that,' said Rob, who turned

and looked up to Zach to see if he had any questions. Zach looked down at Sally for a moment, before shaking his head. Rob turned back to Sally. 'Okay, someone will be down to the hospital to get a full statement once you have had a chance to rest.' He nodded at the paramedics and they started pushing the gurney towards the back of the ambulance.

Rachael saw the forensics officer looking in her direction. He gave her an upwards nod, so she got the team's attention and they all walked over together.

'Fuck, that Sally had a face like a dropped pie,' said Dave. Mark gave a quick snort of laughter.

'Well, she *was* stuck in a cage for two days,' said Julie, one eyebrow raised.

'Still, I can't see it getting much better with rest,' said Dave.

Rachael's mind was working overtime as they walked over. *David, Daniel, Damien. Fuck*. She sprinted through the possibilities.

'G'day, Damien, you found something?' she asked. He nodded. *Phew*.

'Yes, we've got footprints. Magnum work boots. Look like the right size. And a note again. Was folded up under a rock near the van.'

Damien opened up a paper evidence bag and pulled out the note with tweezers so they could see. There was just one word printed on the page. *Care*. Underneath was a black and white image of a man.

Rachael moved closer to have a closer look. 'Fuck,' said Rachael. 'That's Paul King. He owned PK Farm. He died late last year. Shot himself.' She looked at Mark, who was wide eyed, staring at the note.

They were all quiet for a moment, digesting the new information.

Damien continued, 'We've dusted the cab of the van for fingerprints. We've got smudged prints on the steering wheel and door handles. I'm fairly certain they will turn out to be the victim's own prints. Looks like the guy was wearing gloves that smudged the prints that were already there. No prints on the padlock from the woman's cage. We have done a few of the dog crates. Just smudged prints there too, like the van. We'll keep going, but I wouldn't hold much hope of finding anything. The guy is a pro, but we already knew that.'

'Thanks, Damien. Appreciate the update,' Rachael said.

As he walked away, the team gathered.

'Julie, can you run the name Joab through the database and see what we get? It's probably our guy trying to misdirect us, but it's worth a look,' said Rob.

'Will do,' said Julie. 'If we get a ping from the name, we can check it with the woman at PK Farm, the widow.'

'It's another message,' said Rachael.

'How so?' asked Rob.

'Joab was King David's nephew and commander of his armies. He defied the king often and followed his own rules,' said Rachael. 'Just like our guy, I suppose.'

Everyone stood staring at her for a moment. 'Right, okay then. I guess your knowledge of history and religion is why you got drafted by the Cold Case Unit,' said Rob.

'Where the fuck did you learn that?' asked Mark.

'School,' said Rachael, plainly.

Mark was glaring narrow-eyed at Rachael. 'What

sort of school was—?'

'Let's all sit around and reminisce about our teenage years some other time,' said Rob, cutting Mark off. 'What about the other thing he said to her. *Sentience*. What's that?'

'This came up on the cold case I was on before I came on to the Taskforce,' said Rachael. 'Sentience is the capacity for sensation or feeling. In this case he is talking about animals. It isn't about how smart an animal is, but rather about whether an animal can experience emotions like joy, sadness, loneliness, fear, contentment, that sort of thing.'

'So, that's why he's killing people and locking a woman in a cage, is it?' asked Mark. 'Because animals have feelings. Fuck me.' He shut his eyes and shook his head.

Dave gave Mark a sideways glance.

Rachael took a breath. 'Look, if we're going to catch this guy we need to understand the way he's thinking. If we just ignore it, we won't get anywhere.'

Everyone stood for a moment taking that in.

'So, why didn't he kill this woman?' asked Rob. 'Is it a gender thing?'

Julie shook her head. 'We haven't found any dead dogs,' said Julie. 'If he had found a dead dog, I think Sally would have been found dead as well. Also, when she was found guilty on animal neglect and cruelty charges, her court conviction shows that there weren't any dead dogs found on the day this place was raided, just a whole heap of nearly dead dogs. It's eye for an eye, remember. He's doing to them what they did to animals, and Kinnaird locked them up and underfed them—she didn't kill them.'

Rachael nodded. 'It's consistent with his approach. If you kill an animal for sport, you die. Keep an animal locked up and half-starved in a cage, you get the same.'

'Sounds plausible to me too,' said Rob.

'If that's the case,' said Mark, 'shouldn't he have tried to impregnate Kinnaird as well? That's what happens here, isn't it?'

Zach arched his eybrows at Mark. 'I think he made his point with the cage,' he said dryly.

'He's expanding beyond hunters as well,' said Julie. 'It looks to be more about animal cruelty in general with this new victim.'

'Yes,' said Rob. 'Zach, did her description or the name Joab ring any bells for you?'

'Her description was pretty vague. Average white guy. Sorry, I can't think of any animal rights people who stand out based on that. And the name Joab doesn't help. I'll run it by our team and see if rings a bell with anyone though.'

Rob nodded, disappointed. 'Thanks.'

'Shall I organise someone to go see Sally Kinnaird to get a photofit done of our hooded guy?' asked Rachael, looking at Rob.

'Yep, do it,' Mark said sharply, writing notes in his folder.

Rachael ignored him. 'This is why the crime scenes are so clean of hair fibres. The Lycra suit and the hood. Unless he was to lose an eyebrow hair or scratch his face, the chances of him leaving DNA are minimal.'

Rob nodded. 'Okay, Julie, try and find some reference to the name Joab somewhere on the main database, and check with police forces in other states as well. Also, get on to the Sunshine Magistrates' Court and view the CCTV from the day of Sally Kinnaird's appearance. Hopefully they will still have it.'

Julie nodded, making a note.

'Mark, look into this suit and hood lead. See who sells plain black cycling gear and diving hoods in the area we think this guy is living.'

'Needle in a haystack would be easier to find,' said Mark, gruffly.

Rob ignored him. 'Dave, go to the hospital and get her statement tonight. And find a decent photo of a Glock 33 and get her to confirm it was the firearm involved. And see if she has any link to PK Farm. Any link at all.'

'Got it,' said Dave.

'Can you get the photofit organised as well?' he asked. Dave nodded, noting it down in his folder.

'Rachael, as soon as I've finished with the media here, you and I will drive up to see Robert Vassar to see if he can account for his movements. Jonathon Shimmer is now out of the picture as he was in hospital when this woman went into the cage. Can you call Debbie Flint now and update her on what we've found out here tonight? Hopefully, this will help to narrow her profile.'

Rachael nodded, making notes.

36

The media were standing huddled behind the police tape at the gate. They were impatient for the press conference. The television reporters were getting text messages every minute for an update. Their producers wanted to know if they were going to get a live cross in before the end of the six o'clock news. If not, the story would be pushed to appear in updates throughout the evening and coverage on the late news. The newspaper journalists knew their deadlines were looming. The most relaxed reporters were from the radio stations. They would just cross live to the press conference whenever it started and someone in the studio would do the rest.

At six thirty-four, Rob made his way down the driveway towards them. The television reporters wore unhappy expressions. They'd missed the end of their main evening news bulletins by four minutes.

'Good evening. Everyone good to go?' asked Rob.

Once he saw they were ready, he started. 'Good evening. At approximately four-thirty this afternoon we had an anonymous tip that there was a person being held inside a dog cage at this address. Police attended the scene and found a forty-year-old woman locked in a cage. She has been transported to hospital. Apart from being dehydrated, she is in a stable condition.

'The victim was put into the cage two nights ago, early on Saturday evening. We have recovered some evidence at the scene that will need to be analysed over the next twenty-four hours,' said Rob.

A reporter jumped in with a question as Rob was taking a breath. 'Is the victim named Sally Kinnaird? The puppy farmer who was convicted last year of animal cruelty?'

Rob took a moment before answering. Behind him, in the distance, were a large number of cages, lit up by the Major Crime Scene team's lighting rigs. Rob knew there was little point deflecting the question. 'Yes, that's correct.'

'Seeing as the members of the Operation Torchlight Taskforce are here, do you believe that it is the same perpetrator as the two recent homicides?' asked a TV reporter.

Rob looked at the reporter through the glare of the media's spotlights. 'There is evidence at the scene that directly links this crime scene to the other two. We have found notes at all three crime scenes. Each of the notes consists of just one word. At Frogmore Swap, where Steve Lawrence was shot dead, we found a note with the single word, *Humane*, and a chicken feather taped to it. At Bulla, where Jim Camella was killed by an arrow, we found a note with the word, *Pests*. That note had a logo for a company called PK Farm printed on it as well. The note we found here tonight had the word *Care* printed on it. The was also a printed photograph of a man we believe is

Paul King, the former owner of PK Farm, who passed away last year.'

Rob could see the media trying to digest and process all of the information.

'Detective, what do these notes mean?' asked the reporter from Channel Nine.

'We're still analysing the information at the moment.'

'Why are we only now hearing about these notes?' asked a journalist from the *Herald Sun*.

'We were holding that information back because we were not sure if the perpetrator was looking to use the media to relay a message. With this third incident we are releasing the information in the hope that someone in the community will recognise what these clues mean in relation to any of the victims, or the perpetrator, and will call it in.'

A journalist from *The Age* raised her pen. 'Are the three victims linked to Paul King or PK Farm?'

'Not as far as we are aware. We are still to get a formal statement from tonight's victim. We are hoping to get that later this evening.'

'So what do you think PK Farm's connection is here?'

'We are simply not sure at this time. PK Farm is cooperating with our enquiries into this matter.'

'Do you have any indication why this person was left alive, whilst the other two victims were killed?' asked the ABC News reporter.

'No, not as yet. We still need to take a detailed statement from the victim first. That may shed some light on that question,' said Rob.

'Who called it in to police?' shouted out the reporter from *3AW*.

'The call came in this afternoon from a pay phone in Melbourne's CBD. We would appeal for that caller to come forward.'

'A duck hunter who gets shot dead, a horse trainer who shoots deer with arrows and then gets killed with an arrow, and now a puppy farmer who gets locked in one of her own cages. Is the perpetrator sending a message beyond just hunters here?'

'I cannot comment on that at this time. That is all I have. If anyone has any information, please get in direct contact with Victoria Police or Crime Stoppers. Thank you.' Rob turned and walked away from the gate where the media scrum was positioned. Behind him the reporters continued to call out questions in the vain hope he would be tempted to turn back and answer one of them. He kept walking, a grim expression on his face.

Rob had decided to hold back the name Joab. They would first try and run it through the system to see if it had been used as an alias elsewhere.

Time was running out.

37

The photofit sketch was stuck to the whiteboard.

'Fucking pointless,' Mark said. 'He looks like one of those alien sketches with that hood on.'

Rachael nodded. He was right. The image could have probably matched any one of a million people in the state. It showed a plain face, brown eyes, average nose and lips. The eyebrows were a light brown, but could have been a darker blond. Even the shape of the face couldn't be seen, as the edges of the hood hid that as well. Just part of a face in a hood, showing no hair. As a tool to help identify the offender, the image was essentially useless.

Rachael felt sleep deprived and knew the whole crew was feeling the same. There was no switching off from a case like this. You woke up in the morning thinking about it and went to bed the same way.

Mark walked back and rested on the edge of the table, still looking at the photofit. 'The only thing this confirms is that our guy is a white male. How did you go on your field trip to Vassar's place with Rob?'

'Vassar had an alibi for the night Sally Kinnaird was

locked in the cage. He said he was at the supermarket in Castlemaine. Rob and I went and viewed the footage from the supermarket's security cameras that show him entering the store around the same time Sally was being locked up a hundred kilometres away. He's out of the frame.'

'So, back to square one again.'

'Guess so,' said Rachael.

'Hey,' said Mark after a moment, his tone suddenly friendly. 'I noticed that Julie always looks good.'

'Yes, she does,' said Rachael.

'You know, she goes to a bit of effort with her make-up and stuff. I was thinking that you would look okay if you put on a bit more make-up for work.'

Rachael turned wearily and stared hard at Mark.

'Hey, just a suggestion,' he said.

'When make-up helps solve cases, I'll wear it. Got it?'

'Okay, okay, no need to get hysterical.'

Rachael turned to respond. 'Look—' she said, before seeing the flash of excitement in Mark's eye. She realised he was using her tiredness against her. He wanted her to lash out at work over something he would later claim was innocent conversation.

She took a deep breath as Rob Morello walked in with Debbie Flint, followed by Dave and Julie. Looking exhausted, Rob sighed as he sat down.

'Okay,' said Rob. 'Debbie has come in to update her profile based on what we discovered at Sally Kinnaird's crime scene. What do you have, Debbie?'

Debbie Flint opened her folder. 'Okay, Rachael briefed me over the phone on what you found last night. Based on the description from the victim, he is a white male in the age range outlined in the profile we already have. Regarding the new information: the Lycra suit and hood support what I said in the initial profile, that this guy is careful and organised. He is wearing gloves and the hood minimises the chances of him losing a stray hair or even being easily identifiable,' she said, pointing at the photofit image. 'There is nothing really distinctive about the gun. Glocks are fairly common handguns, but I believe that the victim identified the weapon as a Glock 33. Is that right?'

Dave nodded. 'Yes, I showed the victim enlarged photos of a range of Glocks, including the 33. She remembered seeing the number engraved into the side of the gun, next to the logo. My take was that it was a confident ID of the weapon. She seemed sure.'

'I know some of the other police forces use the Glock 22,' said Rob. 'How common is the Glock 33 in Australia?'

'Not very common, but who knows how many illegal guns are out there,' said Dave. 'I'm looking into members of the public who have a licence for 33s right now.'

'Good,' said Rob. 'Sorry, Debbie, go on.'

'No worries. Okay, the name *Joab* is most probably symbolic. As Rachael pointed out to you all last night, it is a biblical reference to King David's nephew, who was commander of his armies. Thanks to Google, I know that he defied the king and followed his own rules, just as this guy is doing. In the first profile I gave, I said that the offender may be an atheist. We may need to rethink that based on the religious connotations surrounding the name we now have. At the least, he will be well read, as the reference is pretty obscure.'

Rachael looked up from writing notes to see Mark staring straight back at her.

Debbie continued, 'It also reinforces my belief that this guy is acting alone, and isn't operating under anyone's orders. The only other thing is the detailed conversation the guy had with your victim. He *wanted* her to know why she was being locked up. This shows how emotionally invested he is in what he is doing.'

'Debbie, do you think he wants to be caught?' asked Rob. 'What I mean is, does he want to be caught so as he can have a forum for his beliefs?'

'Maybe. Maybe not. I wouldn't rely on it though. If he did, I think he'd be leaving longer messages.'

Rob nodded slowly. 'Julie, did you get any hits on the name?'

'No hits on the police databases here or interstate on the name *Joab*. I checked with the Feds as well. Nothing.'

'Did you get hold of Zach?'

'Yes, I spoke to him this morning. No luck there. The name meant nothing to anyone at ICSC.'

Rob sighed heavily, turning to Mark. 'Any luck on the Lycra suit and the diving hood?'

'Not so far. They're sold in a lot of places, including online, so they could have come from anywhere. I'm getting some samples to take to the victim and see if we can possibly narrow it down to a brand or style.'

'Good thinking. Okay, so we have three crime scenes, three notes containing a grand total of three words and some boot prints. The notes all refer to PK Farm, but we don't know what it means. We have a name, which we're presuming is a pseudonym, confirmation he is a white male, some distinctive clothing choices and a Glock 33.'

The rest of the team wore grim expressions. It still wasn't much to go on.

'In the meantime, we need to work out why the words the perp is leaving are so relevant. We have checked with the first two victims' families and friends. No significance to them. The latest victim, Sally Kinnaird, has no idea. Been through the court transcripts for Sally and the second victim, Jim Camella. Nothing there relating to the notes about them. The press and talkback radio are ramping up the pressure. For the last couple of weeks they've been titillated by the case, but now they're starting to get bored and want the case resolved so they can move on.'

Rob nodded at the photofit on the whiteboard. 'And we've got an image of the offender that's not worth releasing because it looks like a quarter of the population of the state. Heck, I can see thirty people in this building who could fit that image. Julie, what do we have from Crime Stopper tips? Anything useful?'

Julie opened her folder. 'Crime Stoppers have given us a list of tips that they got overnight following the press conference. A number of calls came in direct to the main Homicide phone line as well. We'll need to chase them all down today to sort out what's real and what's imagined.'

'And did you have any luck getting the CCTV footage from the Sunshine Magistrates' Court for Sally Kinnaird's court date?' asked Rob.

'Yes, but there's nothing there,' Julie said. 'There were some members of the media in the gallery of the court, as well as the old guy who sells most of Sally's puppies for her. No males that fit the bill inside the courtroom. It was mainly middle-aged female shoplifters that day. We'll speak to them all, but I can't see it going anywhere. There were a few police officers we know floating around the building at various stages, including Mark's old partner, but no one though who looks good for this.'

Mark said nothing and just stared at the table.

Still shitty his old partner jumped ship, Rachael thought.

Rachael's phone vibrated in her jacket. She put her hand in her pocket and pushed the button that would send the call to voicemail. She then stared at the table, suddenly lost in thought.

'What is it?' asked Rob, seeing her expression change. Everyone turned towards Rachael.

'We already checked the first two victims' social media accounts to see if anything they were posting about on their own page was linked to the words on the notes, but we didn't check if they had used those words posting on other people's pages—it could be in comments they made on other pages. We should get into their accounts to look at their activity logs over the past six months or so.'

'Okay,' said Rob, brightening, 'this is good. Rachael, head out west and see the puppy farmer. Dave, go and see Jim Camella's parents: I think they live in Trentham. You can head back home to Bendigo for a night with your wife and kids from there. Julie, you go see the first vic's wife, Charni Lawrence.'

'Good luck with her. She hates cops,' said Mark.

'Mark and I will go through the tips from Crime Stoppers and the ones that came in directly to Homicide,' said Rob. 'Let's reconvene back here in the morning. Good luck.'

Everyone got up and made for the door.

Rachael caught Rob's eye and motioned with her hand for him to stay behind. Once everyone else was gone, she shut the door.

38

'Hi, Rachael. What do you have?'

'I need to chat. Something confidential.'

'Okay, shoot,' Rob said, sitting down.

Rachael laid her hands flat on the table. 'You remember the day I joined the Taskforce I mentioned that I was looking at PK Farm as part of a cold case I was on?'

'Yes, I remember.'

'Let me just sketch in the background.' She filled Rob in on the crash, the make of the second car, and Helen and Grace's activism.

Rachael paused a moment, taking a breath, and continued. 'So as part of the re-investigation I went and spoke with the head of Animal Action, the group the two women were involved with. She said the only reason she could think of for them being up there at that time of the night would be because they had got a tip about animal abuse and had gone to have a look.'

She went on to detail the proximity of PK Farm and King's possession of the right kind of car, and his widow's reaction to their supposed whereabouts on the night of the crash. 'So the alibi is in question, but the person who apparently gave it is dead, so I can't go back to question him.'

Rob leaned forward, placing his elbows on the table and rubbing his forehead. 'What do you mean by *apparently*?'

'Well, it wasn't a signed statement. It was taken over the phone and never verified.'

'Okay,' said Rob, slowly.

'The other thing was that the senior detective on the case told his partner, the day after the crash, that he spoke to Paul King and alibied him. Makes sense he would go there first. Two dead animal activists and a factory farm around the corner, but there is no trace of that statement anywhere, just one taken the next week after the list of Commodore VZ owners came in from VicRoads.'

'So, you think the whole thing is fishy?'

'Well, it doesn't smell good to me. Thing is—.' She trailed off and looked at him.

'Spit it out.'

'Mark Cullen took the alibi.' Rachael paused for a moment as Rob closed his eyes. 'Dianne King also told me she and her husband had been friends with Mark since primary school.'

'Fuck.'

'That's what I thought. Mark's partner back then was Johannes Petra, who is now a detective sergeant with PSC. We went to have a chat with him about the case. Johannes clearly remembers Mark telling him that he had alibied the King couple the day after the crash. He has detailed personal diary notes on the case. He told us they were sure that the victims were up that way on some sort of animal cruelty raid and that PK Farm was the only option within cooee of the crash site. He said that once PK Farm was ruled out, they had nothing. I didn't tell him about the fact there was no record of Paul King being alibied the day after the crash. I was still trying to get all the pieces together when I got called onto the Taskforce, so the case is on ice until I get back.'

Rob was staring at the table, deep in thought.

Rachael continued, 'When I spoke to the woman who runs Animal Action, she also said that Mark told her he'd alibied the people from PK Farm the day after the crash.'

'And now we have notes left at our crime scenes linking these crimes to PK Farm,' said Rob.

'Exactly. And with the photo of Paul King on the latest note, I'm certain now that this killer is also telling us there is a link to the car crash.'

'Are you thinking that the guy committing our crimes thinks that Paul King is responsible for the car crash that killed those women, and that he also killed King? That it wasn't a suicide at all?' asked Rob.

'That's possible, but why make it look like a suicide? If our current perp killed Paul King, I would have expected a note with one word on it, like the others. I reckon someone found out Paul King was involved in the fatal car crash and was putting pressure on him or blackmailing him. Paul then felt cornered, cracked under the pressure and shot himself. He couldn't have known at the time that Cold Case was going to be reviewing the case, so it wasn't that.'

They sat in silence for a minute while Rob mulled the information over.

Rachael spoke again. 'The other issue is the video

cameras. For animal rights investigations to be of any value they need evidence of animal abuse—right?—so the two women would never have gone without a way to record what they found. Emma Jennings from Animal Action is adamant she told Mark that two video cameras went missing the night the victims died, but there's no mention of this in the case file.'

'Is she sure she told Mark about this?'

'She seemed particularly clear about it. The equipment would've cost a couple of thousand dollars to replace, and they aren't swimming in cash. She remembers.'

Rachael silently looked at Rob, as he processed the information. After a moment he looked up. 'I think that we need to bring Julie and the DI across this. I mean, Mark needed to mention how close he was to Paul King and PK Farm on the first day he landed on the Taskforce and saw PK Farm's logo on that second note. That's basic regulations level stuff. Let's arrange to meet with DI Parker and Julie tonight and come up with a plan that works. I'll make a call and get us a quiet room at the South Melbourne station. We'll go through it all in detail again then.'

'Sounds good. Just… one more thing,' said Rachael.

'Fuck,' said Rob, exasperated, rubbing his face with his hands, 'what else?'

'Paul King's suicide. The investigating detectives were Mark and Johannes.'

Rob cleared his throat. 'Right, so we have Mark telling his partner the day after the crash that the King couple have an alibi for that night, but there is no written record of that anywhere. And he also allegedly said the same thing to the Animal Action woman. Then she tells him that two video cameras are missing and he makes no note of it anywhere.'

'Yes.'

'And then we have him investigating and signing off on his mate's suicide.'

'That's about it, yes.'

'What a fucking mess. Why didn't you tell me all this earlier?'

Rachael sucked in a breath. She knew the question had been coming. She looked Rob in the eye.

'I knew that there were plenty of holes in the investigation of the car crash. Once the Taskforce was wrapped up, I was planning to go back and dig harder— build the case and then let Professional Standards know if I needed to. If I made allegations against a senior detective without the proper evidence though, my career would be destroyed. That's why I was holding back.'

Rob slowly nodded his head. 'Yes, fair enough.'

'And until I saw Paul King's photo on the note last night, the links between the Taskforce cases and my cold case could well have been coincidental, just as you said at the first meeting. Now I'm convinced there is no coincidence.'

'Yeah, I agree. Thanks for letting me know,' he said, standing up and making for the door.

39

The next morning Rachael walked into the Homicide office. She poured a coffee in the kitchen area and wandered to her desk.

Mark and Dave sat nearby.

'Hey guys.'

'Hi, Rachael,' said Dave. Mark kept his head down, making notes.

'Where's everyone else?'

'Not sure,' said Dave.

At that moment, Detective Inspector Tom Parker entered the room, followed by Rob and Julie. He walked towards the cluster of desks that the Taskforce was using.

'Good morning, everyone. Can we meet in the conference room?' asked Tom, not breaking stride as he went past.

'No problem,' said Dave. Rachael nodded.

Mark looked up from his writing after a moment. He gave a sigh as he got up from his desk.

They all took their seats, with Tom at the head of the table. He nodded to Rob.

Rob sat forward. 'What is everyone's update?'

'Well,' said Dave, 'I can confidently report that we are as popular as a tiger snake in a lucky dip with the section sergeant up in Bendigo. Dianne King called yesterday complaining that there were reporters and media vans parked at PK Farm's gate after the press conference at the cage woman's place. They were buzzing the intercom every five minutes wanting a comment on the crimes and her connection to them. The sergeant reckons the media were trying to taunt her so she'd crack it and march down to the gate to scream and yell at them for the cameras. So Bendigo have had to send a car and a couple of uniformed officers down there to stand guard and keep them away from the intercom button. I told the sergeant they should lose interest pretty quickly as there are no decent coffee shops nearby. He didn't laugh.'

'Okay,' said Rob, letting out a frustrated sigh. 'I meant an update on the social media hunt?'

'Gotcha, sorry,' said Dave. 'Jim Camella's parents were happy for us to have access to his phone. Checked through his posts on other pages: mostly moronic stuff about pizza, beer, women and hunting, but he also commented a lot on the Animal Action's Facebook page, having a go at people who defended animal rights. Nasty stuff—some of it was quite threatening. He kept using the word *Pests* over and over when justifying his hunting. He made hundreds of comments on the Animal Action page over the past year. I saved off a good sample of them, plus I saved off his login details,' he said, tapping his finger on the file in front of him.

'Okay, that's good stuff. Thanks. Rachael, what do you have?' asked Rob.

'Sally Kinnaird took some convincing to let me on

her computer. I ended up telling her that if we didn't catch the guy he might be back for her and that the other two victims were dead. She gave me her password quickly after that. She was a prolific commenter on an anti-puppy farming page on Facebook; they want puppy farms closed down and outlawed. Her comments on that page there were generally quite feral, but there were also several dozen posts where she was stating how much she loves her dogs. In those posts, she used the word *Care* repeatedly. I pulled a list of the males who commented negatively about her around the same time and who fit our guy's description.' Rachael nodded to indicate that was the end of her report.

'Okay, over to you, Jules,' said Rob.

Julie opened her folder. 'I saw Steve Lawrence's widow. Went through the activity log and found he had made hundreds of comments on an anti-duck hunting page, especially in the lead-up to the season. He was commenting about how great duck hunting was, how it was all about conservation and how it was a family-friendly activity. Apart from abusing the anti-duck shooting people, he did use the word *Humane* a lot when he talked about it. He was not trolling other pages though, just the anti-duck hunting one. I looked back and he was doing the same thing around the same time every year just prior to the duck-hunting season.'

'Did you save his login details?' asked Rob.

'Yeah, told his wife we needed to analyse the posts.'

'Sounds like all three of our victims were internet trolls,' said Rachael.

'I thought trolls were mostly just keyboard warriors, hiding behind their screens,' said Dave.

'That's generally true,' said Rachael, 'but these three victims were also engaged in actions that backed up their online comments. Maybe the trolling made them targets, and then their real-world actions triggered our guy to go after them.'

Rob tapped his pen on the table. 'Mark, what did you find from the Crime Stopper tips?'

'In a word, nothing. Loads of people dobbing in their neighbours. Eliminated most of them based on the race, gender or age of the person being reported. There were three worth chasing, but they all had solid alibis for one or more of the times when the crimes occurred.'

Rob nodded. 'Same with the tips I was chasing. Nothing there. Okay, Julie, give the Tactical Intelligence Officers the usernames and passwords for all three victims' Facebook accounts as well as the three Facebook pages that they were trolling. We'll see if we have any common connections across all of those pages, the anti-duck shooting one, the Animal Action one and the anti-puppy farmer page. There may be white males that fit our profile connected to all three. Our killer may be in that list.'

'Yes, understood,' said Julie.

Tom Parker leaned forwards. Everyone looked down the table towards the detective inspector. 'Right,' he said, 'thanks. Mark, we'd like a word. Everyone else can go.'

Rachael, Julie and Dave stood up, grabbing their folders. Dave hesitated, looking confused, before following the others to the door. As they went out the door, a woman walked in and shut the door behind her.

'Mark,' said Tom when they had the room, 'this is

DI Mary Costa from Professional Standards Command.'

Mary sat down and nodded to Mark, grimly.

Tom continued. 'You are being suspended, with pay, while there is a disciplinary review of your conduct whilst you have been part of the Taskforce.'

Rage rose in Mark's gut. 'What are you talking about?'

'You have a major conflict of interest that you should have disclosed on the first day you arrived here, as soon as you saw that PK Farm was connected to this case.'

'What conflict of interest?'

'Well,' interjected Rob, 'you are childhood friends with the owners of the farm. That is a conflict right there.'

Mark sat silently, his face hot.

Tom said coolly, 'There's some formalities to go through with DI Costa and then you can head off home until further notice. I need to secure your firearm now, and your badge.'

They watched carefully as Mark pulled his gun from his belt—Rob had kept his jacket well open throughout just in case he had to draw his own weapon. Mark put the gun down flat on the table and slid it across, leaving a light scratch on the surface. He then pulled out his badge and spun it through the air, landing it next to the gun.

'Thank you,' said Tom, picking them both up. 'Rob, you can head off now while we get the paperwork sorted.'

Rob nodded and got up. He left the room without looking at Mark.

Rob walked towards his office, signalling for Rachael, Julie and Dave to follow him. 'Close the door, please,' he said to Dave. Rachael and Julie sat in chairs across from Rob. Dave stood, leaning against the door.

'Mark has been suspended from duty, as of right now.'

'Crikey. What for?' asked Dave.

'Conflict of interest,' said Rob. 'He is childhood friends with the people who own PK Farm and he didn't let us know.' Tom and Rob had decided that the suspension would be officially due solely to Mark's relationship with the King couple; the other issues would come out when Mark's review by PSC happened.

'Shit, I had no idea,' said Dave. 'He never told me.'

'Yes, I know,' said Rob.

Rachael looked at Rob. 'So what's the plan of attack now?'

'Dave, I want you based back in Bendigo, working the case from there. The rest of us will stay here. We will teleconference every morning, just like we meet every morning now. It will save people driving all over the place and eliminate your hotel bills down here at the same time.'

Dave looked crestfallen. 'Boss, I swear to you that I really didn't know about Mark and those people from PK Farm.'

'Yes,' said Rob, looking Dave in the eye, 'we know that. It is not related to the thing with Mark. It just makes logistical sense, that's all.'

'Okay then, if that's the case, it's great by me. My wife will be putting you on her Christmas card list,' said Dave, brightening.

Rob went on. 'As soon as the Tactical Intelligence Officers have compiled the list of white males who were on the three Facebook pages getting trolled, we will start rounding them up for interviews. I suspect that they will be scattered across the state. Dave, I'll send through the ones based up towards Bendigo to you. Make sure you take someone with you when you go and see anyone. I'll call DI Martinez at Bendigo CIU to explain the situation with Mark's suspension and arrange someone to back you up.'

Dave nodded.

'In the meantime, Tom has arranged to borrow some detectives from Melbourne CIU to act as floaters. They will chase up the rest of the list down here. I'll be briefing them shortly. Julie and Rachael, once we get the list of possible suspects from the Facebook data mining, I want us to go back to the families of the victims of the cold case to see if anyone sounds familiar to them.'

'Sounds good,' said Julie.

'I also want to have a look at the woman at Animal Action again.'

Rachael went to speak, but caught herself. Rob noticed. 'I know you think she's a dead end, Rachael, but we need to be thorough.'

Rachael nodded. She knew he was right.

'We're getting to the pointy end now, so we need to get this guy soon,' said Rob. 'There's been a lot of attention from the media on the animal abuse links between the victims. The journos are doing their own investigations and finding plenty of dirt on the victims. The Police Media team have been following the press reports as well as social media sentiment, and there is a shift happening in the attitudes of the community. Attitudes are moving negatively against the victims and positively towards the perpetrator of these crimes. This guy is heading for folk hero status in some sections of the community—if we don't catch him soon, the majority of people won't want him getting caught at all. Once that happens, any leads or community support will dry up.'

At that moment they heard a door slam, vibrating the walls. Rachael and Julie turned in their seats just as Mark stormed past the window.

40

Rob looked down at the list of names. Homicide's Tactical Intelligence Officers had taken three hours to compile a list of Facebook users who followed all three of the pages that their case's victims had been trolling.

There were about five hundred people active across all of the three different pages, living in Victoria and active on social media around the time the sites were being trolled by the victims. Luckily, only forty-two of them were white males.

'You there, Dave?' asked Rob towards the speakerphone.

'Yes, here boss.'

'Okay, we've got forty-two people in total that we need to check out. Ten of those people live between here and Bendigo and we need you to chase them down. I spoke to DI Martinez and he said he'd get you sorted with an interim partner.'

'Yes, he spoke to me when I got back. It's all good.'

'We'll need you to also speak to the families of our current victims, Steve Lawrence and Jim Camella, as well as Sally Kinnaird—see if they react at all to any of the forty-two names. I'll get the full list off to you by email in a minute.'

'Thanks, boss.'

'No worries,' said Rob. 'Speak to you soon, bye.'

'See ya.'

Rob hit the button on the phone, disconnecting the call, then pulled his laptop over in front of him and sent the email to Dave.

'Okay,' he said, 'next steps. The four floaters on loan from Melbourne CIU are chasing up the remainder of the list—the other thirty-two people. I'll catch up with them at end of day and review where they're at. I'll let you know if anyone is looking like a suspect. While that's happening, we need to go and see whether any of the forty-two names ring any bells with the families of the two women killed in Rachael's cold case, and also the Animal Action woman. Rachael, what's your impression of her?'

'She's passionate about her cause. She feels guilty about the two women dying while she was away and I doubt she's taken another holiday since. She has a long criminal history due to her activism, mostly for trespassing and break and enters. All of the charges are around animal issues. Magistrates don't tend to let this stuff slide, exactly, but at the same time they probably wouldn't sleep well after sending people like this to prison. She usually gets fines, sometimes big ones. No history of violence against people of course.'

'Who pays all the fines?' Julie asked.

'The organisation is a voluntary one, so the fines are often paid by supporters. They put out a call for donations and people step up. They also get money through merchandise, T-shirts and stuff like that.'

Rob opened his folder and made a note. 'Okay,' he

said. 'Julie and I will go and see Emma Jennings. Rachael, we'll hold you back, as you weren't treating her as a person of interest when you met with her—we may need you to rekindle the relationship at some point if we rule her out completely.'

'Understood. What do you want me working on?'

'Go and see Grace Blackwood's family. Run through the Facebook list with them and see if they react to any of the names. And try and suss out if they think any of her friends might have taken things into their own hands. First up tomorrow I'll get you and Julie to go and see Helen Ng's family and chat to them in the same way. Julie will lead that one obviously.'

Julie laughed. 'Why's that, Rob?'

'Well…ah…'

'You know my background is Chinese, not Vietnamese, right?' asked Julie, smiling.

Rob blushed. 'Yes, sorry. I had a senior moment there. Let's get out of here before I put my other foot in my mouth.'

They all got up. Julie and Rachael shared a subtle smile.

41

Rachael pulled off the Western Highway before Ballarat and negotiated the back roads towards the Blackwood family's farm. She was surrounded by paddocks the whole way, with either sheep or cows in each. A large livestock truck roared past her, shaking her car in its wake. She caught a glimpse through the grates of sheep jammed in, a flash of terrified eyes looking out. Rachael thought of Billy and what Yvette had said about winning the lottery. She couldn't help being reminded of those films showing death trains in Europe during World War II.

As she drove up to the Blackwood house, her mind was still on the truck. She was brought back to the present by the sight of a woman standing on the front porch.

Rachael parked the car and got out. 'Mrs Blackwood. I'm Rachael Schlank.'

'Hello, Rachael,' she said. They shook hands. 'Please, call me Belinda.'

Rachael gave her a subdued smile and walked inside. Belinda gestured Rachael towards the living room.

Once they sat down, Belinda immediately sat forward. 'So, do you have news about the crash? Has someone been arrested?'

'No, no one has been arrested. I'm here because I'm working on another case that may be linked to your daughter and Helen Ng's crash.'

'What case are you talking about?'

'I'll get to that in just a sec. First off, what is your opinion of Paul King?' Rachael watched for any reaction from Belinda Blackwood, looking for any sign that she recognised the name.

Belinda stared down, searching her memory. Rachael looked through the glass coffee table at Belinda's feet. Rachael knew that a person's feet tended to unconsciously twitch and move under stress. Belinda's feet were still.

After a few moments, she spoke. 'The name sounds familiar, but I don't think I know who that is. Why?'

'He was a person of interest in your daughter's death. He died last year.'

'Person of interest? The detective on the case back then said they didn't have any suspects.'

'Yes, well, the case is being re-investigated. Mr King had an alibi back then, which is being reviewed right now. And he was a person of interest, not a suspect. Anyone possibly connected to a case can be a person of interest. It's a long way from being a suspect.'

'But he is dead, you said.'

'Yes, unfortunately.'

Belinda looked down. Rachael took a moment to look around the room. Photographs of Grace hung on the walls. There were other girls of similar ages in some of the photographs.

'Is your husband here at the moment?'

'No, my husband died a couple of years ago. He had a stroke. I found him out beside the tractor.'

'I'm very sorry,' said Rachael.

'He never… *we* never got over Grace's death. It took the life right out of him. We couldn't move on without answers. We'd call the detective in charge, Mark Cullen, every few days at first for an update, then every month, then every six months, then once a year, until I think my husband just gave up on ever getting justice for Grace. It has been almost ten years now since Grace died. The detective would just say the same thing every time. *No new information at this time*. It was almost robotic the way he said it.'

'I am sorry about this. I can tell you that the crash is being looked at again by the Cold Case Unit.' Rachael neglected to say that she was doing that investigation.

'That makes me feel a bit better, knowing she and Helen haven't been forgotten by the police.'

'What are Grace's sisters doing now?'

'Bethany got married and lives in Los Angeles. She generally comes home to visit once a year, or I fly over. She has two children. Cate is a doctor in Adelaide. I see her a few times a year. I catch up with them both every week by video conferencing on the computer. It's not the same as having them here, but it is good to see them and talk in real time.'

'What about Grace's friends? Do you still know them?'

'Yes, I know some of them. Helen was her best friend of course. She had some friends at university, but most of her close friends were tied up with the animal rights movement. She was studying law, but was starting to become disillusioned. She went into law believing in the idea of justice, but the more she saw in the world, the more she was losing faith in the system. She would see the people she knew being charged with property crimes or trespassing for trying to save animals' lives and that upset her terribly. At the same time, people who killed or abused animals for their own enjoyment got a fine, if that. Anyway, to answer your question, most of her friends stay in touch sporadically. They have jobs, families. Some of them are still local, but a lot have moved away.'

'Can I get the names of those people she was friendly with who are still living in Victoria?'

'Sure. We could start with the memorial book, from the funeral.'

Belinda got the book from the bookshelf and they went through the names, with Belinda pointing to each and identifying Grace's friends, as opposed to family members or family friends. At the same time, Rachael was seeing whether any of the names looked familiar from her memory of the list of forty-two names the Tactical Intelligence Officers had data mined from Facebook. None of the names stood out.

'What about relationships? Was she involved with anybody before the crash?'

'No, she was concentrating all of her energies on her studies and her animal lib work. She had a boyfriend after high school for a while, but then nothing serious for years. She would have had brief relationships, I'm sure, but nothing long-term. She would have told me if it were anything serious. We were very close.'

'Yes, I understand. Belinda, this question might seem a bit shocking, and I apologise for that. Do you think any of her friends might have taken the law into their own hands to avenge Grace's death?'

'What—seriously?' Belinda *was* shocked; Rachael was in no doubt. The older woman shook her head. 'Wait. Who exactly would they take revenge against? There were no suspects. Some of the animal lib people thought there was a factory farm in the area, but Detective Cullen told us no one was there that night.'

Dead end. 'Belinda, I know this is going to be a bit laborious, but I need to read you a list of names. Can you tell me if you know or have heard of any of these people?'

'Yes, of course,' said Belinda.

Rachael opened her folder and read through the list of forty-two names, pausing after each name to see Belinda Blackwood's reaction. She knew none of them.

Belinda narrowed her eyes. 'What is this new case you're working on, the one you mentioned when we started talking? Is it that person I've been reading about in the newspaper who's running around killing hunters and who locked that puppy farmer in the cage?'

'Why do you ask that?'

'I just remembered where I had heard Paul King's name before. It was in the paper after the woman was released from the cage. His photo was on the note left at the property, wasn't it?'

Rachael hesitated before answering. 'Yes, that's correct.'

'And you think that case is linked somehow to Grace's crash?'

'We simply do not know enough to say that at present. There has been some evidence at the crime scenes linking the crimes to Paul King. As I said before, he was a person of interest in Grace and Helen's crash. That's as much as I can say right now: the investigation is live and ongoing.'

Belinda Blackwood stared at Rachael. 'Do you think someone is killing these people as revenge for Grace and Helen?'

'We're not sure. That is one possibility, but there are others.'

'I have been following those cases in the newspaper. It got me thinking about what Grace would have thought. Probably she would have hoped you never catch him. I was thrilled when I saw on television that the guy who tortured that poor deer with the arrows had been killed. I clapped my hands and laughed. The justice system just protects psychopaths like him, so all power to the person taking these people out permanently.' Belinda Blackwood was shaking with emotion as she finished speaking.

Rachael looked at her. Grace had inherited her passion from her mother. Belinda Blackwood shook her head, turning to stare out of the window.

'I will need to speak to your daughters as well.'

'Yes,' Belinda said. 'I'll give you Cate's number. If you want, you can Skype with Bethany now. I was just talking to her before you arrived and she wanted me to call her right back once you left. It is around eleven pm there now,' she added, looking at her watch. She got up. 'Let me get my iPad. You can talk to her on that.'

At six pm Rachael pulled into the car park at the Homicide office. She took the lift up and walked over to where Rob and Julie were sitting.

'How did you go with Emma?' asked Rachael.

'We don't think she's involved, although she isn't exactly upset about our vigilante. She had a good laugh about the puppy farmer woman getting locked in the cage. She thought it was a hoot,' said Julie.

'Yes, I thought she would. Grace's mum had some similar feelings as well.'

'We took Emma through the list of names,' said Julie. 'No hits. She said none of them were activists she knew. Her body language was consistent with that as well.'

Rob leaned back in his chair. 'Emma Jennings also confirmed again that she told Mark all those years ago that the video cameras were missing. You were right: she is very clear about it. Decent quality video equipment cost a lot back then and she remembers having to hold a couple of fundraisers to get new cameras.'

'I suppose that will be an issue for Professional Standards to follow up with Mark,' said Julie.

'How'd you go with Grace Blackwood's family?' asked Julie.

Rachael grabbed a chair and sat down. She gave them the condensed version of her chat with Belinda Blackwood.

'What about the sisters?' asked Rob, once she finished.

'Yes, I spoke to them both and went through the whole thing. Neither seemed to know anything relevant.'

'Let's all get a good night's sleep. We'll attack this fresh in the morning,' said Rob, looking out into the darkness through his window. 'I need a drink.'

42

Rachael retrieved the recorder from the Velcro pocket in her jacket and left it on the kitchen bench next to her keys before heading in to run a bath and undress. She locked her gun in the safe.

She scrolled through her music on her phone, clicking on a Miley Cyrus playlist. She slipped into the bath and let the heat of the water do its job, loosening the tension in her body.

An hour later the intercom buzzed. She checked the screen next to the front door and could see Zach standing there, holding up two plastic bags in his hands. She buzzed him into the lobby downstairs.

Two minutes later there was a knock at the door.

Rachel opened the door. 'Hey there.'

'Wow. Nice outfit,' he said, smiling openly at her grey T-shirt and sweat pants.

'Not too casual for you?'

'Heck no. Perfect.'

He placed the food down on the bench, smiled and scooped his right hand behind her back, pulling her body firmly against his, and running his left hand through her hair. He kissed her, softly at first and then more passionately.

'I got us Thai food,' he said.

'Yum. I love it.'

'You've got a microwave, haven't you?' he whispered, leaning in against her neck. Rachael felt the words vibrate on her skin, radiating warmth within her.

Rachael pushed away slightly and then grabbed at his shirt. She gently pulled him as she walked backwards to her bedroom, all the while looking into his eyes. She laid down on the bed and pulled her T-shirt off, throwing it to the floor. Zach pulled his shirt over his head and threw it on top of hers. He then lay hovering above her, supported by his elbows.

They shared a passionate kiss before Zach started to move down her neck towards her breasts. Rachael cradled his head against her body. She could smell that his hair had just been washed. He was kissing her breasts as she started to push him slowly down the length of her body.

An hour later they sat at the kitchen bench, eating Thai food and drinking a beer each.

'What's the deal with the recorder?' asked Zach, pointing with his beer at the equipment on the bench.

Shit. Shit. Shit.

Rachael screwed up her face. 'I've got a small confession to make.'

'Darn, I didn't bring my handcuffs,' he said, smiling. 'Okay, out with it.'

'I have a crap memory. I use the recorder to tape interviews so I can go back and review them later if I need to. I get too busy watching the body language of the interviewee. This way I can concentrate on the person and also capture all of the information. I've got a microphone that sits under my lapel, with a switch to turn it on and off.' She neglected to say that it was only the secondary reason for the recorder.

'Is that legal?'

'Well, it is kind of a grey area,' she said, smiling coyly, 'but I just do it for my own purposes. I don't use it directly as evidence.'

'So, how long has this been going on?'

'About fourteen years,' said Rachael, suddenly feeling exposed.

'Crikey, that's a serious hobby you have there. So what do you do with all the recordings?'

'I've got a box of hard drives. We're talking terabytes of data over the years.'

'Sounds like you're your own spy agency. That will make a nice archive for a historian one day.'

'It is just a back-up, just in case I ever need to go back to it, but do me a favour and don't mention it to anyone.'

'Your secret is safe with me. You aren't recording anything right now, are you?' asked Zach, an eye towards the bedroom.

Rachael laughed. 'No, the apartment is clear of recording devices of all types. You're safe.'

'Good to hear. So, how is the Taskforce going?'

'Round and round in circles. Mark Cullen got suspended this morning.'

'What? Why?' asked Zach, stunned.

'He has been friends with Paul and Dianne King

from PK Farm his whole life, and he should have disclosed it when he joined the Taskforce, but didn't. So he was suspended for having a conflict of interest.'

'Wow, big day then.'

'Dramatic, yes. I brought it up with the bosses yesterday. I was worried it would jeopardise the current case somehow. There are a heap of other red flags that have come up in my review of an old case Mark investigated in 2007, but they're being left to another day.'

'Like what?' asked Zach.

'It's a long story and I don't want to sit around all night talking about work.'

'Come on,' he said, 'don't leave me hanging.'

'Okay, I'll give you the condensed version. Before I joined the Taskforce, I was working a cold case, the deaths of two animal activists in a car crash in 2007. The crash happened right around the corner from PK Farm.'

'Yes, I'm familiar with it. Emma Jennings reminds people of it before they do raids. She was very close to the two women who died.'

'She sure was. Anyway, I think that the perp in our current Taskforce cases thinks they know what happened out there in 2007 and is pointing us at PK Farm. What I do know is that the original investigation was shoddy, at best.'

'How so?' he asked.

She ran Zach through the inconsistencies in Mark's report.

'Shit,' said Zach at the end of it. 'So, do you think Mark was covering for Paul?'

'It looks like it.'

'So there is a suspicious alibi, conflicting stories

about the video cameras, and Mark investigating his friend's suicide,' said Zach.

'Yes, that's about it.'

'Have you let Professional Standards know yet?' asked Zach.

'Kind of. Mary Costa, the DI at Professional Standards, knows about Mark having been lifelong friends with the King couple. She was there today when he got suspended, I'm not sure if Rob told her the rest. I am guessing not, as PSC play things straight down the line.'

'Does Paul King's suicide look suspect to you?'

'Maybe, maybe not. Bullet in the side of the head in the middle of the night last November. No note, no alcohol or drugs in his system, no apparent signs of depression beforehand. Gunshot residue on his right hand, gun beside him on the ground. Strange situation, but open and shut. His wife was in Europe at the time. She had a long plane ride home alone.'

They sat silently for a moment.

'What made you suspect this guy, Paul King, in your cold case?' asked Zach.

'It was simply because the victims of the crash were animal rights activists and he had a factory farm around the corner. Simplest answer is usually the correct answer. What's that called again?'

'Occam's razor, I think,' said Zach. 'Any new leads on the Taskforce cases?'

'Yes. We now believe that the words on the three notes found at the scenes are linked to the Facebook accounts of the victims. We think this is how they are becoming targets. They were trolling animal rights-type Facebook pages and our perp has seen what they were writing.'

'Sounds promising.'

Rachael nodded. 'Hopefully we're getting closer.'

'So, what's Mark been like with you, up until him getting suspended this morning?'

'Same as always. We have never got along, ever since I was in uniform. I was having coffee with Julie a few weeks ago and, from what she told me, it sounds like Mark's been spreading rumours about me to whichever departments I've worked in since I left Bendigo CIU nine years ago.'

'What, like to sabotage you?'

'Exactly, he spread a rumour around Homicide that I was an informant for PSC. I went and checked with Amit, and the rumour when I got to the Cold Case Unit was that I had botched a homicide case.'

'Fucking prick.'

'That sums him up nicely.'

'Do you want me to beat him up for you?'

'Sure, sounds good,' said Rachael, smiling. 'Let's get back to bed.'

43

Rachael and Julie pulled off the Calder Freeway, heading towards PK Farm after an early finish to the morning meeting. Dave Boucher had given his update over the phone from Bendigo, reporting that he was working through the list of Facebook users he had, speaking to five of them since the previous day, and was in the process of verifying alibis. No one was looking like a good candidate so far.

Rob had decided Rachael and Julie would reinterview Dianne King while he went to interview the Ng family. The women had grinned in memory of Rob's cultural misstep the day before.

Rachael looked out the car window as they drove, taking in the sights of the countryside. She saw a large group of kangaroos standing together near the base of a hill, taking in the autumn sunshine. She could see a couple of the roos had joeys, their small heads sticking out of their mother's pouches.

They pulled up at the gate outside PK Farm. The media had obviously given up; the road was empty once more.

'It looks like Dianne King has guests,' said Rachael, looking up the driveway. There was a black Ford Falcon parked outside the house.

'How inconvenient for her,' Julie said, obviously delighted to be intruding. 'Hope she's not embarrassed having the police arrive unannounced during morning tea.'

Julie pressed the remote and waited. After twenty seconds, Dianne King answered.

'Yes?'

'Mrs King, it's Detectives Wang and Schlank here to see you. Can you open up?'

'What do you want?'

'We want a chat,' said Julie, flatly.

There was silence from the intercom as the gates started to open slowly.

Julie drove quickly towards the house, coming to a stop beside the Falcon. They walked to the door and knocked.

Dianne King opened the door. A number of strands of her hair were loose and hanging across her forehead. Her skirt was almost straight, but not quite. If it had been the first time Rachael had met her, she might not have noticed any of this, but there was a discernible difference from her last visit.

Julie spoke first. 'Mrs King, I am Detective Senior Constable Wang and you know my colleague, Detective Senior Constable Schlank.'

'Yes, yes, what do you want today?' Dianne King was standing across her doorway, as if guarding it.

'May we come in?' asked Julie.

Dianne hesitated. 'Yes, of course,' she said finally, standing aside so they could enter.

As Rachael and Julie walked into the living room, they saw Mark standing there glaring at them both. For a moment they all stood silent, staring at each other.

'Hi, Mark,' said Rachael finally, upbeat and friendly.

'What are you two doing here?' asked Mark.

'We're working on the investigation.' Rachael was looking directly at Mark's eyes and smiling, knowing it would unsettle him.

'Dianne asked me to give her a hand fixing some stuff around here.'

'I didn't ask why you were here,' said Rachael.

'Right,' he said.

'Okay then, we need to have a chat with Dianne,' said Rachael.

Rachael and Julie watched Mark. They could tell he was running the situation through his mind. 'I'm done here anyhow. See you, Dianne.'

'Thanks for helping out, Mark,' said Dianne, as he walked towards the front door.

'No problem,' he said.

'Bye, Mark,' said Rachael, to his back.

Dianne shut the door behind him.

They sat down as they heard Mark rev his car's engine three times before spinning the tyres on the crushed granite of the driveway and speeding away from the house.

Julie snorted. 'Crikey, he needs to get a new muffler. That sounds like a plane taking off.'

'So, Dianne.' Rachael smiled kindly across at her.

'Yes, detective.'

'How long have you been sleeping with Mark

Cullen?'

Dianne immediately blushed and looked around the room as if she could find an answer in the furnishings. 'How could you say such a thing?' she stammered.

'One of his shoelaces was untied,' said Rachael.

Dianne hesitated for a moment as her mind scrambled to come up with a response. In the end, her shoulders slumped slightly and she let the façade fall. 'We've been seeing each other for a few months. There's no crime in that, is there? I've been alone for a while now.'

'It would have been pertinent to mention it when I spoke to you the first time and asked you if you knew Mark. Remember?'

'Yes, I do, but I didn't see how it was relevant then. Or now.'

Julie jumped into the conversation, speaking quickly. 'Mrs King, it is relevant because Mark took the alibi that Detective Schlank asked you about last time she was here, the one from your husband in 2007 when the car crash occurred. You claimed to have never been to Tumut, the very place your husband alleged you both were when two very young women were violently killed just down the road. So either your husband lied in his statement or you are lying about not having been on a caravanning holiday in Tumut.' Julie left out the obvious third option: that Mark had invented the alibi himself.

Dianne sat staring at Julie. Rachael was impressed by her friend's interviewing style. Julie wasn't letting Dianne out of her grip.

'Come on, Dianne. You were here the night of the crash, weren't you? You and your husband? Why'd he

S.D. Rowell

give the false alibi? Did he chase after those women that night and it all went wrong?'

'No.'

'Well, it seems like the most obvious answer here, doesn't it?'

'No.'

'Was he worried he'd be seen as a suspect?'

'No, I mean, I don't know. As I told her,' Dianne said, pointing at Rachael, 'I can't remember that far back.'

Julie continued. 'How many vehicles use this road per day?'

'I don't know, maybe five to ten.'

'So, on a quiet night on your quiet back road, you didn't hear two cars flying past at high speed, or one of them crashing head-on into a tree? Then in the morning, half the emergency services from Bendigo came by your house, the first couple at least with their sirens blaring, and you heard nothing. Is that what you are trying to say?' asked Julie.

Dianne had composed herself a little by then. 'No, that's not what I'm saying. I'm saying that I don't remember. Maybe I did go to Tumut, as the alibi said. Maybe my memory isn't as good as I thought, but I certainly don't recall hearing all that noise at any point. If I was here, I am sure I would recall it.'

Rachael sat forwards. 'Dianne, why are we finding notes referencing PK Farm at our crime scenes?'

'I don't know.'

'Do you believe your husband committed suicide?' asked Rachael.

'What...? Yes, of course. What do you mean? Why, what do you know?' Dianne's voice sounded anxious now, and she hugged her arms around herself to keep steady.

'Well, someone is committing crimes right now and leaving notes for us pointing right back at your company and at Paul. So now I am asking myself whether someone else shot Paul and staged it as a suicide.'

'Why would the police have said it was suicide if he was murdered? Are you saying the police got it wrong?' Dianne half smiled, as if she had found a way out of the interrogation.

'Maybe,' Rachael answered, and watched that smile vanish again. 'We might have to look and see who investigated your husband's death and talk to them.' Dianne immediately turned red again. *She definitely knows that Mark investigated the suicide.*

'But how do you fake a suicide?' asked Dianne. 'There was only one bullet fired and there was gunshot residue stuff on Paul's hands.'

'There are ways to do it, but I cannot go into details with you. The real question then is, why and who could have done this? Do you have any ideas?'

'Me. Why…do you think I had something to do with this? I was in Paris when it happened.'

'Yes, we know where you were. Did your husband have any enemies?' asked Rachael.

'Paul, no, he had no enemies. Business was good. Everything was fine.'

'What about your marriage, how was that going?'

'Our marriage was great.'

'So Paul didn't have any girlfriends on the side?'

'No, Paul was a good man.'

'And what about you, Dianne? Did you have any

outside interests?'

Dianne looked at Rachael defiantly. 'No, I did not.'

'And how long was it, did you say, you had been seeing Mark?'

'A couple of months. And no, I wasn't sleeping with Mark before then.'

'So who would want your husband dead?'

'No idea.'

'Did you know that ninety-seven per cent of murder victims know their murderer?'

'No, I did not know that.'

'Well, the situation is this. We have someone going around targeting people who are animal abusers of some kind or another and he is leaving us notes linking it all back to Paul and PK Farm. Two animal activists were killed in a road rage-style event just down the road using a model of car that was the same as one you and Paul owned. To me, a potential scenario is that somebody killed your husband as revenge for chasing those women down the road and into a tree. What do you think, Dianne?'

'It sounds like you are trying to retrofit the facts to back up your theory,' said Dianne.

'The other option is that somebody else was also involved in causing the crash and they silenced your husband because he had a guilty conscience and was going to talk to the police,' said Rachael.

Dianne sat silently for a long moment, staring intently at the coffee table.

'Or someone threatened to expose your husband and that's why he took his own life. Which is it, Dianne?'

Dianne King remained silent. Rachael and Julie both knew to say nothing. If she was going to crack and tell them anything, it was now.

Dianne looked up. 'I think this conversation is over, detectives. If you want to continue, I'll get a lawyer and shut this fishing expedition down.'

Rachael smiled broadly at Dianne, as if thrilled by this statement. 'Okay then. Thank you very much. Again, it's been insightful.' She and Julie stood up.

Julie caught on and also smiled triumphantly at Dianne. 'Thank you so much,' she added.

Dianne looked bewildered as she stood up and walked them to the door.

'We'll be in touch,' said Rachael, walking past, still smiling.

Dianne said nothing, closing the door firmly behind them.

As they got into the car, Julie turned to Rachael. 'Good catch on seeing Mark's shoelace was untied.'

Rachael laughed under her breath. 'It wasn't. I just knew her reaction to me saying it would give us the answer.'

Julie grinned as she started the car.

44

The dairy farmer stood leaning against the temporary cattleyard he had constructed of steel panels, butted up to the gate to the paddock next to his house. Inside, four tiny calves stood, wonky and confused, on their gangly legs. They were only a few days old, as big as medium-sized dogs. In the paddock next to the yard, eight cows stood watching as the calves tried to find a way back to them. The older cows were getting more and more agitated as Joab approached.

He had rung Gary Burn two days prior from a pre-paid phone and asked if he could come out to learn how to dispose of dairy wastage. Gary had agreed, saying he had one or two that needed doing and that there were a couple of other cows due to give birth.

Joab had parked behind a pair of large shrubs, just down the road, his car out of sight of Gary's house. He was walking up the side of the house, towards where the temporary yard was set up. The four calves were huddled together and, Joab now saw, another calf lay dead on the ground at the back of the yard.

'G'day; you Joe?' asked Gary.

'Yeah. Couldn't wait, eh?' Joab said, pointing at the

dead calf.

'Thought I'd get a practice swing in first,' he said, laughing. 'What's the deal with the get-up you're wearing? You look like one of those forensics guys off the TV.'

'Nothing that fancy. They're just coveralls, you know, for painting the house. Got them for a couple of bucks at the hardware store. I presume this can be a messy business.'

'That's actually a really good idea,' Gary said. He turned towards the house. 'Hey, Candy, come have a gander at this.'

Joab quickly pulled the hood up over his head and yanked the drawstring tight.

The screen door at the back of the house creaked as it opened. A blonde woman walked around to the side of the house.

'Have a look at this bloke. Jumpsuit for painting the house. How good's that? He'll be cleaned off in no time after this.'

'Not much of a fashion statement,' said Candy, as she looked Joab up and down. 'But it looks like a good idea, given the occasion. The gloves are a nice touch.'

Joab gave her the thumbs up sign with one of the fluorescent yellow dishwashing gloves he was wearing.

'I'll leave you boys to it. Have fun,' she said, turning to walk away.

'Right, let's get in there,' said Gary. He climbed over the panel and into the yard. Joab did the same.

'What you want to do is grab the calf by one of its back legs and pull the leg back and up. The calf will be off balance then and that will allow you to ram its body against the fence. Use your knee to hold it there. Then you bring the hammer down into its forehead. If you do it right, it should die fairly quickly. If not, just smash 'em again with it. Got it?'

'Yeah, all makes sense. What's the deal with those ones standing there?' Joab asked, pointing at the bellowing cows, who were straining against the fence.

'That's their mothers and some others. Once the first calf is killed, the other calves freak out and run over there to get to them. It makes them easier to catch them that way, all huddled together. Okay, grab the first one.'

Joab grabbed a calf by the leg as gently as he could and pushed it against the side of the yard. Once he had it held there by his knee, he nodded to Gary to give him the hammer. Gary passed it across and Joab took it in his right hand.

'Okay, show me where to hit it again?' Joab asked.

Gary came around to the front of the calf and pointed to a spot on its forehead. 'Anywhere around there should do it.'

Joab lifted the hammer high above his head, before suddenly releasing the pressure of his leg. The calf jumped up and away, knocking Gary off balance. Joab drove the hammer swiftly into the middle of Gary Burn's forehead. He fell immediately to the ground, one leg twitching. Joab dropped the hammer into the dirt beside him. He grimaced, looking across at the calf Gary had killed before he arrived. The four surviving calves stood on the side of the yard closest to their mothers, crying out in panic.

Joab opened the gate between the yard and the paddock and the four calves ran through, back to their mothers, who licked their faces.

45

Rachael and Julie were back in the office late in the afternoon, giving Rob a blow-by-blow update on their meeting with Dianne King and their encounter with Mark Cullen.

'Makes me even more glad that we suspended him and got him off the case,' said Rob. 'I'd better let the DI up in Bendigo know as well.'

'How did you go with the Ng family?' asked Rachael.

'Okay. They are Buddhist and seem to have come to terms with things. Although there was still sadness in their eyes when they spoke about Helen, they seemed at peace, you know. Reincarnation and all that stuff. They were proud of her achievements, having a Master's degree, and that she was finishing her PhD. All of Helen's friends they could remember were also Grace's friends, mostly tied up with Animal Action. I took them through the list from Facebook. They didn't know any of them. Her parents couldn't think of anyone who might be seeking revenge. Said they didn't even know where you would start looking.'

'That's similar to what Grace's mother said. The person who ran them off the road is a nameless ghost to them.'

'Hopefully not for ever,' said Julie.

'How are our floater detectives going with the list of Facebook possibilities?'

'They're getting through it quickly,' said Rob. 'A lot of the people on the list use Facebook to post photos and they have geo-tracking enabled on their phones, so their locations are recorded as well. So we can see where they were at different times by searching through their feed and matching it to the times our crimes happened. That has effectively eliminated about twelve of them already. Of the rest, so far they all have alibis that are checking out for at least one of the crimes.'

At that moment, Rob's phone rang.

'Morello here.'

'Rob, it's Dave. We've got another one.'

46

Rachael called Zach as Julie drove the car out of the Homicide car park.

'Hi there, sexy,' he said.

Rachael blushed as Julie laughed beside her. 'Hi yourself,' said Julie, leaning across towards the phone at Rachael's ear. 'But Rachael also wants to say hi.'

'Whoops,' said Zach.

'Hi, just a quick call,' said Rachael. 'I can't catch up tonight. We're on our way to another homicide, so I'll be working late. It's up on the outskirts of Shepparton.'

'Oh, okay. I'm stuck at work myself. Stay safe and drive carefully.'

'Yes, will do. Bye.'

Julie smiled in Rachael's direction as she turned on the siren and they made their way through the after-work traffic. Once they were on the Hume freeway, the pace quickened. The lights and siren caused most of the cars to give them room as they approached. After two and a quarter hours they pulled up outside the dairy farm. There were five police cars on site and a Major Crime Scene forensics van, as well as Dave Boucher's unmarked car.

An ambulance was parked with its lights off.

Dave approached them as they were getting out of the car. 'Hey, you made good time. Where's Rob?'

'He's following us up. He wanted to bring Tom up to speed before he left. What have we got?'

Coming from the paddocks all around them was the sound of cows mooing, waiting to be milked. Dave motioned for them to follow him as he walked towards a yard, off to the right of the house. 'One deceased male, thirty years old, married. Hammer wound to the forehead. Not pretty. His wife is here; she came out and found him. The ambos are checking her out now.'

'Is there another note?'

'Yeah, in there next to the body with a rock placed on top of it,' Dave said, pointing towards the edge of the temporary yard. 'A senior constable saw the note folded up under a rock and was smart enough to leave it alone.'

Rachael looked into the yard. She could see the body there in the darkness. 'Okay, what's the deal with the victim?'

'The vic's name is Gary Burn. He comes from a long line of dairy farmers. Most of the local police know him from around Shepparton.'

'Has he got form with us?' asked Julie.

'No, they know him from the local football club.'

They walked up to the yard and saw the body of Gary Burn laid out on the ground, a wound directly in the centre of his forehead. Beside the body was a hammer covered in blood and brain matter. The note was sitting under a rock next to the hammer. The Major Crime Scene team were finishing setting up lighting rigs to illuminate the scene. One of them hit a switch and the whole area was suddenly bathed in bright light.

As their eyes adjusted to the glare, they all saw the other body at the back of the yard. 'What the fuck is that?' asked Julie. 'Is that a dead dog?'

'No, it's a calf,' said Dave, motioning for them to follow him.

The three of them made their way along the side of the house, skirting around the yard where the bodies of Gary Burn and the calf were lying. In the backyard, a woman sat having her blood pressure taken by a paramedic. She was sweating and breathing heavily.

'Mrs Burn. I'm Detective Dave Boucher, and these are Detectives Rachael Schlank and Julie Wang. We are very sorry for your loss. Are you able to take us through what happened? You can take your time—it is crucial we get as much information as quickly as we can, but we don't want to upset you further.'

The woman's eyes were red and more tears were forming. Her voice was slow and monotone; shock was already setting in. 'A guy called a couple of days ago, said he wanted to start a small dairy and could Gary show him how to get rid of dairy waste soon. Gary told the guy to come out tonight to have a go. He came decked out in a white jumpsuit thing with a hood. And bright yellow dishwashing gloves. I went back inside and came out an hour later to see where Gary was—I called triple zero.'

They knew now was the time to ask their questions, before the full realisation of what had happened kicked in. At that point she might become catatonic.

'What did this guy look like?' asked Dave.

'Average. Like six foot; just under. Couldn't see much.'

'What about his build?'

'Strong. Like a footballer. You know, fit.'

'How old do you think he was?'

'Maybe thirty,' said Candy.

'Did he have an accent?'

She stopped and closed her eyes. 'Dunno. I don't think he talked.'

'Did he look like this?' Dave held out the photofit image.

She studied it for a moment. 'Yeah. Except the hood was white.'

'Tell us about the suit he was wearing.'

'White. Hood with a drawstring. Like a forensics person on the TV.'

'Did Gary mention what the guy's name was?'

Candy sat staring at the wall for a moment and then shut her eyes again. 'It was Joe,' she said finally.

'Do you know how he found your husband?'

'Gary said he'd got our number from one of the stockfeed suppliers in town.'

'Do you have any idea who would have targeted your husband like this?' asked Rachael.

'No.'

'Anyone you owe money to? Any drug issues? Anything.'

Candy rallied a bit. 'No, we just live a simple life here. No enemies. Nothing.'

'What did you mean when you said *getting rid of dairy waste*?' Julie asked.

'He was dealing with the bobby calves.'

'What does that mean, exactly?' asked Dave.

'We trucked most of them off last week, but these

ones were born late. Wasn't worth getting the truck back for five of them so Gary was dealing with them himself.'

Julie was frowning, not understanding the answer. 'You mean he was killing them?'

'Yeah.'

Candy saw the momentary look of horror on Julie and Dave's faces. 'Can't have milk without the cows having been pregnant,' she said, her voice lifeless. 'Can't have milk if the calves drink it.'

'So, killing them with a hammer is normal?' asked Julie.

'It's just business. The ones we put on the trucks are sold off for veal.'

Rachael could sense Julie and Dave had many more questions, so she jumped in to get everyone back to the crime at hand. She'd direct them to some good websites on the way back to town. 'There is only one calf in the yard; it's dead. Were there more when you saw the man out there with Gary?'

'Yes, there were four others, still alive.'

'So, did you let the other four calves into the paddock when you found Gary?'

Candy shuddered; they didn't have much longer. 'No, it was just Gary and the one calf in there.'

'Okay,' said Rachael. 'Mrs Burn, have you ever had anyone threaten or harass you or your husband over the killing of calves?'

'No, we keep it pretty quiet. Even family don't really wanna know. You reckon it's about the calves?'

'It is too early to say, but we need to look at every possibility. Mrs Burns, we'll need to prepare a statement. Are you up to doing that now?' asked Julie.

'Yes, I think so.'

Rachael wrote *Facebook?* on a page in her folder and showed it discreetly to Julie, who nodded.

Julie sat down with Mrs Burn to write her statement. Rachael and Dave walked back past where the bodies of Gary Burn and the calf lay in the yard and into the driveway area.

'Well, that puts me off cheese.'

'Sorry, what?' asked Rachael.

'The calves. I had no idea.'

'Yeah. I just learned about it recently myself,' she said. They were silent for a moment. 'Fairy tales.'

'What?' asked Dave.

'Oh, just something someone told me recently. That people like to insulate themselves from uncomfortable truths, and rather than change their behaviour and stop buying the products, they prefer to pretend it's not real or would never happen here. A fairy tale for adults.'

Dave was staring back at the dead calf.

'You should know,' she said, 'that we found Mark today at PK Farm when Julie and I arrived unannounced to do an interview with Dianne King. He said he was just there fixing some things for her, but she admitted once he was gone that they had been seeing each other for a few months.'

Dave just shook his head. 'Fuck. I had no idea,' he said, angrily.

Rachael turned back towards the yard. The spotlights illuminated the horror with stunning clarity. It looked like a theatre set, with the colours exaggerated in the artificial brightness. Rachael looked at the patterns on the skin of the dead calf, the dark reflection of the blood on the hammer and the man lying on his back. Only then did she notice the single cow in the paddock behind the yard. The cow was moaning deeply, staring desperately at the dead calf inside the yard. *The mother*.

47

Rob Morello arrived at the scene. He leaned against his car as Rachael, Julie and Dave gave him an update on the crime and what the victim's wife had said. Over Rob's shoulder, Rachael noticed Damien from the Major Crime Scene team looking in her direction. She put up a hand and waved him over.

'Hi, Damien—are you now our exclusive forensics officer?' asked Rachael, when he arrived.

'Yeah, after the horse trainer, our boss decided it would be best if there was consistency with any crimes that looked connected to your guy. So, here I am.'

'So what have we got?' asked Rachael.

'A single blow to the forehead with a hammer. Hard. There are prints on the hammer, but they are smudged, so I'd guess they are going to be from the victim. Looks like the killer wore gloves, which smudged over the vic's prints, like with the cage woman,' said Damien. 'We have boot prints which look like a match for our guy based on a quick visual, but we are taking measurements and an imprint casing to be sure. And, as you know, we have another note. Same font as the others.' Damien looked down at the digital screen on the back of the camera he was holding. He used the zoom function to increase the size of the image, and turned the camera so they could all see the screen.

Hammertime.
Once Cullen is off the crew and charged, I will stop.
Grace and Helen deserved better.

There was silence as the four detectives processed the information. Damien looked at each of them in turn.

Rob looked at Damien. 'You know who Cullen is?'

'He's the other detective on the Taskforce, isn't he?'

'Yep, that's him. Damien, can we rely on your confidentiality here? It's important we don't broadcast this information to anyone until we work out what's going on.'

'Yes, of course. Understood.'

'Can you email me that photo? Just to me?' asked Rob.

'Sure, I'll do it right now.'

'Thanks, mate,' said Rob. Damien gave them a nod and walked back towards the crime scene.

'Well, that absolutely confirms the link to the cold case,' said Julie.

'And it sounds like it's a cop,' said Rachael.

Rob was looking down at the ground. 'Yes, using the word *crew* is fairly telling. So, it's likely to be a police officer linked to Mark. Or a former officer he worked with. Who'd he work with before you, Dave?'

'His partner before me was Johannes Petra, for years. Before that, we'd have to look it up with HR, or speak to my DI in Bendigo.'

'The victim's wife said the guy who called said his

name was Joe,' said Rachael. 'It could be short for Johannes.'

Rob placed his hands flat on the hood of the car. 'Okay, listen up. As you all know Johannes Petra is with Ethical Standards or Professional Standards or whatever the hell they're calling themselves this week. We need to tread very fucking lightly here. Talk to no one about this. No one. I'll speak to Tom and get his advice, but I'd say we'll be speaking to the deputy commissioner tomorrow morning. Then we'll be seeing the DI in charge of Professional Standards Command, and pulling Petra in for a chat soon after that.'

They were all silent for a moment.

'So, if the perp is Petra,' said Rachael, 'it may be because he discovered Mark gave Paul King a bullshit alibi for the 2007 car crash and now he wants to bring Mark down. Plus, Mark and Johannes were the investigators of Paul King's suicide.'

Dave crossed his arms. 'Can someone tell me what the frickin heck is going on here? I haven't heard any of this about Mark creating fake alibis and investigating King's suicide. What's going on?'

Rob put up a reassuring hand to calm Dave. 'That was information that has just recently come to hand and we were trying to work out the best way to play it with Mark. We suspended him based on the conflict of interest of being friends with the King couple, but there is much more to it than that. We didn't want you to feel compromised, since he's your partner. That's why we hadn't told you yet. I'll give you the full brief on all that in a couple of minutes. Okay?'

'Okay,' said Dave reluctantly.

'Hold on a second,' said Rachael. 'Julie, didn't you say you saw Johannes Petra in the CCTV footage from Magistrates' Court on Kinnaird's court date?'

'Shit, I forgot about that,' said Julie. 'Yeah, Petra was in the building, but he wasn't in the actual court room where Sally Kinnaird's case was happening. Those were the people I was concentrating on.'

Rachael stared up into the night sky, shaking her head.

Rob said, 'What is it?'

'Petra was in the army,' said Rachael. 'I just remembered. My sergeant and I went to see him when we were reviewing the cold case and I saw a tattoo on his arm. He was in some sort of commando regiment. The tattoo had a dagger with a scroll written in Latin across it. I asked him what it meant and he said it translated to *Without Warning.*'

Rob rubbed his forehead. They all looked at each other, their minds racing.

'Jules, did you get access to the victim's Facebook page here tonight?' asked Rob.

'Yes,' said Julie.

'Okay, go back and see if you can find the word *Hammertime* or something similar. Look for a page where the victim might have been acting like a troll.'

'Got it,' said Julie, walking towards the house.

'Rachael, locate the closest mobile phone tower and organise a dump from an hour either side of five pm, when the killer arrived. That will give us a list of all the phone numbers that were around here then. We'll see if Petra's number pops up.'

'Will do.'

'Don't we need a warrant to get that info?' asked Dave.

'Not at present. If we're looking at a specific tower for a specific block of time and we're only after metadata, in this case phone numbers, we're good. If we want to track an individual phone number, then we have a dozen more hoops to jump through.'

'Good to know,' said Dave.

'Dave, once we're done here, find out from the local police who owns the local stockfeed companies and call them tonight to see if any of them sent the killer here like he said. You'll need to get hold of their staff as well. It's unlikely, as I reckon he would've found this guy on Facebook, like the other victims, but we need to check it off anyhow. Also, get in touch with the owners of any hardware stores in Shepparton and see if they sell these white jumpsuits the victim's wife described. Who knows, he might have bought it locally with a credit card.' Rob's tone told them how unlikely he thought that this would be.

'Got it,' said Dave.

'Rachael, when Julie comes back, we'll team up with some local uniforms and do a canvass of nearby residents to see if any neighbours saw an unfamiliar car or anything suspicious tonight.'

He turned back to Dave. 'Okay, let's get you up to speed on Mark.'

48

Rob Morello and DI Tom Parker walked into the conference room. Rachael and Julie were updating Dave on the speakerphone about the unsuccessful canvassing of Gary Burn's neighbours the previous night.

'Good morning, everyone,' said Tom. 'Is that Dave on the phone?'

'Good morning, Detective Inspector; yes, it's me,' said Dave.

'Okay, Julie, do you have an update on what you found on the latest victim's Facebook page?' asked Rob.

'Yes, Gary Burn had been trolling the Facebook page of Animals Australia for at least a year. Hurling abuse in all directions. To paraphrase, he was saying how he would love to see how these *city hippies would cope when it's Hammertime in the paddocks*, or variations on that. He loved using the term *Hammertime* when talking about killing the calves, as it got a lot of negative reactions from people, but there were also some other dairy farmers who were encouraging him. He seemed to be doing it every time there was a story about dairies and the killing of the calves. At other times though, he would comment that no calves were ever killed and that it was all propaganda, and that the dairy farms kept all the calves, living happily together with their mums. So he seemed to flip between bragging about the killings or declaring it all *fake news*.'

'Okay,' said Rob. 'As of this morning, we have two distinct lines of investigation. One is looking hard at Mark's old partner, Johannes Petra, which we will discuss in a moment. The other is looking at the list of males who were upset by the trolling by our first three victims and see if any of them were also active on the Animals Australia Facebook page when Gary Burn was trolling it. That should reduce the list by quite a bit. Rachael, can you coordinate with one of our Tactical Intelligence Officers to get that done this morning?'

Rachael nodded, as Rob continued, 'Any posters who were active on all four pages will be the priorities. Send any Melbourne names to the floaters. If there are any regional names, send them to Dave. Also get the Tactical Intelligence Officer to try and see if any of them is a cop or has any relationship to the police force.'

'Got it,' said Rachael.

'Thanks,' said Rob. 'Okay, back to Johannes Petra. Tom and I met early this morning with the deputy commissioner and Detective Inspector Mary Costa, who heads up Professional Standards Command, to discuss the developments last night. They agree with our hypothesis that, based on what was in the note, signs are pointing to a serving or former police officer and that the person has a direct relationship with Mark. So, we're looking first at Johannes Petra, as they were partners in 2007 when the car crash occurred.'

Rachael tapped her pen on her folder. 'When we interviewed him about the cold case, he did come very prepared. He even brought his personal diary from that time and was able to answer specific questions from 2007 very easily.'

'The other thing,' said Tom, 'is that Petra applied to join Professional Standards just after the Paul King suicide. Literally two days later, to be precise.'

They were all silent as they took that in.

Rachael looked up at the whiteboard. It was covered in information and photographs. Johannes Petra's name was nowhere to be seen. She squinted at the photofit prepared from the description that Sally Kinnaird gave. *It could be Petra.* 'So, are we saying Petra felt somehow threatened by Paul King's suicide,' she said, 'and went to find sanctuary within the walls of PSC? Or are we saying that he was involved with Paul King's death, and that PSC was a good place to go and stay out of sight?'

'Hopefully we'll find out more when we interview him this morning,' said Tom. 'As it's a sensitive situation, the interview will be conducted by Rob. Julie, you will be there as well, as will DI Costa, who'll attend to make sure everything we do is up to code.'

'Having his boss in there with him for the interview is a bit odd,' said Julie.

'Yes, that's what we said, but the deputy commissioner was insistent,' said Tom. 'The whole situation is odd. We are now investigating a police officer who investigates police officers. He said the other option would be to call in IBAC,' referring to the state anti-corruption commission, 'but I don't think now is the right time for that. Rachael, you will be observing via the monitoring room. Petra has met you before and if he sees you here it might give him the heads up about what we suspect and give him time to prepare his answers. For all he knows, you're still working away in the Cold Case Unit. Julie can text you when they're nearly back here with Petra so you can get out of sight. All good?'

'Yes, no worries,' said Rachael.

Rob looked down towards the speakerphone on the desk. 'Dave, did you get anywhere this morning with the stockfeed stores?'

'Yes, I've spoken to them all. No one had given Gary Burn's name or number out to anyone.'

'What about the jumpsuit lead? Any luck with the local hardware stores?'

'The only local store that sells the house painting jumpsuits is the Bunnings Warehouse in Shepparton. I checked with them and they sell a number of them every month. Usually to DIY home painters. I've got them going through their sales in the past month from all of their stores in Victoria and the southern part of New South Wales. We'll be able to see who purchased using a credit card, but anyone who paid cash will be anonymous. I was going to go through the security tapes from the store, but they hadn't sold any in the two days leading up to the dairy farmer getting killed, so I've left that for the time being.'

'Okay, it was always a long shot, seeing as how organised this guy is. Dave, I want you to go and see the families of our three homicide victims and that puppy farmer woman, Sally Kinnaird, and very subtly find out if they have ever heard of Johannes Petra. Write down about ten other made-up names as well and ask about them too, just so they don't get fixated on Petra's name. Check out their body language as well. Let me know straight away if anyone reacts at all. Go to Sally Kinnaird first and take a photo of Petra to show her. I'll get one to you by email, with a hood Photoshopped on. We don't want her knowing Petra is a police officer, else it will be in the press by noon.'

'Got it,' said Dave, through the phone.

'Dave, the other thing is that, with the Tactical Intel people here hopefully narrowing down the Facebook users, you may have to jump on one of those leads if one comes up. If it does, you'll need to get significant local back up before going to interview them.'

'Yes, understood,' said Dave.

'Rachael, any news on the tower dump of mobile phone data?'

'Still waiting for it. Should be here any time. I'll check my email before your interview to see if Petra's phone number is there. I can run it against the list in a minute or two.'

'Sounds good. Julie and I will drop by and see DI Costa and then we'll go and get Petra. We should be back here by ten-thirty.'

'Good luck,' said Rachael. *We're getting closer.*

49

Johannes Petra sat alone, slouched in the interview room. He stared at the corner of the room, strumming his fingers across the tabletop. Rob, Julie, DI Tom Parker and DI Mary Costa stood watching him on the bank of television screens in the monitoring room.

'I can't tell if he is actually bored or trying to appear bored,' Julie said.

Rachael opened the door. 'I received the phone data from last night. No luck, I'm afraid. Petra's phone wasn't anywhere near the dairy farm.'

Rob nodded. 'Okay, still doesn't mean he isn't our man. He would be smart enough to have left his phone at home. Are you ready?' he asked Detective Inspector Mary Costa.

'Yes. As agreed, I'll sit off to the side and say nothing, unless you guys overstep. Okay?'

'Agreed,' said Rob, gesturing towards the door to the hallway.

Rachael and Tom watched the screens as Rob, Julie and Mary entered the interview room. Johannes Petra looked up at the three of them, only giving a nod of acknowledgement to his boss.

'So, the suspense is killing me. What is this all about?'

'We'll get to that soon enough.' Rob hit the record button on the desk. 'Recorded interview between Detective Senior Sergeant Rob Morello and Detective Sergeant Johannes Petra, conducted at the City West Police Complex on Friday 7 April. Also present, Detective Senior Constable Julie Wang, along with Detective Inspector Mary Costa of Professional Standards Command. Do you agree that the time is now eleven-oh-five am?'

Johannes looked casually at his watch. 'Yes.'

'I intend to interview you in relation to the death of two women in a collision in April of 2007, as well as some more recent investigations. Before continuing, I must inform you that you do not have to say anything, but anything you say or do may be given in evidence. Do you understand that?' asked Rob.

Johannes stared at Rob for a few seconds, unresponsive. Rob held his gaze.

'Yes,' he said finally.

'First question. What size shoe do you wear, Johannes?' asked Rob.

'Sorry?'

'Your shoe size. What size do you wear?'

Johannes looked across at Julie, who was leaning over, peering at his feet under the table. 'Eleven. Why?'

'Thank you. We wish to ask you some questions in relation to the deaths of two women in a car crash in 2007. The women who died were named Grace Blackwood and Helen Ng. Are you familiar with this incident?'

'Yes, of course I am. I was one of the detectives assigned to the case.'

'Can you take me through what you remember about it?'

'My partner was Detective Sergeant Mark Cullen. We were called out early one morning. There had been a twin fatality south of Bendigo on a back road in the early hours of that morning. It was a narrow dirt road and the crash occurred at high speed. The team from Major Collision Investigation noticed some strange tyre tread patterns on the dirt road. They determined there had been a second car involved and it was likely that the car that hit the tree had been forced off the road by this second car. After analysis, the techs found that the type of tyre was most likely from a Holden Commodore VZ manufactured in the previous two years, and, as we had no other evidence like paint transfer, we started looking at all Commodore VZ owners in the area. We came up with nothing.'

'You've got a pretty clear memory of an investigation from a long time ago.'

'Is that a question?'

'No, just an observation. Tell me, were you happy with the way the investigation turned out?'

'No.'

'Why's that?'

'Well, we didn't find the person or people who drove those women off the road. So, no, it was not successful and I was not happy with that outcome.'

'Do you still think about that investigation much?'

'Yes, from time to time.' Johannes shifted in his seat and looked at Rob. 'Am I a suspect here?'

'No, Detective, we are simply looking to fill in a couple of gaps. What was your working relationship like with Mark Cullen?'

'Mark was my partner for a number of years. We had a decent working relationship, but I would not call it a partnership in the true sense of the word. He was the boss and I worked for him. He would usually take on the easier tasks and leave the grunt work for me.'

'In relation to the Blackwood and Ng investigation, did he leave the grunt work to you there as well?'

Petra was silent for a moment before responding. 'No, with that one, Mark had his sleeves rolled up and was hard at it.'

'Did that surprise you?'

'Yeah, a bit. It was unlike him. I remember he took the lead on getting the car rego records from VicRoads, which would usually be a pain in the arse. And when he got the records he divided them up and worked pretty hard on the follow up. We got nowhere with the investigation though.'

'What about Paul King?'

Johannes stared at the video camera set up behind Rob and Julie for a moment, looking confused. 'Paul King was a friend of Mark's from school. I only found that out after Paul shot himself late last year and Mark and I were out at his property on the morning he died. Mark was pretty cut up about the suicide. I think he took a week off to help out the guy's wife. They had a chicken business.'

'Yes, that's right,' said Rob. 'The factory farm right around the corner from the site where the two women, who were animal activists, died.'

Johannes looked at Rob. 'What are you implying?

That Paul King and that crash were connected?'

'I'm not saying that. Are you?' asked Rob.

Johannes was silent for a moment. 'I don't know. I mean, I don't know anything about that. Mark spoke to the King couple as part of the investigation the day after the crash. They had been away on holidays and there was no one else staying at the property.'

'Did you know that there is nothing in the case file about Mark taking a statement from either Paul or Dianne King the day after the crash?'

'What?' Johannes looked stunned, staring at Rob. 'No, I didn't. Look, I was a new detective back then and Mark was in charge. He was managing the case file, and I was running back and forth trying to keep up with his orders.'

'After you and Mark got the list of Commodore VZ owners from VicRoads, did you read each other's reports on the follow-up interviews?'

'No, I don't recall doing that. Not thoroughly at least. There were about a hundred of them and they were monotonously similar. Almost all the people reported they were asleep at the time. A couple of them were away on holidays.'

'Did you know that Paul King's name was on the list of Commodore VZ owners?'

'What? No, I didn't know that. Mark gave me the names starting with *L* onwards. I never saw the rest of the list.' Johannes sat up straight in his chair. 'Once I had finished my share of the statements, Mark and I sat down and decided none of the people we interviewed were viable as suspects, so Mark filed them all away and we moved on. I never looked at them again. I didn't have a reason to.' Johannes rubbed his face with his hands, as if trying to wake himself up.

'Did you know that the statement Mark took from Paul King almost a week after the crash said that the King couple were on a caravanning holiday in Tumut in New South Wales when the crash occurred?'

'Well, yes I did. Mark told me on *the day after* the crash that he'd spoken to the King couple and that they were on holiday, towing a caravan through New South Wales. He also said there was no one on the property on the night of the crash.'

'Do you know that Paul's wife, Dianne, has since told us that she has never been to Tumut?'

'No, I didn't,' said Johannes, going red in the face.

'What about the video cameras and phones from the crash?'

'What about them? We didn't find any at the scene.'

'The head of Animal Action clearly remembers telling Mark that two video cameras went missing from their offices the night of the crash, but there is nothing in the case file about that. What can you tell us about that?'

'What? Nothing. Mark never told me that.'

'Do you know of any reason Mark Cullen wouldn't have included that in his notes?'

'No, I don't. I can't believe it's true. I mean… why wouldn't he? It makes no sense.' Johannes shifted uncomfortably on his seat, before continuing. 'Why are you talking to me and not to Mark?' He looked across at Mary Costa, who was looking down, taking notes in her folder.

'Someone will be talking to him soon enough, Johannes. So, why did you leave Bendigo CIU?'

'There was a role at PSC, so I went for it.'

'Why then? You applied to Professional Standards Command two days after Paul King's suicide.'

Johannes took a deep breath. 'Look, I don't know. The timing was coincidental. I just needed a change and Mark wasn't going anywhere.'

'That's not really good enough. From what I've heard, Mark has always been the same pain in the arse to work with, so why then?'

Johannes was silent for a moment, staring at his hands. He then spread his fingers wide on the table. 'Look, when his mate topped himself, I felt sorry for Mark and offered to take him out for a beer. You know, as a gesture. I was surprised when he said yes, and we went down to the local pub. He was kind of in shock and was drinking scotch like it was water. I was just there to sit and listen, you know.'

He looked up. Rob and Julie nodded back at him, silent.

'After about half an hour he started getting a bit agitated and was muttering under his breath. He said, "Those stupid bitches," and that Paul was a coward. Stuff like that. I asked him who he was talking about and he said no one, but then a few minutes later he started up again. It was as if I wasn't there and he was alone, talking to himself. Then he said, "Those fucken greenies," which was what he called any lefty he didn't like, but then he whispered, "Showed those greenie bitches." Then he basically passed out at the pub and I drove him home.'

'The next morning I asked him about what he'd said, but he claimed to have no memory of the conversation. I was torn, because I knew there was something there, but I would be essentially fucking myself in the department by telling anyone. And I didn't really have anything except some drunken slurring about something I didn't really understand. So I was trapped. I decided to apply to join Professional Standards Command, and as soon as I officially got the job, I became a *persona non grata* in the Bendigo CIU. I don't think Mark said more than two words directly to me again after that, but no one else there did either. Anyway, a crew from Cold Case are reviewing the crash now. They came to see me. Hopefully they'll get somewhere with it. It's been nagging at me for a long time.'

'So, why didn't you just organise someone to review the case at PSC when you had been there a while?'

'Yeah, good question,' Johannes said. He looked again across towards Mary Costa, who still had her head down, taking notes. 'I think I was worried that if Mark had done something wrong, which was just theoretical to me at that point, he would try and pull me down with him. He's a shifty sort of bloke. He would go down throwing shit at everyone around him, trying to make something stick. I didn't have enough evidence to take that risk.'

'Where were you on Sunday 19 March at seven-twenty am, Johannes?'

'What? I can't remember. In bed most probably.'

'Anyone able to verify that?' asked Rob.

'Not if I was alone in bed, no.'

'Right, so what do you know about Steve Lawrence?'

'The duck hunter? Nothing. Why?'

'Did you know him?'

'Er, no.'

'What do you think about duck hunting, Johannes?'

'Nothing really; it's not something that interests me. I like ducks myself.'

Rob turned a page in his folder. 'Where were you early on Thursday 23 March, around seven am?'

'No idea—at home I would say. Having breakfast.'

'What about Jim Camella? You know him?'

'He's the guy who got killed up near Bulla, with the arrow.'

'That's the one. You know him?'

'Only what I read in the news.'

'What about Sally Kinnaird?'

'No.'

'You were at the Sunshine Magistrates' Court the day she was before the magistrate on animal cruelty charges—3 December last year. You remember that?'

'No, I do not.'

'Why were you at the court that day?'

'That's almost five months ago; I'd have to check.'

'Okay. The person we're looking for killed the duck hunter, a guy who was both a horse trainer and a deer hunter, and a dairy farmer late yesterday afternoon. In the middle of all that, he locked up a puppy farmer in one of her cages and left her there for a couple of days. Do you think the punishments handed down by the courts to animal abusers are adequate?'

'Probably not, but I could say that about more than half the punishments handed out across all crimes. Most police would say the same.'

'Would you call yourself an animal lover, Johannes?' asked Rob.

'Sure, wouldn't most people?'

'So what do you think about someone going around hurting people who abuse animals. Would you want to see them caught?'

'Yes.'

'Are you saying that as a police officer, or as an everyday person?'

'Both.'

'Where were you yesterday evening around five o'clock, Johannes?'

Johannes hesitated before responding. 'I was driving back to Melbourne. I was interviewing someone about an ongoing matter out in the Yarra Ranges. I was still in traffic around five.'

'So, nowhere near Shepparton then?'

'No.'

'You live alone?' asked Rob.

'Yes, now I do. Getting divorced. I'm renting an apartment in Port Melbourne at the moment.'

'There was a note left at the crime scene last night. It said that the killings would stop once Mark Cullen is charged. What do you think about that?'

Petra's eyes widened. 'Well it sounds like Mark is linked obviously. Other than that, I don't know.'

'The other thing is that it sounds like the person who left the note is, or was, on the job.'

'A cop? Why?'

'There was some language used in the note that indicates it was written by a police officer. So, we think that it's someone closely linked, either currently or in the past, to Mark through work. Also, as you probably heard, the notes have all referred to PK Farm.'

Petra sat back. 'I can tell you all I had nothing to do

with any of this. I can also say it feels suspiciously like a stitch-up by a taskforce that is spinning its wheels. Now I definitely want a lawyer.'

Rob looked across at Mary Costa, who had stopped writing in her folder and was now looking up at Rob.

'Interview suspended at eleven seventeen am, Friday 7 April, in order to make further enquiries.'

Johannes Petra looked across at DI Costa. 'What now?'

'Let's chat back at the office, Detective Sergeant.'

'We'll be in touch,' Rob said to Petra.

'You are off course here,' said Johannes as he left, followed by Mary Costa.

Rob and Julie walked out of the interview room and into the monitoring room, where Rachael and Tom Parker had been observing. 'What do you think?' asked Rob.

'He sounds truthful to me,' said Tom. 'I saw no indication that he was lying and what he is saying sounds plausible. What about you, Rachael?'

'I agree,' said Rachael, 'but we've all met expert liars before.'

Rob was looking at his phone. 'I got a text from Dave while we were in the interview. He has seen the puppy farmer, Sally Kinnaird, and she didn't react to Petra's name or his photograph.'

'Darn,' said Julie.

'He's on his way to Ballarat to see the first victim's wife.' Rob looked up from his phone. 'Okay, well right now Petra is heading back to Professional Standards Command with DI Costa. She will then suspend him formally with pay until the case sorts itself out, one way or another. Rachael and Julie, follow him and see where he goes. He will still be at work for at least thirty minutes while they go through the motions relating to the formal suspension.'

An hour later, Rachael and Julie were parked on Beach Road outside Johannes Petra's first-floor bayside apartment in Port Melbourne. Through the floor to ceiling window, Rachael and Julie saw Petra enter the apartment and sit on the couch. He'd been sitting there staring at the wall ever since. Occasionally he would shake his head, as if in a conversation with himself.

'Well, he doesn't appear to be rushing off anywhere to get rid of evidence,' said Julie.

'Yeah, true. But surely he knows surveillance is looking at him right now? He's Professional Standards Command, for goodness' sake. If it were me, I'd be standing on the balcony staring at us right now. Either he is in shock and hasn't thought about it, or he is acting innocent for our benefit.'

Julie's phone buzzed. 'It's Rob,' she said, looking at the display. 'Hey, boss,' she answered, putting the phone on speaker.

'Hi. Any movement on Petra?'

'No, nothing. We can see him through the window from here. He's just sitting on his couch staring at the wall.'

'Okay, stay put. The Tactical Intel Officer here reduced our Facebook list down to five names of white males who fit the age range and who are living in Victoria, and who interacted with Gary Burn on the Animals Australia page. Two of them made posts on Facebook from interstate when one or more of the crimes occurred and another was overseas. That leaves two names. Both live in Melbourne, so I'm taking the floater detectives and we're going to go and chat with them now,' said Rob. 'I'm still waiting on a trace of Petra's recent movements through his mobile phone. It will probably be tomorrow before I know more on that. I'm arranging a surveillance team to watch him; they'll take over from you at two. So, we now have three persons of interest, Petra and these other two. Hopefully one of them is our guy. Rachael, you should take off early today to recharge, since you did the all-nighter outside Vassar's farm. I'll call you if we have any serious movement in the case.'

'Sounds good to me, thanks,' said Rachael.

'Oh, and I spoke to Dave. He's seen Charni Lawrence, the duck hunter's wife. No reaction to Petra's name or photo. He's en route to Shepparton now to see the dairy farmer's wife.'

'Okay, thanks for the update.'

Julie and Rachael both said goodbye and ended the call.

'Good news about getting off early,' said Julie.

'Yes. It's been a long couple of weeks. Might see what Zach is up to,' Rachael said.

'Good idea. Make love while the sun shines, I say.'

'I think the expression is *make hay while the sun shines*.'

'I prefer my version,' said Julie, smiling, staring up at Johannes through the window.

Rachael pulled out her phone and dialled Zach.

'Hi.'

'Hi there,' he said.

'You know how you told me you had today off?'

asked Rachael.

'Yeah.'

'Well, I just got given the rest of the day off too and I thought I might drive down the Peninsula for a visit. What do you think?'

Zach laughed. 'Sounds like the best idea I've heard this week.'

'I want to go to the beach and walk barefoot in the sand. I need a big dose of fresh air.'

'I know just the place,' said Zach. 'I'll text you the address and see you there at four. And maybe we'll go to Wombat Café in Dromana tomorrow. They do a great breakfast. All plant-based, unbelievably delicious.'

Rachael laughed. 'I didn't mention staying over at your place tonight. That's a bit presumptuous.'

'Maybe I am a presumptuous sort of guy,' he said. They both laughed.

'We can discuss their menu when I see you. Bye,' said Rachael.

'See you soon.'

Rachael ended the call, smiling to herself.

'Don't forget to pack a toothbrush,' said Julie.

'Any update on when you are going to stop looking so pleased with yourself?' asked Rachael.

'At the wedding, I'd say,' Julie replied, grinning broadly.

50

Rachael took the exit off the Mornington Peninsula Freeway. She'd spent an hour and a half racing a wave of Friday afternoon traffic, and breathed a sigh of relief.

She allowed the GPS to guide her through the back streets of St Andrew's Beach, and came to a stop at a dead end near a walkway that cut a path through the large sand dunes.

Rachael could hear the waves crashing in the distance. The steep sides of the dunes were as high as the houses nearby, sheltering them from the ocean winds. She could see that the wooden path was being reclaimed by sand, appearing and disappearing at intervals along the way.

Looking at her watch, she saw she was fifteen minutes early. Rachael kicked off her shoes and got out of the car. She would sit on the beach and watch the ocean.

She was halfway down the curved path when she stopped walking and half turned back, listening. She could hear the low rumble of a car coming from where her car was parked. She remembered the sound distinctly from when she and Julie were at PK Farm. *Is that Mark?*

She quickly calculated she was at least three hours'

drive from Bendigo. *This is no coincidence.*

Rachael felt exposed standing on the path and walked quickly towards the beach. She adjusted her lapel, clicking the button to turn on the digital recorder in her jacket. After a minute, the path opened up to reveal the ocean. Waves from Bass Straight crashed against the beach. She realised that with the wind in her face she couldn't hear much behind her. Rachael stopped and turned.

She flinched. Mark was standing there, a gun pointed at her chest. Rachael saw it was a Glock pistol. *Fuck.*

Rachael mind raced. She took a few steps backwards onto the beach. She wanted to draw Mark off the path, from where he would be able to see Zach coming when he arrived. Mark stayed at the end of the path.

'Stop fucking moving,' he said.

Rachael stopped. 'What are you doing here?' she asked, trying to remain calm.

'I came to see you, obviously.' He was smiling.

'How did you know I'd be here? Are you tracing my phone or something?'

'I attached a tracker to your car a few weeks ago. Sends your location to my phone. Technology, eh? Seems like old dogs can learn new tricks.'

'Why?'

'You know why. I heard about the note at the dairy farm. One of my old mates from the Shepparton station was the first on scene and he had a look at the note before you guys turned up. He called me about it when he saw my name printed on it. Somebody is out for me. I've been racking my brain and the only person I can come up with is you. You've worked out what happened all those years ago with that crash, so I decided to get more proactive in my approach. So, voilà, here I am.' Mark gave an exaggerated flourish with his free hand, as if he were conducting an orchestra.

Rachael could see that Mark's eyes were red and he had bags under his eyes. She knew his decision-making ability would be even more compromised if he was sleep deprived.

'What do you think I know about the crash, Mark?' asked Rachael, knowing she needed to buy some time.

'First things first. Use your left hand to pull out your gun, nice and slowly, and throw it that way.' Mark gave a quick flick of his pistol towards the surf.

Rachael hesitated.

'Hurry the fuck up,' he snapped. Mark was leaning back every few seconds to look up the path to make sure no one was coming. Rachael could see no one was on the beach.

'Okay, okay.' Rachael took out her gun with her left hand and threw it away, onto the sand.

'That's a good girl. I've got to give you some credit. I didn't think you'd have a snowball's chance in hell of working it out.'

'So, why'd you do it?' yelled Rachael, over the wind.

Mark lowered the gun slightly, pointing it toward Rachael's stomach. 'Those girls were trying to fuck up Paul's business. If the videos from inside the chook sheds had got out and on television, who knows what would have happened. People might have got all upset about it and then the supermarkets might have been forced to cancel their contracts with Paul and Dianne. They would have been screwed financially. It's not as if their place is any different from any other. It's free range. It's certified. Paul had been my mate ever since primary school. He called and said that there were some hippies traipsing about. I drove out there and we saw these two girls running towards the fence, all in black, carrying video cameras. I got Paul to give me his car keys and we took off after them. It didn't take long to catch up to them. They were maxing out that old Ford and I just overtook them and cut in. That was it. They shouldn't have been there.'

'So, trespassing is a capital crime now?'

'You're in no position to be a smart arse right now, princess.'

Rachael was desperately praying that Zach would arrive, but she was also worried Mark would see him coming down the path and shoot at him.

'What about the video cameras and their phones? The woman from Animal Action told you the victims had video cameras on them. You left it out of the report.'

'That was easy. I pulled the phones and video cameras out of the wreck just after the crash. Took the SIM cards from their phones and snapped them in two. Burned the video cameras and the phones that night. They were smoke long before the first patrol arrived on scene.' Mark was waving the gun around as he gestured. She could see that his finger was firmly on the trigger.

'Did your old partner Petra know what went on?'

'No. He was raw. I was still working out what sort of copper he was planning on being when it all happened.'

'What about Paul? What happened to him?' asked

Rachael. She kept her hands out to her sides, palms open, defenceless.

Mark sighed impatiently. 'He called me last November and said some guy had come to the house and told him to confess or else. I went out there and he was freaking out. I was not going down for his guilty conscience. If he had confessed, they would have locked him away for twenty years and he would have taken me down with him. I put a bullet in his head and put him out of his misery. I replaced the bullet in the gun and fired a shot off into the wilderness using his finger on the trigger. One bullet in his head, gunshot residue on his hands, one body. Suicide. Simple.'

Rachael prayed Zach was close by. Mark confessing everything to her meant she didn't have long. 'Wasn't he your friend?'

'Yeah, but it was his fault. He gave me no choice,' yelled Mark, over the wind.

'Did Dianne know you killed Paul?'

'No, she thinks he got a case of the guilts and shot himself.'

'But she knew you and Paul killed those girls in the crash?'

'Yeah, but she thought they deserved everything they got. She even gave me the fucking matches to burn the cameras and phones. She wouldn't have wanted Paul running off and confessing either. She'd have been implicated as well.'

'I gotta tell you, Mark, I only suspected you had given your mate a dodgy alibi and I couldn't even prove that—Paul's dead.'

'Stop playing coy with me. It was you who set up

the note at the dairy. You fed the crim the info.'

'What the fuck are you talking about? You think I am the mastermind behind all this, that I've got someone killing people and leaving notes about you? Seriously?'

She saw his eyes harden further. Mark slowly raised the gun slowly.

'Listen, Mark, it isn't me,' said Rachael, as calmly as she could. 'We interviewed Petra today—we reckon it's him. He's under surveillance right now while we run his phone records.'

Mark's head reeled back. 'Fuck,' he said, looking over Rachael's shoulder for a moment.

'He said he was never comfortable with the investigation and thought you were covering up for Paul.'

'That fucker,' growled Mark.

'Mark, there is no one here to corroborate what you've said to me, so you still have choices. You can stop all this and get charged for leaving the scene of an accident in 2007. No one can prove you had anything to do with Paul's death, and that case is closed. You'd probably get a suspended sentence for the car accident and walk away. You could say you didn't mean for those women to die. It was just a situation that got out of your control.'

In her peripheral vision, Rachael could see Zach come into view, on top of the large sand dune behind Mark. He was frantically looking for a way to get to the ground quickly without making any noise. Rachael renewed her focus on Mark.

Mark laughed. 'As if I would be charged with leaving the scene of an accident. It was premeditated, and you know what that means. I am not going down for murdering those girls, and they'll never prove anything once you've disappeared. There will be no trace left of you. I'll make sure of that.'

Mark swung the gun up towards Rachael's head. Zach was halfway down the face of the dune.

'Hey,' he yelled.

Mark's head spun instinctively towards the sound, swinging the gun around as well. Zach was completely exposed.

Rachael quickly ran forwards and kicked behind Mark's knee, sweeping his leg from under him. Mark fell backwards, his head smacking hard against the wooden pathway. His gun fell away from him. Rachael ran across to pick up her gun up from the sand nearby.

When she looked up, Zach had Mark's gun in his hand, pointed at Mark, who was unconscious. He looked up momentarily at Rachael, who shook her head and put a finger to her lips. She grabbed at her lapel, turning the digital recorder off.

'Okay, it's off now,' she said.

'Dead or alive?' asked Zach, his voice breaking with rage.

'What? Alive—fuck, I want this prick rotting in jail for Grace and Helen,' said Rachael.

'I want to deliver him to hell for Grace and Helen,' Zach said, his voice shaking. His arm quivered with adrenalin.

He looked up at Rachael and everything fell into place. She saw it reflected in his eyes.

Rachael slowed her breathing. 'Zach, he's a police officer who deliberately killed two women in a crash and shot another man last year. He'll get life without parole. I have the recording, and it will convince the Director of Public Prosecutions. I don't know if it will be admissible in court. You'll need to testify as to what you saw and heard here. Then he'll go away forever. Zach, look at me. This guy needs to go down. I need to have him suffering for a long time in jail. He and I have a bad history. I need you to do it for me, Zach.'

He held the gun steady, still aimed at Mark's bleeding head.

Rachael spoke slowly. 'You shoot him and you'll be the one going to jail. I will not stop that. Do you hear me?'

For a few moments there was silence as Rachael stared at Zach while he continued to stare down at Mark.

'Better cuff him then,' he said eventually, moving his aim slightly away from Mark's head.

Mark was still unconscious as Rachael walked across, reaching behind her and taking her handcuffs off her belt. She pulled his arm out from under him and cuffed both his hands behind his back.

'I need to call this in. Put the gun down, Zach. Please.'

Zach stood still, gun still pointed at the ground near Mark. Rachael could see by the look in his eyes that his mind was somewhere else. 'Zach, put it this way: if he somehow gets off the charge or gets out of jail, you will be able to find him easily enough, so let's do it the right way for now. He isn't getting away. I need this, okay?'

Zach looked at Rachael and slowly started to nod. 'Okay,' he said, putting the gun carefully on the wooden path a few metres away.

Rachael patted Mark's body down, checking for any other weapons. In his pocket was a pack of zip-ties.

Rachael shuddered.

'I'm turning the recorder back on. Zach, do you understand?' asked Rachael, holding on to her lapel.

'Yes, understood,' he said flatly.

Rachael clicked the button on the lapel of her jacket. She pulled out her phone and called Rob.

Rob answered immediately. 'Rachael.'

'Hi. I've got a situation here. I have Mark under arrest.'

'Wait, what? Do you mean Mark Cullen?'

'Yeah. He followed me…threatened me…look it's under control now—I was meeting Zach and we overpowered him together. But Rob, Mark admitted to deliberately killing those two women in the cold case, and he has also admitted to shooting Paul King and staging it as a suicide. He is currently unconscious and cuffed. I don't have my radio on me, but I will need an ambo down here to take him to hospital and an officer to guard him on the way. We're at St Andrew's Beach. I'll text you the address.'

'Okay, got it. Stay put, the cavalry is on its way. I will need to bring Professional Standards in now there's an officer under arrest.'

'Yes, understood. See you soon.'

Rachael hung up and realised how cold she was. It had started raining minutes earlier and she hadn't noticed. They were getting soaked. Zach was standing off behind Mark, looking out at the waves.

'You okay?' she asked.

'Yeah,' he said, turning to look at her. He was about five metres away, but she could clearly see the sadness in his eyes.

'Heads up,' said Rachael, and threw her phone to him. 'I need you to text our address to Rob.'

'Okay,' he said.

Mark started to come to. He rolled around on the ground trying to sit up, facing Rachael. 'What the fuck is going on?' His head was cut, and a trickle of blood ran down the side of his face. Mark rolled himself into a sitting position, facing Rachael, who stood staring down at him. He shook his head, as if to try and get his bearings. She reckoned he was concussed from hitting his head. He wasn't looking around for Zach.

'Mark Cullen, you are under arrest. You are going to be charged for the murders of Grace Blackwood, Helen Ng and Paul King. You do not have to say or do anything unless you wish to do so, but whatever you say or do may be given in evidence. Do you understand this?'

Mark stared at Rachael. 'Go fuck yourself, bitch.'

Rachael continued, 'I must also inform you of the following rights. You may communicate with or attempt to communicate with a friend or a relative to inform that person of your whereabouts. You may communicate with or attempt to communicate with a legal practitioner. Do you understand?'

Mark said nothing.

'Okay, we can do it again later.'

'You're fucked now, Schlank. Assaulting a detective sergeant. Good luck dealing with that in court. I'll sue you and the department for millions, and you'll go to jail. And then when you get out, I'll be there waiting for you.'

'And then what, Mark?'

'Then I'll take you out into the woods and finish what I started all those years ago.'

In a flash, Zach came at Mark. Rachael looked up and could see him bursting with rage. She stepped forwards and put a hand up. 'Zach, don't. Leave him,' she shouted. Mark's head spun around just as Zach stopped, centimetres away, his arms quivering. 'If you don't shut up right now, I will tear you to pieces. Do you fucking understand me?' he yelled into Mark's face.

Mark just stared up, his mouth open.

'Do you understand?' Zach roared, louder again, his tone primal and terrifying.

Mark was leaning his body away from Zach. He nodded. Zach looked up slowly towards Rachael. She looked pointedly down at the lapel of her jacket. Zach nodded in understanding.

In the distance she could hear the first of the sirens making their way towards the beach. *Two police cars and an ambulance.*

51

The ambulance had driven away with Mark handcuffed to the gurney, heading to the secure ward for prisoners at St Vincent's Hospital in Melbourne. A senior constable was also on board to guard him. Two other police officers were on scene, one at the top of the path near the road and one at the beach end, guarding the crime scene. Any curious locals who had followed the excitement of the sirens to the beach were being turned around quickly.

Zach was sitting on the edge of the path, his back against the sand dune. Rachael walked up and sat down close to him. 'Guess that's the end of our evening.'

'You're probably right there,' whispered Zach.

The approaching sound of a helicopter made them look up. They both stood as they saw a blue and white POLAIR helicopter landing on the beach, but turned away as the sand was blown in every direction. Rachael squinted back towards the helicopter and saw Rob, Julie and DI Mary Costa running awkwardly towards them across the sand. The helicopter increased thrust and took off, banking out over the ocean swell.

'Just stick to the facts of what Mark said and did. Nothing else,' yelled Rachael into Zach's ear, over the noise of the helicopter. He nodded.

Rob ran ahead of the others, up the pathway to where they were standing. 'Rachael, are you okay?'

'Yeah, I'm fine. Mark is on his way to St Vincent's, handcuffed and under guard.'

'What happened?' asked Rob, as Julie and Mary caught up.

'I was going to meet Zach at four to take a walk on the beach. I was a bit early and was walking down the path towards the beach when I heard a muscle car from behind me. It reminded me of when Julie and I heard Mark's car at Dianne King's place—it's very distinctive. When I got to the end of the path, I turned around and there was Mark with a gun pointed at me.'

Rachael pulled the digital recorder out of the inside of her jacket. 'I have it all on tape,' she said, hitting play. Rob, Julie and Mary all looked at the digital recorder with surprise.

For the next few minutes they all huddled around and listened as Mark made his admissions about the car crash, Paul King and his threats to kill Rachael.

Rachael continued, 'For the last bit, Zach was there. When he arrived, he saw Mark holding a gun and made his way to where we were along the top of the dunes,' said Rachael. 'You heard him drawing Mark's attention away from me.'

'Thank goodness for that,' said Julie, patting Zach on the arm.

Rob looked at Rachael. 'How did you know he was going to come after you?'

'I didn't. What do you mean?'

'The recorder. You must have known if you had it on you, ready to go.'

Rachael bit her lip and shut her eyes briefly before responding. 'I have actually had this on me every day for years, since I was a rookie detective. I had some trouble early on and it was my word against his. My complaint went nowhere because there was no proof. Ever since then I have had this on me at work, just in case.'

There was silence for a moment as Rob and Julie just stared at her. She knew they were contemplating the fact that she had been taping their conversations. Mary gave the smallest of grins and nodded her head.

Rachael continued, 'It helped when I was reviewing statements taken from crims and witnesses. I only turned it on with other police when I was being hassled or abused. The rest of the time, it's off. There's a button sewn into the lapel that I click to turn it on and off.'

'It was Mark, wasn't it?' asked Julie. 'The trouble you had years ago? It was from Mark up at Bendigo CIU. Is that what he meant when he talked about finishing what he started?'

Rachael hesitated, looking down at the sand and then up at Julie. She was conscious that Zach was standing next to her, unaware of the story.

'It was at a work Christmas party at the pub. He… assaulted me, grabbing at my breasts in a corridor to the bathrooms, but I kicked hard down along his shinbone and ran. I was lucky. The DI was supportive when I first told him, but Mark's side of the story was that I was coming on to him and that I assaulted him. He had photographs taken of a massive black bruise on his leg. No CCTV. No witness. All over.'

Rachael looked across at Zach, who was now staring back down the path towards the ocean. She could sense his regret for not having killed Mark.

'Well, I'm glad you were recording it,' said Rob. 'I don't know if it will be admissible in court, but it will convince Prosecutions that he committed those crimes.

They'll throw everything they can at him.'

Rob looked at Zach. 'I'm grateful you arrived in time. Were you able to hear what he was saying to Rachael?'

'Yes, the last bit at least,' said Zach. 'As you heard, he was bellowing at her, so it was pretty loud.'

'Good, because we'll need you to testify. Okay, you will both need to come in and give statements right now,' said Rob. He nodded at Mary Costa. 'Professional Standards will be all over this as well.'

'We will need to arrest Dianne King,' said Rachael. 'As an accessory, at least. She may flip on Mark for a deal and strengthen the case against him.'

'I'll arrange for the police up in Bendigo to go arrest her and transport her to Melbourne now,' said Rob.

Rachael looked across at DI Mary Costa, who gave her a reassuring smile.

'That was the other thing,' said Rob. 'Julie had a thought after you both finished surveillance duty outside Petra's place, and checked his Facebook page. He was in the Yarra Valley yesterday like he said. He stopped at a winery to buy some wine on the way back and uploaded a photo of himself with a peacock in the background at four-forty pm. We phoned the winery and they have a credit card transaction in his name at that time. So he's out of the frame now.'

52

Rachael awoke to the screech of her alarm. She groaned. It had felt like she had only just closed her eyes.

Once she had been interviewed and given her statement, she had finally collapsed into bed at two am. She had got Julie to let Zach know she would call him in the morning. She knew she needed to spend the night alone.

The sun streamed across her bed as she grabbed the laptop from the bedside table. She opened her email. There was nothing there about Mark. Understandable. He was probably still under guard in hospital, handcuffed to the bed.

She rang Zach, who picked up after one ring.

'Hi,' he said.

'Morning. How'd you go giving the statement?'

'No problems. Had to go over things a few times. You?'

'Same. Felt weird sitting on the other side of the table,' she said, looking out over the bay.

'Where's Cullen?' he asked.

'Probably still under guard in the hospital. I'm

heading into the office soon to see where things are at.'

'Are you okay?' asked Zach.

What the fuck are you talking about? Am I okay? What sort of alternate reality are you living in? She felt her anger growing.

'Yes, all good,' she said, her jaw tight. 'What about you?'

'Yeah, I'm okay. It took me a while to come down afterwards. It was a close call. I kept thinking, if I were a minute later—'

They were both silent for a few moments. *He's right. I was almost killed yesterday.*

'You there?' he asked.

'Yes, just had a bit of a reality check. You know we need to talk, don't you?'

Zach was silent for a moment before answering. 'Yes.'

'I'll come to your place late this afternoon. Okay?'

'Yes.'

'What's your address?'

'Oh right, of course.' Zach gave her his address in Mount Eliza.

'See you then.'

Rachael hung up the phone. Her stomach was setting like concrete.

53

Mark Cullen sat in an interview room at the Melbourne Assessment Prison, across the road from the Homicide offices. He stared straight ahead, his hands resting on his knees. A bandage covered a wound on the back of his head where he had struck the wooden path. A guard opened the door and Dave Boucher walked in.

'Hey, Mark,' said Dave cautiously.

'What are you doing here?'

'Just thought I'd come across and pay you a visit. Heard you got released from the hospital this morning.'

'Yeah, then straight off to the Magistrates' Court for a filing hearing. Loads of fun.'

'Are they treating you okay?'

'Yeah. I'm in protective custody.'

'Have you got a lawyer yet?'

'No, not yet. The Magistrate basically told me I was stupid for not having one in court this morning. I told him I didn't need one because I was innocent and being framed. Where's the rest of them?'

'They're all back in the office. Working away.'

'Pricks. I can't believe that Schlank and that prick Zach are trying to frame me up for this. I can only imagine what sort of crap they're going to say.'

'Yes, that's kind of why I'm here. There's something you need to know before they start formally interviewing you. She was wired up. They have it all on tape.'

Mark stared at Dave a few moments in silence. 'What?' he asked, drawing out the word, his voice low.

Dave pulled his phone out of his pocket. 'Just listen. I recorded it on my phone under the desk, so the quality isn't great.' He touched the screen and the recording started playing.

Mark sat wide-eyed as he heard his own voice coming through the phone. He could also hear Rachael, Rob and Julie talking in the background. The recording was muffled in some parts, but it was clear to Mark that he was finished.

He sat stony-faced, staring at Dave's phone. 'Fuck. So why are you letting me know? Is this some sort of trick?'

'No. Look, you're still my partner and you were stressed out. I would want you to back me up if the boot were on the other foot. Just don't let them know you know about the tape or that I told you, else I will be fucked as well. Professional Standards will go through me like a knife through butter.'

'So why was she wearing a wire to start with? She didn't know I was coming.'

'She was wearing it the whole time. Every day. Rachael was working undercover for Professional Standards.'

'That fucking bitch,' Mark yelled, slamming his hand flat against the table. 'Was she targeting me all that time?'

'I don't know who she was after. They aren't saying too much about it, at least not in front of me. They've been keeping me in the dark as well. All I know for sure is that they want you to plead not guilty and fight the charges. They see this tape as a way to bury you for good.'

Mark set his eyes on the table and slowly shut his eyes.

'Look, I felt an obligation to let you know,' said Dave. 'I have no interest in you being in a deeper hole. At least now you can get a lawyer and find out how to get the best deal you can. The Police Association will organise a barrister if you ask them.'

Mark was silent for a moment. 'Thanks for telling me.'

'Best I can tell, all you tried to do was help your mate out and everything just snowballed from there, that's all.'

'Yeah,' said Mark, staring at the table in front of him.

Dave stood up. 'I'd better get back or they'll wonder where I've gone.'

'Yeah. Hey, thanks for letting me know.'

'Anything else you need?'

'No,' said Mark.

'Okay, I'll see you soon.'

'Right. See you later,' said Mark.

Dave knocked on the door to be let out.

54

'Did he buy it?' asked Rachael, standing with Rob and Julie on Spencer Street outside the prison.

'Not sure,' said Dave. 'We'll see when he's first interviewed, I suppose. Muffling some of the sound helped sell it a lot. His eyes opened wide when he heard everyone at the office discussing what he was saying over the top of the recording.'

'The admissibility of Rachael's tape is the only issue worrying me on this one,' said Julie. 'If we get the wrong judge on the right day, they could rule it off the table and he could possibly walk on the main charges. A guilty plea is our best bet here.'

'He's due to be interviewed again later this afternoon,' said Rob. 'He'll get a chance to make an admission before he gets started answering questions. We'll see which way he goes. We have Dianne King waiting to be interviewed back at the office.' He looked at Rachael and Julie. 'Dave and I will take the lead on this. You will both be called as witnesses against her based on what she told you in the last interview and we don't want them to claiming it's some sort of conspiracy against her.'

Rachael and Julie nodded.

Half an hour later, Rob and Dave walked into the interview room. Dianne King was seated with a uniformed officer standing guard. Rob gave the female officer a nod and she left the room.

'Mrs King, how are we today?' asked Rob, cheerily.

Dianne King looked up, her face cloudy with anger. 'Why am I here?'

'We'll get to that, but we need to do this formally.' Rob and Dave sat down. Rob turned on the recording devices. 'Recorded interview between Detective Senior Sergeant Rob Morello and Mrs Dianne King, conducted at the City West Police Complex on Saturday 8 April. Also present, Detective Senior Constable Dave Boucher. Do you agree that the time is now three pm?'

Dianne nodded impatiently. 'Yes, yes.'

'Mrs King, you are under arrest for two counts of accessory to murder. I must inform you that you do not have to say or do anything, but anything you say or do may be given in evidence. Do you understand that?'

Dianne stared straight ahead at the wall, not making eye contact with Rob. 'Yes, I understand.'

Rob continued, 'I must also inform you of the following rights. You may communicate with, or attempt to communicate with, a friend or a relative to inform that person of your whereabouts. You may communicate with, or attempt to communicate with, a legal practitioner. Do you understand?'

'Yes, and I want a lawyer.'

'Interview suspended at three-oh-one pm, Saturday 8 April.'

Rob and Dave picked up their folders. Rob gave

Dianne a knowing smile. He and Dave started towards the door.

'I don't know why I'm here. I did nothing wrong,' said Dianne.

They stopped and turned.

Rob gave her a condescending look and then spoke quickly. 'You are here because we have Mark Cullen on tape telling us you knew all about two women being deliberately run off the road by him and your late husband Paul, and that you said they deserved everything they got. You know he's locked up right now, don't you? So basically you knew about a double murder and didn't do anything about it. Then you gave Mark matches to help him burn evidence, the video camera and the phones. That's why you are looking at two counts of accessory to murder. It seems kind of obvious, doesn't it?'

Dianne looked as though she had just been slapped.

Rob opened the door, and he and Dave walked out. The female uniformed officer came back into the room and stood by the wall.

Rachael looked up from her desk as she saw a constable walking through the Homicide office, heading towards Rob's office. 'Looks like we're up,' she said. Julie and Dave looked across from their desks as the officer arrived at Rob's door. They got up and made their way there.

'Dianne King's lawyer wants to see you,' the officer said through the door to Rob.

'Thanks,' said Rob, a look of relief on his face. He got up and met the team at his door. 'Let's go see where we're at.'

Rob and Dave walked into the interview room and saw that Dianne King had been crying. There was a box of tissues on the table in front of her.

A grey-haired gentleman in a tailored suit stood up to shake their hands. 'Detectives, I am Peter Smiker, Mrs King's lawyer.' He was smiling as he shook their hands. 'Before we begin, we're interested to hear if you're looking to do a deal on these charges.'

'In exchange for what?'

'In exchange for testimony against Detective Sergeant Mark Cullen.'

'Give us a minute,' said Rob. He and Dave left the room and met Rachael and Julie in the hallway.

'Best get Public Prosecutions on the phone,' said Rob, a broad smile across his face. 'Mark is finished.'

55

As Rachael drove out of the car park at the Homicide offices, she could feel her elation evaporating fast and a feeling of dread returning. Like driving from sunshine into thick fog.

Rob had seen how exhausted she looked and had told her to go home to rest. He said he would let her know what happened after they had interviewed Mark.

She headed towards Zach's house at Mount Eliza. She drove in a daze, trying to make sense of the feeling she'd had yesterday when she looked into Zach's eyes at the beach.

After just over an hour of driving she got off the freeway and pulled over, a couple of streets from Zach's house. She needed to compose herself. She was sweating despite the cold outside. *Breathe, just breathe.*

She checked her watch. It was five-fifteen. She wanted to turn around and go home. Or go back in time. Anything but this.

Rachael's mind raced over details of the previous weeks, looking for clues. Why hadn't Sally Kinnaird recognised him? He was standing right in front of her when she was questioned after coming out of the cage.

Rachael shook her head. *He was hiding in plain sight.* If the puppy farmer had looked up and said that the guy was Zach, no one would have believed her. Plus, the image in Sally's mind was of just a partial face. At worst, she might have said that the guy looked like Zach. It would hardly have been a compelling accusation.

Her heart was beating hard in her chest. Mark had been right about one thing. She had been feeding the perpetrator information towards the end, even if she didn't know it. She shook her head and banged her palm against the steering wheel. *Fuck.*

Rachael reluctantly pulled the car away from the curb.

She parked in Zach's driveway. As she walked to the front door, Rachael instinctively felt for her her gun, handcuffs and pepper spray.

She knocked on the front door. Her legs felt like jelly. There was no answer. She knocked again. Nothing. A feeling of desolation overcame her.

Rachael panicked and grabbed at the door handle. It was unlocked. She walked quickly into the house. She went into the large open-plan dining and living areas, calling his name. No answer. An open fire was well alight in the living room. She then went from room to room, calling out.

She jogged into the backyard, past a large chicken run, and took a breath before tentatively opening the shed. Nothing. *Thank god for that.*

Her phone buzzed as she was walking back into the house. She answered it without looking at the screen.

'Hello.'

'Hi Rachael, it's Rob. Mark has made full admissions. It will be a guilty plea. Well done.'

Rachael breathed heavily, unable to find words.

'Rachael, you there?'

'Yeah, sorry. That's great news. Thanks for letting me know,' she said slowly.

'I've decided we're going to have to make a shift in tactics with the taskforce case. Now Mark is out of the picture, my instinct is that our guy is going to stop the crimes, as he said in the last note, and go to ground. It's probably the right time to give the press a full briefing on everything we have and make a public appeal while things are fresh in people's minds. The commissioner is going to speak to the premier about a reward.'

'Sounds like a good plan,' said Rachael, sounding vacant.

'You okay?'

'Yeah, sorry. Just feeling a bit exhausted by everything.'

'Understandable. Take it easy and rest up.'

'Thanks, boss; see you later.'

Rachael ended the call and dropped the phone on the dining room table. Overwhelmed, she started crying, her body heaving as the emotion swept through her in waves. After ten years, there would be some justice for Grace and Helen. Mark was going to prison.

She took a couple of deep breaths as she slowly recovered.

Looking up, she saw Zach standing by the front door.

'You only made one mistake,' she said.

Zach walked over and embraced her. She felt her legs go weak as he hugged her tightly.

'No, there were no mistakes,' he whispered, his mouth close to her ear.

56

'Mark has confessed to everything,' Rachael said. 'I just spoke to Rob.'

'That's good news,' said Zach.

'It means it will be a guilty plea. We won't need you to testify about what he said at the beach at his trial.'

Zach just nodded.

'Tell me everything,' she said. 'Start at the beginning.'

Zack took a deep breath. 'I had been undercover in Animal Action for a month or so when I first heard about the crash. Emma Jennings told me what she knew; about PK Farm couple's alibi, the missing video cameras, and the detective who didn't seem that interested. She would talk about it a lot, like she was keeping their memory alive by talking about them. I started having a quiet look around and found out about the Collision team's report and that the car that caused the crash was probably a Commodore VZ. I rang a mate at VicRoads and got him to run me a report on registrations from that time. There was Paul King's name and I became convinced that he was involved.'

Rachael nodded. 'Then what?'

'So, one night last November I went and confronted Paul King at his farm. I told him I knew what he'd done. He denied it, but it was obvious he was lying. I told him that if he didn't go and confess, I would finish him, permanently. He knew I meant it.'

'Did he know you were a police officer?' asked Rachael.

'No, I didn't tell him. I couldn't just arrest him. Cullen had alibied him back in 2007 and I had no evidence to contradict that. I needed him to go in voluntarily and confess. I waited outside the Bendigo Police Station that night for him to arrive, but he didn't appear. I went back just before dawn the next morning to drag his arse in myself and found him lying there, dead. I was fucking furious. I wanted Grace's and Helen's families to see someone charged and finally put away after all those years and now that wouldn't happen. The front door was wide open and I went inside the house to look to see if he had left a note confessing what he had done. I checked everywhere, but there was nothing.

'I was so angry. I had almost helped give Grace and Helen some justice, but I'd failed them in the end. Then one night I saw some vicious comments on a Facebook page and decided to do something about it. Those monsters live out there, oblivious, selfish and destructive. I am not sure if there is a God, so I decided to come for them myself.'

He looked up at Rachael. She gazed back, not quite believing what she was hearing.

'Judge, jury and executioner,' she said quietly.

'I suppose so, yes. When I was in the police

academy they drilled into us that we were being trained to fight to protect the innocent. That there is right and there is wrong. I do not believe that people who go around hurting defenceless animals are redeemable. Even if they're charged, there is no justice in a suspended sentence or a fine. The law does not protect the animals, so I did instead. These types of people only understand violence, so that's what they got. It's no coincidence that the percentage of psychopaths in society and the percentage of hunters are about the same.'

Rachael continued to stare at him, silent.

Zach continued, 'Over the past month, there have been almost no hunters out there. They're now scared of being hunted themselves. Talkback radio has been flooded with ordinary people saying puppy farms should be outlawed,' he said. Zach pointed to the newspaper folded on the coffee table. 'Today's paper even has an exposé on dairies and the killing of bobby calves. People's eyes have been opened a little as to what goes on in the world.'

Zach stopped for a moment. Rachael sat hunched over, looking down at her hands clasped tightly together in front of her.

'It wasn't my plan to deceive you or involve you in this at all,' he said. 'It was just coincidental that we met. Yes, I knew Jules was on the Taskforce and I wanted to see where she was at with the case. But what we have is real, you know that, right? I never even knew you were working on Grace and Helen's case until the other day.'

Rachael sat thinking. *He's right. They hadn't spoken about the cold case until then.*

'When you told me Mark had probably given Paul King a false alibi, it rang alarm bells for me. That's why I put his name in the note at the dairy. I wanted to increase the pressure to get at the truth. And we did.'

'He came to kill me because of that note,' she said. She could feel her face getting flushed. She breathed in sharply, trying to keep her emotions in check.

'Rachael, you need to do whatever you need to do, but you should know that I don't feel any guilt for what I've done. This was all in memory of people who would have done so much good, but the past needs to be put to rest now. I need to set Grace and Helen free.'

Rachael nodded as she thought of her own ghosts, the ones she wanted to set free. Grace and Helen were among them. She felt an overwhelming desire to collapse.

'Who else knows about this?'

'No one knows. Except you.'

Rachael looked at Zach. 'In the note left at the dairy you said you would stop once Cullen was charged. Did you mean it?'

'Yes.'

'Why?' she shot back.

'The people responsible for Grace and Helen's deaths would be accounted for. I didn't know Mark was driving the car that night: Paul King didn't tell me. I thought that if Mark had given King a fake alibi, then he had assisted King to get away with it and I wanted him charged for that at least. That way, I would have closure and could stop. Plus, all the hunters and animal abusers out there would have still have a bogeyman running around inside their heads. Someone to fear. They would know there is always a possibility someone might come for them next, and that would make many of them think twice.'

Zach paused for a moment, before adding, 'Plus, I killed Gary Burn on the 6th of April. So I feel…finished.'

Rachael shook her head slowly, confused. Then it suddenly dawned on her. *Fuck. Grace and Helen's anniversary.*

They sat in silence for a few moments, each lost in their own thoughts.

'So, would you ever have told me if last night had never happened?' asked Rachael.

Zach looked in to her eyes. 'No, I didn't plan on it. I wanted the case to go into the unsolved box and act as a warning to others. Then we could've just gone forwards together.'

Rachael put her hands behind her hips and stretched back, subtlety feeling behind her for the handcuffs attached to her belt.

She stood, and walked away from the dining table and into the living room, shaking her head. Rachael remembered the dream she'd had when she had staked out Vassar's farm, the look of deep sadness on Grace's and Helen's faces before she woke up. *They knew what was coming.*

'I didn't thank you,' said Rachael.

He blinked. 'For what?'

'You saved my life last night. If you hadn't been there, Mark would have definitely killed me,' she said. 'And who knows what else beforehand.' She thought of the zip-ties. 'Thank you.'

Zach looked into her eyes. 'I desperately wanted to finish that bastard off. He killed Grace and Helen and I let him live. I did that for you, not for me. I have to live with the fact that he's still alive.'

Rachael nodded, looking at his face. *What if it had been the people who killed my parents? Would I have given up the chance for revenge?*

'It's all over now though,' she said.

Zach slowly nodded. 'Yes, I know.'

Rachael walked towards the fireplace, feeling the heat on her hands and face. She reached inside her jacket and tore open the velcro pocket holding the digital recorder. Pulling it out, she looked down and saw that the recording light was glowing red. She turned slowly back towards Zach, showing him the recorder in her hand. He looked at it solemnly, nodding.

'There are some things you can't come back from,' she said. 'Sometimes our fate is sealed and it can't be changed. We just have to find a way to live with that.'

Rachael looked into his eyes, seeing that he was resigned to her decision. She removed the memory card from the recorder and stared at it for a long moment. Then she tossed it into the fire and watched it burn.

S.D. Rowell

Acknowledgements

I am extremely grateful to a range of people for assistance, including:

Kate O'Donnell, my very talented editor, whose insight and guidance helped set this book free.
Tom Flood, who assisted with valuable directional advice on earlier iterations.
Kate Ryan, whose keen eyes and clear focus gave the story it's final polish.
David Spencer, from Victoria Police's Film and Television Office, who assisted with my many specific questions relating to police operations.
Margaret Bosidis, who gave me valuable feedback on an early draft.
Martin Beaumont, from Magnetic Websites, who was fantastic in building the book's website.
Adam Neylon, who generously gave me permission to use one of his photographs for the cover design.

Special thanks to Karen Rowell, who patiently read countless drafts and gave me thoughtful advice throughout the process. Without her support, there would be no book.

their

hts

e